Praise for *What's Coming to Me*

"A class, wage and grief struggle tight as a garrote, Francesca Padilla's *What's Coming to Me* is devastating in its familiarity: where an ice cream shop becomes the world, and all of the people in it." —K. Ancrum, author of *Darling*

"Raw and unflinching . . . a beautiful story about the uncertainty of adolescence, the burden of grief, and all the ways love can surprise you. I so enjoyed spending time with Minerva Gutiérrez, and Francesca Padilla is a writer to watch."
—Brandy Colbert, award-winning author of *The Voting Booth*

"Nuanced, complex, and deeply emotional, Padilla's novel skillfully delves into the personal impact of trauma and loss, as well as the damage violence and inequity can inflict on a larger community. The high-stakes narrative, as told by a grieving girl desperate to both flee and find meaning in a place that's taken so much from her, is equal parts tense, heartbreaking, and ultimately healing. A must-read."
—Stephanie Kuehn, author of
We Weren't Looking to Be Found

"Justice and morally gray areas collide in a story of haves and have-nots." —Mindy McGinnis, author of *The Last Laugh*

"To say I enjoyed it was an understatement . . . You can't help but feel for Minerva as she wades against a cold, dark tide of things beyond her control. It's rare that you are able to slip so easily into someone's difficult emotions and with Minerva, you feel her every step of the way . . . *What's Coming to Me* is a great revenge fantasy against 'that boss' wrapped around a tender grieving heart."
—Sarah Nicole Lemon, author of *Done Dirt Cheap*

"If you're longing for a book that's gritty (but not exploitative), that's honest (but not cruel), and that will have you screaming as you turn each page . . . Francesca Padilla's *What's Coming to Me* is for you. This sharp, realistic noir illuminates the nuanced journey of Minerva, whose anger is always right on the surface. A masterful debut and one hell of a ride." **—Mark Oshiro, author of *Anger Is a Gift***

"Unexpected and suspenseful. *What's Coming to Me* is a ride fueled by anger and loss, in a car driven by teens who've had enough. Padilla has written a gripping story about survival and injustice. About young women taking back what's owed to them with both hands and without remorse. There be no good girls here—and I'm grateful for that."
—Isabel Quintero, author of *Gabi, A Girl in Pieces*

"Gripping and real. A layered story of grief, justice, and revenge told by an unforgettable narrator."
—Caleb Roehrig, author of *Last Seen Leaving*

"Propulsive, fearless, and filled with heart-aching revelations, *What's Coming to Me* is a beautiful debut by a scorching new voice in YA fiction. This is a thrill ride of a coming-of-age story, one that grabbed me by the throat but most of all moved me to the core."
—Nova Ren Suma, *New York Times* bestselling author of *The Walls Around Us*

"Unfortunately, in this world, there are too many bosses like Anthony whose toxic masculinity goes largely unchecked, in a society that makes it difficult for young femmes to speak up about workplace predators—especially when, like Minerva,

they are navigating responsibilities that require economic stability for survival. Minerva won't settle for the idea that that's just how things are. Anyone who has had to navigate anger and grief simultaneously while continuing to believe in the promise of tomorrow will root for Minerva's perseverance and determination to get what's coming to her."
—**Elisabet Velasquez, author of *When We Make It***

"A delicious story of revenge, unlikely friendships, and claiming your place in an all-too-unfair world. Francesca Padilla's brilliant prose dazzles as Minerva navigates thrilling heists, quiet moments of grief, and all the sparks of joy in between. Minerva is a triumphant underdog, and her savviness, wry humor, and perseverance will win your heart."
—**Angela Velez, author of**
Lulu and Milagro's Search for Clarity

"*What's Coming to Me* by Francesca Padilla perfectly evokes the salt air, gasoline, and desperation of a seaside town. A vivid and truthful book that delves into grief, denial, and finding your way back to yourself."
—**Alexandra Villasante, award-winning**
author of *The Grief Keeper*

"Minerva is all of us. If all of us were smart, cynical, hurt but brilliant young women working for just a little bit of dignity and a little bit of joy in the midst of so much turmoil. I can't imagine a reader who wouldn't fall head over heels for Minerva. Get ready for a journey."
—**Erika T. Wurth, author of *White Horse***

WHAT'S
COMING
TO ME

WHAT'S COMING TO ME

FRANCESCA PADILLA

Published in the United States by Soho Teen
an imprint of Soho Press, Inc.
227 W 17th Street
New York, NY 10011

Library of Congress Cataloging-in-Publication Data
Names: Padilla, Francesca, author.
Title: What's coming to me / Francesca Padilla.
Description: New York, NY : Soho Teen, an imprint of Soho Press, Inc., [2022]
Identifiers: LCCN 2021060848
ISBN 978-1-64129-335-8
eISBN 978-1-64129-336-5

Subjects: CYAC: Grief—Fiction. | Anger—Fiction. | Poverty—Fiction. | Mothers—Fiction. | Dating (Social customs)—Fiction. | Dominican Americans—Fiction. | LCGFT: Novels. Classification: LCC PZ7.1.P323 Wh 2022 | DDC [Fic]—dc23
LC record available at https://lccn.loc.gov/2021060848

Interior design by Janine Agro, Soho Press, Inc.
Printed in the United States of America

10 9 8 7 6 5 4 3 2 1

To my mother, with love

WHAT'S COMING TO ME

CHAPTER ONE

Anthony's going to kill us.

For the third time this week, the register is short, and somebody has to tell him about it. It's been decided that person is me, the newest employee at Duke's Ice Creamery.

Everyone else is too busy. One of the other girls, either Jordan or Jamira, sits cross-legged on the sherbet freezer, counting tips. The other finishes up an order for a woman at the window with a fistful of old coupons. Then there's Eli, who's the assistant manager and happens to be the only guy, walking back inside from emptying the mop bucket. Which everybody acts like he's a big hero for doing but in my opinion is still preferable to most tasks, because it takes place away from the counter and the infinite demand of customers. A monster that refuses to stop feeding.

Somebody turns off the lights inside to hint that we're closing. My eyes throb, trying to adjust after a double shift's worth of white fluorescent tubes. I grab the register money in its fat envelope and continue toward Anthony's office, tucked away in the very back of the ice cream stand.

On the way, I open the side door and step out. I'm

immediately hit with the scent of Nautilus in summer—a mix of grass and dust and air-conditioner exhaust.

I came out here to procrastinate but also to look for my ride home, which isn't here yet. I scan the cars in the weedy lot behind Duke's, even check the picnic tables on one side of the stand, where the coupon woman has split the two-for-one sundaes among a gaggle of children. It's almost midnight.

My neighbor CeCe should've been here at least fifteen minutes ago. We haven't been friends that long—in fact, I'm not sure we're friends now—but she sells weed, meaning she always has some on her, and being in her apartment is better than home.

Assuming my shift ever ends, how the hell am I supposed to get out of here? I might have to grab one of the last buses or—much worse—walk.

The envelope is heavy in my hands, the paper thin and smooth from being used so often. The feel and weight of the cash inside is so specific. It's the most money I've ever seen in my life.

Same as the last time I had to deliver the cash to Anthony, I picture running off with the envelope, leaving Nautilus altogether, and starting over somewhere beautiful and busy. The daydream always evaporates the second I hand it over. Stays just that, a daydream.

Our boss Anthony calls me "Space Cadet." But only when he's in a good mood. When he's in a bad mood, which is most of the time, he calls me "this one," like I haven't been working at the Ice Creamery for an entire six months. I'm pretty sure he's forgotten my name.

The thing is, everyone here believes that I'm a space cadet. Sometimes I want to tell them all I read books (trashy ones most recently, but still). That once I stayed up until 3 A.M. googling *osmosis*. That I'm an advanced student.

Was, corrects a nasty little voice in the back of my head. *Was* an advanced student.

There are only two good things about working at Duke's Ice Creamery. The first is getting paid in cash; I add as much as possible to an old coffee can I call the "Probable Orphan Fund." The second is that nobody at Duke's knows or cares about who I used to be, the Minerva from Before and her fuckups. Eli's the only one who goes to the same school, but we don't know each other, and he just graduated.

So, here, I'm Space Cadet.

A van comes hurtling around the corner, appearing to pull up to the sidewalk in front of the ice cream stand. I bet we'll have to take their order, too, even though we already turned the lights off.

The silver lining is that it'd buy a few more minutes for CeCe to show up.

"Come *on*," I hear Jamira shouting to everyone as I step back inside. It turns out she was the one sitting on the freezer. "Just tell them we're closed."

I'd handle it myself—last-minute orders mean higher tips—but I've already held on to the envelope too long. I shut the door behind me, finally ready to go to Anthony's office and tell him the register was off, when somebody screams. I bolt toward the sound.

This turns out to be a mistake.

Two people—two *figures*—have managed to hop the counter and get inside. Both are wearing black-and-white cat masks. Both hold long, thin knives.

"Stop what you're doing," says one of the masks. He has a faint lisp, although it might be the cheap plastic.

I still have the money.

This is a robbery, and I have the money.

I tighten my grip on the envelope. Fear pulses through my fingers. It's like I'm holding a bag of airborne poison, and if I move an inch, it might escape and kill us all, starting with me.

The two figures stand before the ice cream cake freezer, its display now the main light source. The rest of us have slowly gravitated together to cower by the toppings station.

"Come on, guys," Eli starts, but the first robber takes a step forward, pointing his knife's tip at each of us. He lingers on Eli the longest.

"I will slice all your pretty faces in two seconds or less," he says. "Do you want to see?"

We sink to the tiles.

"Stay the fuck down," the other one says, also with a kind of lisp. Has to be the mask. "And do *not* move."

My eyes, now fully used to the dark, return to the floor and the graveyard of items left behind by Eli's mop: a toothpick, a shrunken hair tie, flattened sprinkles like confetti from a long-dead party.

"Hey," blurts one of the robbers, "she's got something there."

The other mask tilts in my direction. "Give it here."

Time actually stops while I hand over the envelope. Outside, moths bounce against the awning. In the light of the cake freezer, I sneak a look at my coworkers. Eli's face is pale and stony, his glasses smudged and glaring. Jordan and Jamira clutch each other and sob—they've styled themselves similarly tonight, in perfect winged eyeliner and high ponytails spilling out above their Duke's visors. Jamira is Afro-Honduran-Columbian, and Jordan is some kind of white, but they look related. Even their tears are stunning.

"Okay now," one of the robbers calls out, like we're all just little kids misbehaving, "there won't be any problems at *all* if you just *listen*."

They tell one of us to open the cash register and the rest to keep our heads down. Nobody explains that the cash register is empty and that the robbers already have its contents in the envelope. I shift my focus to my feet, my white sneakers and socks that sometimes make me feel more innocent than I am. I suck in my breath and try to erase myself from the moment—pretty easy after all the practice I've had this past year.

The cash register opens. The till lifts.

I brave another look. The envelope I was just holding changes hands, knives still out. One of the robbers counts the envelope money while the other taps his non-knife hand against his thigh. I make out white fingers and wrists. Their clothing is dark and heavy despite the heat.

"Where's your boss?" one asks.

Eli's the one who answers. "He should be back there."

"*Should be?* That's not what I fucking asked."

"I mean, I thought he was." Eli falters and turns to me. "Min? Weren't you just back there?"

Foolish kid, thinking I've been gone this whole time doing my job. This might also be the most Eli's ever spoken to me. While he's never been mean, he's never been anything *else* to me, either.

"I don't— I didn't—" I shake my head at him, then at the knives, then at the masks behind them.

"Leave. All of you."

Nobody needs to be told twice. We spill out the side door

and scatter into the night, which has broken into a sloppy drizzle. I cut through the lot to the sidewalk on the other side. My heart beats so hard I can feel it in my legs as I run for my life.

A car engine starts. Then another.

Somewhere close to my ear and across the ocean at the same time, there's muffled crying.

What about the coupon woman and all those kids?

And what happened to my ride?

I can't think about any of that. All I can do is run, a task I actually understand. Run and keep running until the blood—my heartbeat—is the only sound left in the world.

CHAPTER TWO

Running through Nautilus at night makes the town feel bigger than it is. The spaces between the closed storefronts, scattered buildings, and houses widen. The sidewalks narrow and disappear. Cars pass a few minutes apart, their headlights washing over me. Every time, I hunch my shoulders until they're long gone again.

I consider stopping to dial 911 on my busted, low-battery phone. But I'm sure another Duke's employee has already called. Someone more important than me. Which is anyone.

I make a turn at the church at the end of Nautilus Avenue, with its mossy statues out front. The trees swallow up most of the light. The street lamps are either physically broken or simply nonfunctioning from the hurricane last fall.

This part of Nautilus is a left-alone carcass given too much time to air out. Every dark pocket and unknown corner reminds me of the masks and their plastic hissing, their promises to slice us open with those awful knives. These follow me in the dark as I cut through streets I'm not sure I've ever seen before, which I didn't think was possible.

The moon, about half of it, appears from behind the trees,

wrapped in deep purple clouds. I don't know when, but it stopped drizzling at some point.

This is the second time I've walked home from work. The first was during the in-between period after I got the job and before I was expelled from school. Nautilus felt so unfamiliar close-up that I never did it again. After that, it was only the bus or a ride in CeCe's pitch-black Pontiac when I could get her to come out.

My phone vibrates in the back pocket of my shorts. I startle as if I've done something wrong—*the envelope, the envelope, you thought about taking the envelope before it was taken from you*—but there's no way. My gut trembles like it doesn't believe me.

ELI FROM WORK, the screen blares.

I slow down and stare at the object in my hand. Normally, I'd be fighting butterflies, even though all he ever does is inform me of my schedule. And now—I suppose—checking if I'm alive. But I can't talk to anyone right now, including the crush I'd rather keep pretending doesn't exist.

Predictably, the moment I go to decline the call, my phone dies. I picture Eli relieved to not have to talk to me.

If I'd waited a few more minutes with that envelope of register money—procrastinated just a little longer—*I* would possess a shift's worth of cash right now. It feels related, like the Universe-with-a-capital-U, as my ex-best friend Mary calls it, provided a clear opening.

I didn't take the opening. And now somebody else has it.

The faded tan brick of my apartment building rises into view around the next corner. I'm still holding my dead phone. I should go into my apartment, where the landline was cut just the other week, and charge it. I should call someone. Even if it's not the police.

If Mom were around, I would've called her first. She'd pick me up off Nautilus Avenue, buy a bunch of snacks from the closest gas station—sunflower seeds and salt-crusted chips and three kinds of chocolate—and then we'd find a spot to watch the water, to eat and toss our empty shells.

Who else?

There's Mary, but I stopped answering her calls and messages too long ago.

There's CeCe, who I still have to ask about my ride, even though I already know it's because she got too high and forgot.

I should call someone.

I should, I should, I should.

I don't.

THE APARTMENT BUILDING where I live, the Beach Blossom, is made up of one hundred and fifty-six apartments spanning two stories. Most of the windows are still lit up, but since it's late and everything is wet, there's no activity outside. Crossing through the parking lot, I don't even bother glancing up at my apartment. I know the lights are off, and the nearest light bulb in the walkway has gone out.

Before the Beach Blossom, when I was little, Mom and I lived with my grandparents in a house in the center of Nautilus. When they died within a year of each other from a combination of illnesses, Mom couldn't afford their house on her own.

I was too young to remember any of that—just the excitement of moving and how fancy the name sounded. *Beach Blossom*. Of course, it turns out every other building in the housing complex has an equally fanciful name: the Sand Dollar, the Lily, the Seastar. All of them are gray and squat,

painted brick on the outside and gummy linoleum and car-
peting on the inside.

Mom once explained that all these buildings used to be
part of a hotel, back when Nautilus Point was a place for
rich people who had nothing else to do but vacation at the
seaside. At one time, the grounds were lined with cobblestone paths and carved railings.

"To help the young ladies keep their frilly dresses clean,"
she scoffed while surveying the webs of rust and algae and
walkways people had turned into makeshift balconies.
While our part of the walkway has been empty for a while,
others have toys, extra lamps, lawn chairs, even mini grills
on theirs.

A few steps behind the Beach Blossom, there's a ditch that
fills up when it rains too long, which Mom used to threaten
would sweep me out to the ocean. She was trying to scare
me away from playing in it, but sometimes lately, I wish it
were true.

The hint of a stream smells faintly of eggs, enough
water flowing to be heard over the traffic. This is where
I hop over to the woods—which are more like a cluster
of trees sparse enough to see the road on the other side.
However, if I walk parallel to the Beach Blossom and keep
going just short of the defunct train tracks, it becomes
private enough.

I stop at a massive tree ripped from the ground by a
tropical storm many years ago. The upended roots make
a decent platform above the creek bed. I sit on the flattest
part I can find.

A breeze hits the back of my head. I remember my sweaty
Duke's Ice Creamery visor and rip it off.

"Okay," I say out loud. "Now cry."

But the tears won't come. They haven't for about three months.

I force myself to think about the masks, the knives. The flecks of ice cream and objects on the floor. It still doesn't feel real, but to be fair, neither does anything else in my life. I think about missing school and probably not being allowed back in the fall. About my mother in the hospital and her own heart giving up on her, and how I'm basically going to be an orphan. Because even though I know who my father is—a guy Mom met her first year of college, before dropping out to have me—he refuses to claim me, and what good is a parent who doesn't want to be one?

The tears still won't come. My brain simply turns away from all this like, *I know*.

"Hey! Where you been?"

I turn around. CeCe makes her way through the trees with the help of her phone's flashlight. She must have spotted me walking past her apartment. Her dog, Large Marge—who's actually about the smallest a pit bull can get, way too friendly, and not very smart—barrels into the clearing first.

"The Ice Creamery was crawling with cops and fire trucks," CeCe says. "What the hell happened?"

I tell her, and she hisses at the ground, her head shaking slowly in awe. I watch Large Marge do her usual circling of the perimeter before returning to sit on my foot.

"Damn, Mini-Mart. That is *fucked* up." CeCe turns off the flashlight and pockets her phone. Her hair, in its usual short ponytail, looks like a wet paintbrush between her shoulder blades. "I always thought that place was kind of off. I thought maybe it was all those white people who run it. But I didn't want to say anything, seeing as how you work there."

"Thanks," I grumble. "And don't call me Mini-Mart."

She ignores me. "They know who did it yet?"

"It just happened. Why were you late picking me up, anyway?"

"Car wouldn't start." She sucks her teeth. "I think it's really done. I finally borrowed my cousin's car, but you were gone by the time I got there. Plus all the cops. You know."

I scratch Large Marge behind the ears, because I need something to do with my hands. "Did you bring anything?"

"You already know." CeCe gives the tree root a light kick, then remembers the limited-edition boots she won't admit to this day how she acquired. She sits at last, briefly examining her shoe, then produces a pipe already fully packed with weed.

She hands it to me, a bright green spot in the dark. The sound of a helicopter rises somewhere above us. I take a hit and nod at the sky. "You think that's because of the robbery?"

CeCe shrugs. "Could be. Or not. You know how it is here."

She means the crime, which is supposedly the worst it's ever been. The local news has a whole segment devoted to crime in Nautilus, specifically the Point—I've watched enough in the hospital waiting room to know.

According to CeCe, though, just as much shadiness happens in the wealthier parts of Nautilus. As the resident weed dealer, she'd know better than me.

The smoke between us drifts upward and hoops around the branches. The helicopter is louder now. If they were trying, they could probably find us among the trees. It's just weed, but people have been taken in for way less.

"Maybe we should go back," I say. CeCe knows I mean

her apartment. The thought of having to go back to mine makes me stop scratching Large Marge. She nudges me with the cold tip of her nose to keep going.

"Actually, I have a drop-off."

"At midnight?"

"Don't be so naive, Mini-Mart."

She tosses the last embers into the creek bed and tucks the pipe away. When she takes her hand back out of her pocket, she's got her phone again. The case is matte red, the colors of the screen popping from where I sit on my trunk platform. As always, I can't help staring; my phone comes from the government, and I've had to share it with my mother for most of the time I've had it.

"Can you drive me?" CeCe asks suddenly. "Don't you guys have a car you don't use anymore?" She points in the general direction of the Beach Blossom, I guess meaning the parking lot.

"The Boat?" I pivot to face her. "That's my mom's car. You know that."

The Boat is a Grand Marquis, a car they don't make anymore. It's long and white with a navy-blue top. It used to be a taxi in the 90s and still smells like cigarettes from before Mom claimed to have quit smoking. When I started working at Duke's, I asked her if I could use it to drive to work, and she said no, claiming the bus was perfectly acceptable and would make for good homework and studying time.

But Mom stopped using the Boat altogether way before things got bad, around the time she had to leave her job at the bank. It's been sitting in the parking lot sprouting rust ever since.

Which, admittedly, doesn't seem fair.

"I'll give you something if you give me a ride."

CeCe either means weed or money. The latter is especially

enticing, since I never got my tips tonight. I was so busy thinking about handing over the envelope—the feel of the money, the cat masks floating above us, the weight of the bills there and gone so fast. Happening and not happening, real and not real. All of it mixes together, sinking to the bottom of my stomach like greasy fast food.

"I had to walk home." I feel terrible the second I say it, knowing it wasn't CeCe's fault. Just bad timing, the general shittiness of life at the Beach Blossom.

"Damn, Mini-Mart. I didn't realize. I'm sorry." CeCe stands up, exposing the jagged roots underneath. They look like no one should ever be sitting on them, but we've been to this spot enough times to know every surface like the furniture in our own homes. "I'll just be in and out," she says. "There and back."

There and back. That's what she always says when she drags me somewhere. Except there's about a fifty-fifty chance it won't be. One time, during what was supposed to be a "quick drop-off" in West Babylon, I got stuck watching her play video games for about three hours with some guy who was trying too hard and entirely in vain to get into her pants.

I look up as if the answer of what to do next is floating in the sickly purple sky. The helicopter seems to have drifted off when I wasn't paying attention.

"Fine," I say at last.

Back at the Beach Blossom, I dash into my tomb of an apartment to fetch the car keys and change into a dry shirt. For all my complaining, the truth is that I'm glad to postpone going to bed here. Not to mention, I actually like to drive.

I might even love it, if I'm ever capable of feeling that deeply again.

• • •

TECHNICALLY, MOM STARTED teaching me how to drive when I was eleven. But the day I turned sixteen, she revealed she'd signed me up for a driver's ed course at a community center the next town over. Driving has always felt natural to me. It's the expansive feeling of it, the movement, that you don't always need a specific destination. You could keep going forever if you wanted.

If you really wanted.

CeCe's drop-off, though, is barely a ten-minute drive. She's in and out just like she said. But soon she wants to swing by two other houses and then the corner store for wraps and Takis. "Really fast," she promises, but we're gone for another hour.

I complain, but really I'm happy for a reason not to go home yet and be alone with what happened at work.

When we finally get back to the Beach Blossom, CeCe tries to give me a few bags for free. I stare down at them, a vague sense coiling inside me that maybe I should try and do better. Start fresh. Maybe even go to summer school, quit my job for good.

Maybe that's what the robbery is trying to tell me.

Before I decide, she hands me a twenty-dollar bill on top of the weed. An unexpected addition to the Probable Orphan Fund is the best kind of surprise.

Maybe it's her way of telling me everything will be okay.

"You said there were cops at Duke's?" I ask.

CeCe scratches at a mosquito bite on her arm. "Yeah, like a lot. Firefighters and shit, too."

Heat, as if from an invisible fire, rushes my face. "What do you think will happen next?"

The thing is, I'm not even sure what kind of answer I expect, or even what I mean by that question.

And this is when I know. I want somebody to say the robbery happened for a reason. Maybe even that it means I won't have to deal with my leering boss, bad music, or slack-eyed customers anymore.

Somehow.

But CeCe shrugs and reaches for the car door. "No idea, kid."

As soon as CeCe and Large Marge disappear in the direction of their apartment, I restart the engine of my mother's car—more and more I'm loving the sensation of this, like a flame in my hand—and peel out of the Beach Blossom, hands shaking. I need to see what's going on at Duke's.

CHAPTER THREE

A block away from Duke's, I spot emergency lights strobing into the dark blue sky. I run into a police barricade soon after and double back to look for a parking spot down the street, which is lined with more cars than usual. I park the Boat and walk over to get a better look.

Red-and-white emergency vehicles surround the ice cream stand, enough to obscure the tiny structure. A crowd of people has materialized from around corners, other stores, apartments, and houses. The pink cursive DUKE'S ICE CREAM-ERY sign, usually neon and spinning, is off and stationary. Instead, the lights of the vehicles brighten everything in turns.

I count five police cars and two fire trucks altogether. They must have been here for hours.

Maybe the place will close.

The thought sends my brain on multiple round trips from deep relief to panic and flailing. This is the first job I've ever had in my life. The first time I've ever had money. Anthony likes to remind us that, even though he pays us below mini-mum wage, it's off the books and "balances out," as if it's a favor to us and not shady tax-dodging. What's more, I only recently started getting evening shifts, which puts me at the mercy of Jordan's and Jamira's dictatorial musical choices but is worth the tips, which are so plentiful that the jar has to be emptied several times each night.

The reality is that my job was immensely hard to get. Either Jordan or Jamira once claimed there were more than two hundred applications for my spot alone. The only reason I got it was that somebody in our family knew a former Duke's girl, who put in a good word with Anthony. Also, because during my interview, I'm pretty sure my bleached hair, along with the piss-yellow light in his office, caused him to mistakenly believe I was a *very* tan white girl. Same with Jamira and probably a bunch of others over the years.

Anthony only hires girls he thinks are cute. Jamira told me this during training like it was the most inevitable fact in the world, but there was a hint of irony in her demeanor as she went on reviewing the popular flavors, station of multicolored toppings, and cake freezer, which, as low-ranking staff, I was allowed to access only in the event of urgent cake-related matters. Jamira, who is Duke's longest-running employee, has the sole privilege of decorating the cakes. The way she and everyone else acted, I still don't know if I was hired because of, or despite, Anthony's rule.

There's another, more official policy at Duke's, which grants free ice cream of any kind or size to police, firefighters, and sometimes EMTs. Not all of them are exactly polite about it.

One time early on, one of the visiting cops leaned over as I was pre-mixing powder and water for shakes and told me I was "doing a *real good job*," his tongue peeking out from his thin gray lips. I stared back at him, imagining what it might feel like to punch a grown man square in the face.

Not only does Anthony get friendly visits from the police, but he also collects old police badges the way normal people collect seashells or souvenir magnets. Rows and rows of police badges line the wall around the mounted double monitors on his desk. There's a framed photo of him with the police department, another with volunteer firefighters.

It's weird seeing Anthony's buddies in the context of a real emergency, how they stand around under the awning and talk to one another and into their walkie-talkies.

None of them are eating free ice cream.

I'm stopped by a woman whose high ponytail looks like uncooked ramen noodles. "Any idea what happened?" She squints painfully into the colored lights.

I shake my head, glad to have changed out of my Duke's shirt when I grabbed my mother's car keys.

"I heard some kids robbed the place," she says, proud of thinking she knows more than I do. Her mouth stays open like she's trying to drink in as much of the scene as she can. "Tried to set fire to it, too."

Fire? Did it happen after we left, or is it an exaggeration? "Do they know who did it?"

"Nah, they got away." She squints again, drunk or mesmerized or both.

"Do you know what they stole?"

For some reason, this question snaps her out of it. "How should I know? All I know is it happened in the first place."

I leave the crowd and blinking vehicles and swarm of people talking too loudly. A few of them even laugh. The feeling rises again, growing from the back of my mind like one of those plants filmed and played back at high speed, spiraling wider and wider into existence.

I wish I thought to rob Duke's Ice Creamery.

Down the road, near where I parked, there isn't a single person on the street. Like all the life force in Nautilus has been funneled toward this one event. The rain and mist have made a comeback as a gusty wetness, and the night clouds are the same sick purple as the Duke's visors and T-shirts we have to wear when Anthony's around.

If that part about the fire is true, I think, *they should've planned better.*

They should've burned it all to the ground.

I imagine the robbery happening again, this time with Anthony inside the ice cream stand and—just for added fun—Mr. Duke himself. All the doors and windows are mysteriously bolted from the outside. Anthony with his pale eyes and sandy, close-cropped hair and beard. The shadows created by those horrible office lights, giving him an almost ghoulish quality at certain angles. At my interview, I thought maybe he was just serious about ice cream.

As for Mr. Duke, he has no face. Whenever I think about him, he wears a suit and tie. But really, he's so rich he could probably wear whatever he wants, living his very best life off the spoils of teenage labor.

Duke's Ice Creamery is one of those places that's always been around. Beloved and corny. But that's why people like it: it's a token from the golden days of Nautilus. Because the Nautilus of today is a joke. Because anyone who actually still lives here is a joke. It's so much easier to live in the past, before the hurricanes and empty condos and everyone with money fleeing back to the other side.

A cop strolls past. He notices me and pauses, his hand drawn to his belt. I swallow burning salt, but I'm not doing anything wrong by sitting in a parked car.

The emergency lights strobe away behind him, and for

a moment, he's the same cop who licked his lips at me, the cop who was laughing and talking shit with Anthony a few minutes later. I knew with my entire gut their laughter that day was about me.

But right now, his face is a shadow. He's all of them.

"Better get on home, honey," he says. "Some dangerous people out here. This place isn't what it used to be."

CHAPTER FOUR

I noticed the cameras about a month after I started at Duke's. They were tiny black plastic things, smaller than my thumbs. One was resting just beneath the counter, one hung from the underside of the cone shelf, and one was fixed above the toppings station. One in front of the cake freezer. One behind it.

Avoiding their gaze became a doomed mission that involved sidestepping and dipping and bending in new ways I wasn't even sure made a difference.

Jamira confronted me in the middle of my shift. Apparently, I was moving all funny around the counters. "You look like you're square-dancing or some shit," she said plainly.

I told the other girls about the cameras—whispered it, in case Anthony was watching in that moment. They just stared at me. It was Jamira and this corn silk–blonde girl named Annelise who barely spoke and was about to leave for softball camp. I was her replacement.

Annelise lowered her Duke's visor almost completely over her eyes, and Jamira crossed her arms. Then it clicked. It took me a minute, but I got it.

"You both knew?"

"Everyone knows," Jamira said. "It's not really a secret."

I said we could report him and that it was sexual harassment. Jamira reminded me about his cop friends.

"Besides," she said, "some girl already tried that."

When I asked her what she meant, she told me to never mind and that she forgot the girl's name anyway. She went back to unwrapping a blank ice cream cake she'd eventually cover in flowers or cartoon animals and balloons. She seemed determined to move on. "Not everything has to be some big crusade," she said. "It's just ice cream."

I looked at Annelise, who shrugged and said, "It's messed up."

Jamira went on. "He's just a weird old dude. There's nothing you can do, Minerva." She didn't bother to lower her voice much; I'd come to find out later the cameras didn't pick up sound. In addition, everyone assumes the cameras don't record, so it's at least safe if Anthony isn't in his office.

But I couldn't stop thinking about how it was near impossible to tell whether Anthony was in his office at any given time, watching. Not from the counter or anywhere else inside the stand.

After that, everyone faded back into work. Or—since it wasn't yet the busy season—pretending to work. We had all gotten very good at pretending.

CHAPTER FIVE

I wake up to the sounds of clanging dishes and running water. The first thing I think of is Mom coming home from the hospital without telling me first, a dozen or so times in the past year alone. Sometimes in the middle of the night. The hope and dread warring in the pit of my stomach: hope that everything would be normal again, whatever normal meant, and dread that she had more bad news from her doctors.

Sorry, she'd whisper, hugging me tight. *I didn't want to get your hopes up.*

But it's not Mom. The realization hits along with the memory of last night. Mom isn't here, Duke's Ice Creamery was robbed by creeps, and I had to walk home.

The activity in the kitchen is Mom's cousin, Nicole, who's been "taking care" of me in my mother's absence. Nicole is ten years older than me and ten years younger than Mom. When she's not over here scolding me, she lives across town in Nautilus proper. She even sleeps over sometimes. It's been about three months of this, and every time I have to see her is somehow the worst.

Nicole is on her hands and knees, cleaning out the

refrigerator. She has earbuds in and doesn't hear me enter the kitchenette.

I tap her on the shoulder, and she jumps. The surprised look on her face hardens to annoyance. I notice her new tan, offset by a deep blue ruffled sundress, and remember her saying something about a trip to Florida. She must have left and come back at some point.

I've been spending so much time at CeCe's and Duke's that I didn't realize she was gone. Being home, especially sober, draws memories as easily as if they were just under my skin, each one trying to burst out and outrun me.

"Do you know how much of a disaster this kitchen was when I got here?" Nicole stands up. "It took me an hour just to clean out this fridge. You were supposed to do this before I left."

"Maybe you shouldn't have left, then."

Mom's and my tiny apartment always looks different when an outsider is present—and Nicole is most definitely still an outsider. In her presence, I suddenly become too aware of the clutter. The papers and books and curled-up copies of the *Weekly Wave* I won't let her throw out. The empty fruit bowl on the kitchen table, in which the fruit went dusty and soft before she got her hands on it. The pens and markers in every random drawer. The wrong time on the microwave from the last daylight savings time.

I maneuver past her petite frame to grab a container of apple juice and a newly cleaned glass. "There was a robbery at Duke's last night."

Nicole shakes her head in the open fridge. "That's, like, the third one around here this month."

The cold juice is the best thing I've ever tasted. I finish it in five seconds and reach for the bottle again.

"I don't get why your mother chose to stay here," Nicole rambles. "There are apartments everywhere."

Me, I answer in my head. *I'm the reason she had to stay.* "I'm fine, in case you were wondering."

Nicole unscrews a container of milk. "What? Of course I'm glad you're—" She stops talking when the smell of dairy rot fills the room, gags theatrically, and pours it down the sink. I make a point to act like there isn't puke simmering in the back of my own throat, like I don't notice myself how disgusting the kitchen is.

Nicole turns on the faucet and yells above the water. "I hear you've been skipping summer school."

"Jesus Christ. How'd *you* know about that?"

My second glass of juice goes sour. I back out of the kitchen and fall into a chair at the dining table Mom shoved way into the corner of the living room, near the best window in the apartment. Outside, you can actually see the ocean above the treetops.

"Leave Christ out of this. And you know your mom put me down as a contact for school."

"Summer school is bullshit." I wrap my arms tight around my head and sink to the table. It's nice and dark and safe in here.

"If I didn't know any better, I'd think you were trying to get kicked out of school. Again."

"I'm not trying—"

"That's exactly the point. You're not *trying* to do *any-thing*. Do you know how lucky you are? I would've killed for a fraction of your opportunities."

"Maybe you can kill me now. Take my place."

"That's not funny." Nicole's voice is closer. I don't need to look up to know she's glaring at me, but what she doesn't understand is that her potential for intimidation is tragically weak compared to Mom's.

"You think it's so cute," she says, "skipping school and making jokes while your home is falling apart? How could you do this to Sunny?"

I finally lift my head to look at her. My hands reach for something solid and wrap around the empty glass in front of me. I picture myself throwing it at her. Or pushing her against the fridge until she apologizes for bringing Mom into this. The apartment is so small it's no more than three steps to reality.

When the feeling passes, we're still on opposite sides of the room. The vision leaves me dizzy.

"Do it." Nicole's voice is low, dangerous. "Attack me just like you did to that white girl at your school. If only I could *suspend* you from this apartment."

"Stop talking about—" My fists ache from squeezing so tightly. "Just stop talking."

"No. You don't get a say in things anymore." She takes out her phone.

"What are you doing?" I ask, but Nicole pretends not to hear me, and I remind myself I don't really care. Caring about what she thinks or does opens a door to a new world of things to care about. Besides, if I put up too much of a fight, she'll only watch me closer. Which is the very last thing I need right now.

I escape back to my room at the end of the hall, where the sunlight pouring in through the blinds cranks up the dial on my lingering headache and illuminates the hills of dirty laundry, unread textbooks, half-read novels, and candy wrappers scattered all over. The only semblance of order is the small arrangement of makeup on my dresser, the majority of it stolen from Mom and some pushed on me by Mary. I can't even pinpoint the last time I wore any of it, except that it was Before.

Last night I slipped in and passed out cold, more tired than I've been in months—since before I started working at Duke's, even. CeCe warned me something like that would happen because of the adrenaline from experiencing the robbery.

Looking around my messy room in daylight, I wish I could sleep another twelve hours.

I kneel on the carpet and feel around in the far corner of the closet, behind clothes that don't fit and several single flip-flops, until my fingers grasp the old coffee can labeled PROBABLE ORPHAN FUND in black marker. If last night had gone as normal, I'd be adding my tips to the meager amount that's already there. I use a coffee can because of how satisfying it is to feel it grow heavier—usually right before it gets light again. Also because you need all kinds of paperwork to open a bank account, and I wouldn't even know where to start with that.

At the moment, the Probable Orphan Fund is a couple of twenties, a five, and a bunch of ones. I've had to dip into it more than a few times. Fast food, weed, chipping in for beer and wraps at the convenience store where CeCe knows the cashier, and the occasional dumb tee from the Goodwill.

But it was the rent that really did me in. Half a month's rent, which Mom promised was a singular occurrence. I haven't been able to bring it back up since.

I count the money again and shove the can back into its hiding place. I sit hunched against the closet door, keenly aware of the shower I still need to take. Then I lock eyes with Jason Newhouse, the bass player of Astral Kingdom, me and my best friend Mary's favorite band. I found their photo in a magazine in the hospital waiting room the first time Mom was hospitalized and carefully ripped it out. It's taped to the wall beside my pillow and surrounded with the highest concentration of glow-in-the-dark stars.

Mary was into Astral Kingdom first. When I finally listened past a couple of songs, I loved them, too. It was my idea to follow them on tour, to drive as far away and see as many new places as possible. Once I got the job at Duke's, it became more than just a possibility. Mary would record us, posting alongside her best fan art, and I'd become Jason Newhouse's muse. That was our plan.

Then I got into a fight with the girl Mary had just started dating. And expelled. And we haven't spoken since. Or, more specifically, I haven't answered her messages or calls, and then she stopped trying.

Jason Newhouse's shining brown eyes and chiseled jaw convey a mixture of disappointment and concern. For the skipped shower but also the misplaced rage. For fantasizing about stealing envelopes of money. For wishing my job had burned to the ground, and then panicking about finding a new one.

Jason Newhouse can honestly take his pick.

Anybody else would probably just be grateful to be alive after what happened. Whatever the appropriate response is when your evil boss gets robbed, I bet my coworkers have it and I don't.

I keep coming back to the money. As if there was something I could've done with it anyway.

Once, when I was alone in Mom's hospital room, I watched part of a show on the History Channel about how different versions of us exist in alternate realities. Somewhere in a parallel universe, another Minerva kept the money without anyone ever noticing and is counting her own Probable Orphan Fund right now. One giant step closer to her own perfect little apartment in New York City. Or Los Angeles. Or Montreal. Anywhere but Nautilus.

It's like the robbery showed me a glimpse of that alternate reality—the start of escaping a trap I didn't even know I was in.

Nicole knocks on my bedroom door. "Are you there? I was gonna visit Sunny soon."

I can't go to that place. Can't acknowledge its existence on the other side of town. I open my mouth to tell Nicole this, but the quiet closes in. Through the cheap board material of the door, I feel everything we're not saying in the moment. Everything I've been running from. First as a space cadet at work, and now as a mess—a disaster—at home.

Mom might say I'm too smart to think that's true. But I'm also too smart to believe there isn't truth to it.

"Last call to visit your mother," Nicole says.

Now it's my turn to pretend I can't hear.

CHAPTER SIX

When Duke's still doesn't reopen the next day, Nicole, who slept on the couch and shows no sign of leaving, tries to guilt me into going back to summer school. I explain that I've already missed the whole first week. I don't say how I never had any intention of returning.

Nicole's voice rushes at my back. "After everything your mother's done for you?"

Mom got me into Greater Nautilus High School, the same school she attended as a kid, through a special program for out-of-zone kids who each had to jump through flaming hoops in the form of grades, tests, and interviews.

Before that, she had me apply for scholarships at every private school within an hour of Nautilus. I barely remember middle school, but I remember the extra work she made me do. The essays, the vocabulary words, the test bubbles, and the endless tours of schools I'd only ever attend in my imagination. One of them made me take an IQ test, but we never got the results. It was like skipping a stone into dark water.

None of those private schools offered me a scholarship. But Mom was still convinced I was special; I was smart like her. It only made me feel worse.

I always suspected she pulled some strings at Greater Nautilus, talked to somebody she grew up with, even resorted to bribery. It didn't matter in the end. The county shut down the high school in the Point after deciding there weren't enough teenagers in this part of town to warrant a whole building.

Then Mom got sick, and everything imploded.

If she were next to me now, she'd snap that *I* got *myself* into the special program at Greater Nautilus, but for once Nicole is right. Mom did all that work so I wouldn't end up stuck here like her.

So I get dressed and wait for the bus.

School is more than thirty minutes away by bus. It'd be eight minutes by car, depending on the traffic or construction. I could probably drive the Boat, but it's low on gas, and I don't want to break into the Probable Orphan Fund.

Besides, I don't mind the bus. It's the closest thing to working like it should around here, like a faucet someone forgot to turn off.

The Beach Blossom lies at the end of the route. Or the beginning. Either way, it's good for getting a window seat, because the bus is empty when I board. It takes a roundabout way back to the main drag, avoiding all the "affordable housing," and slips farther into the woods before returning to the rest of the world.

I settle in for the view of the overgrown trees and bushes and wait for them to give way to water, then to the boardwalk where it's still intact. After that come the condos, about half of which aren't finished. Finally, what remains: a few smaller apartment buildings, houses, and businesses—somewhere in there Duke's—until the bus crosses the bridge over the canal.

For a second, the inside of the bus is filled with the light reflected off the water before entering a small no-man's-land of docks and shrubbery and a few gas stations. Nicer buildings and houses start to appear. The part people like Nicole jokingly refer to as civilization.

A voice inside me asks what the point is of going back to school. I can still turn around and go to CeCe's apartment—well, CeCe's mom's apartment, but she's usually either not home or zoning out to true crime in bed. CeCe would be pissed at me for waking her up before noon, but she'll forgive me quickly. Then I'd get to hang out with Large Marge instead of doing this.

The latter sounds more and more tempting, but I've taken too long to decide, and now the bus has arrived at school.

OUT OF HABIT, I head straight for the main office, where information is exchanged without the guilt that's unavoidable with teachers and counselors. The hallways are quiet, the air thin and moist and oddly cool despite the lack of air-conditioning.

Now that I'm here, this feels doable. Maybe I can, in fact, start over again.

I tell the woman at the front desk my name and that I was supposed to start two weeks ago. "Technically, a week and a half," I add, as if it makes one iota of difference.

"Hang on a second," she says. She eyes me up and down. "Are you Second Starts?"

I resent the assumption. But also her assumption is right, and I hate her a little bit for that as well. I look down at my outfit: cutoff shorts—actual jeans I cut above the knees that are now fraying admirably—and a thin cotton T-shirt with a watercolor of a mongoose on the front, my most prized dollar-bin clothing item.

She sets down the phone she was holding. "They'll have more information for you in the guidance office."

My Second Starts counselor is a woman with a fake tan, helmet hair, and a comically raspy voice that rattles the outdated papers on the bulletin board above her desk. She insists on being called Mrs. Delgado.

"Please always say 'Mrs.' Never say 'Ms.'" She emphasizes this as *Miz* while skimming my file on her computer screen, probably for the first time ever. Somewhere inside, among the data and pixels, is an alternate-reality Minerva Gutiérrez, a version they think they know, whose actions are of a lot more importance than those of the one sitting in this chair.

Minerva Gutiérrez: formerly gifted, currently poor, and a total degenerate.

Before everything changed, my favorite subjects were chemistry (I liked the balance of it), my debate elective, and sometimes language arts. Before everything changed, I was going to take AP classes. If I couldn't get into college in New York City, I'd go to school as far away as reasonably possible.

The plan was supposed to be Greater Nautilus High School, then college, then a job. I didn't realize how fragile the plan was all along, how comforting it was to have until I got in trouble. Then a piece was taken away, and the entire plan collapsed.

"Minerva," Mrs. Delgado intones, "what happened to your attendance?"

"I haven't been feeling well."

This feels true enough; I couldn't sleep, and then I found a sleeping pill in Mom's room, and it hit me like a hand forcing my head underwater. I remember that numb, wavy feeling just before the blissful loss of consciousness and yearn for it now.

"Well, I must say you look exhausted," she quips.

I bite down on a response; it feels like a trick invitation.

"You've missed quite a lot of days this summer term. All of them, as a matter of fact." She moves on, clicking through more information. She squints at the page as if to make sure of the number, then widens her eyes, impressed. "Absent sixty-two days in the past school year." She peers over at me expectantly.

"Yep."

She clicks again. "I remember you now. Assault and attempted robbery of a fellow student. You could've been charged for real, you know."

"I know." That's not really what happened, but I've learned with most adults it never helps to try and set things right, especially when it comes to one's own good name.

"I see you didn't attend the tutoring sessions during your expulsion period," she says. "Why?"

She means the tutoring sessions forced on me by the school district, intended to keep me caught up. These were scheduled at the Nautilus Point Library, two trailers back to back on a lot behind an older building that used to be a real library until the hurricane before last. The one time I went, the college student volunteer didn't know what a homonym was, which caused me to question the validity of the entire system. Mom would've come to the same conclusion.

Mrs. Delgado moves on while I'm still trying to figure out how to answer. She locks her hands over the desk. "I know you've been through a lot, Minerva. I hope, very much for your sake, we can find a place for you."

She waits for me to respond, but all I can think is that

Second Starts is supposed to be the place for me. Mom saw to it when she last met with the school. That, plus Mrs. Delgado is one of those people who uses names like punctuation marks.

"Yeah, me, too," I mumble.

She half nods as if that'll suffice. "We only want the best for all of our students from Nautilus Point. Give them the support they need to become productive members of society."

I could scream at the words, the lipstick smile, the fake reassuring tone. Why can't she just talk to me like a person instead of a brochure?

"Some people," she continues, "might be better suited for alternative programming."

At this my temples sting, which used to signal tears coming. "What's that mean? Alternative programming?"

"Well, the local Opportunity Center has a wonderful high school equivalency program, for instance."

A cold wave knocks me over. "Are you saying I have to drop out?"

"There are only so many resources we can provide in Second Starts. *Some people*," Mrs. Delgado repeats, her voice thinning, "just aren't a good fit."

The words are thick in my throat. "But I'm here. I'm here now."

She looks directly into my eyes. "I'm afraid it's too late."

All I can think about is Nicole, insisting that I haven't been trying. I clench my hands, containing the heat of what feels like all my seventeen years. Deep breaths. Count to ten, fifteen, twenty.

None of it makes a difference.

"Does this make sense," Mrs. Delgado asks, "what I'm saying to you?"

"No." I shake my head. The cold wave has turned me upside down. "I mean, yeah."

"Wonderful. I'll be sending some paperwork in the mail for your parents—I mean, whoever—to review. You take care."

CHAPTER SEVEN

I'm too sober. That's the problem.

To make matters worse, summer school lets out at the exact moment I leave the office. People flood the halls, nobody I recognize.

I try not to make eye contact as I traverse what feels like the longest hallway of my life. The last time I was here was my expulsion hearing, later downsized to suspension. It's nothing worth being all sentimental about, let alone remembering.

I spot Eli near one of the exit stairwells. For a moment, my brain short-circuits at seeing him outside of Duke's. The last time we saw each other, we had weapons shoved in our faces and were made to run for our lives. He sees me at the same time, an expression on his face I can't read.

Before working at Duke's, I didn't know Eli existed, much less that we attended the same school. But in that three-month overlap between getting hired *and* expelled, I realized he had been all over the place. Running track, doing sound for every school production, filing in at assemblies. The latter is how I learned he's going to college in the fall on full scholarship.

"Hey," he says in his customary minimal way. Maybe he's in a hurry, and maybe he's desperate to get away from me.

My best friend Mary—before we stopped talking—said Eli seems uninterested because I've already projected to the Universe that I don't deserve his love.

I told her I just want to kiss him and how none of this is about love.

"In any case," she insisted, "you're doing something to signal you're not interested. I'm sure of it."

What I didn't (and still don't) understand: if Eli Ronan looks through me like a heat ripple in the distance, and it's my fault for making it happen, does that make it better or worse than if it weren't my fault?

He's wearing a white T-shirt with a black cartoon outline of a disembodied brain in massive headphones. The contrast of his tan forearms in pale cotton, specifically *not* a Duke's uniform, has all my attention.

I fold my arms, as if Eli can somehow tell I was kicked out of school five minutes ago for not being a good fit.

Instead of what I was going to say, which is something about Duke's, I blurt, "You're in summer school? Didn't you graduate?" Eli doesn't seem like the type to have failed anything.

"It's for college credit," he explains.

Of course it is.

He checks his phone for the time and starts walking again. "What's up?"

I try to keep up with him in the stairwell. "I was hoping you'd tell me what's up." My eyes catch on the delicate pattern of birthmarks on the back of his neck as we make our way down the last flight of stairs. "Is Duke's closed now?"

"Oh." He slows down and looks at me like I only just

appeared. "Yeah. Sorry. Just for a couple days. We should be back up and running by Friday."

"Should I show up then?"

"When, Friday?" He looks at his phone again. "Yeah. I'm pretty sure you'll be on opening shift."

"Opening?" I repeat, holding back a sneer. The tips are nonexistent that early in the day.

He shrugs. "We need somebody at that time."

"Do you think I'll get any more evening shifts?"

"You gotta take it up with Anthony." Eli speeds up again as we reach the ground floor, but I race ahead and hold open the door to outside. The sunshine hits us both.

"Hey." I let the door slam behind me.

"Hey."

"We got robbed the other day."

"I know," he shoots back. Then he kind of smiles, which makes me smile. Soon we're both smiling at each other about the robbery. With some notable exceptions, including the robbery itself, it's the strangest moment of my life.

"I tried looking for you that night," he says. We're standing at the gate right outside the doors, slightly jostled as more people stream out of the building around us. He nods, his lips slightly parted. Just a hint of that chip in his front tooth, which I've always found intriguing. "You didn't have a ride, right? I was wondering how you got home."

"Huh?" The heat of the day hits me at once. "You were?"

"Yeah. Were you okay?"

Not really. "I think so. What about you?"

He nods slowly, as if surprised to be doing it. "Actually, I don't know."

Actually, I don't know.

What?

Eli pulls a pair of headphones from his bag as large as the ones depicted on his shirt. He says, "If you ever want to talk about it . . ."

"Sounds like I'm the one who should be saying that to you."

I think the joke might've gone too far, but he actually laughs.

"At least you didn't have to tell him the register was off." He slips the headphones around his neck and with his other hand checks his phone again. The whole time, he glances back at me as if to make sure I'm still there. It's like entering a room for the thousandth time but using a brand-new entrance. Every angle looks different. I feel like laughing again.

I watch him make his way toward the student parking lot. Was he flirting with me or just being nice? Was it both? He offered to talk.

Why would anyone lie about that?

CHAPTER EIGHT

This summer was supposed to be my second chance. But as I stand outside the school, any concerns I may have had about feeling exposed or running into anyone else dwindles to the reality that I've been away from school for too long and have become a nobody.

The hair, I think. *Maybe no one recognizes me with this hair.*

But no. Mary bleached my hair *before* the expulsion. Before I attacked Vera. Before Mom had to come down to the school and deal with the extra stress, which was all my fault.

Before before before.

It wasn't just getting expelled—it was the way things were going for a while. When I cut class and sometimes got Mary to cut with me. The drinking, and times like when I rolled a clumsy joint with her dad's special Cuban cigars, and we almost got caught. Or maybe her parents did find out and Mary never told me, which is exactly the kind of thing she would do.

The thought of this is even more embarrassing.

Before we stopped talking, Mary mentioned taking

summer art classes at the community college, so I probably won't run into her around here like I did Eli. I make the leap and text her.

Hi.

She answers right away. Stranger!

The exclamation point seems friendly enough coming from her. But why would she act as if I haven't ghosted her for months?

Suddenly I want to give up and put the phone away. I want to delete the conversation, just like the unanswered texts from her a while back. At the same time, the possibility of Mary not hating me fills me with hope, and a kind of dumb bravery, too.

Before I change my mind, I type I'm sorry and hit SEND.

For...

All right. She doesn't hate me, but she hasn't forgotten that I beat up the girl who eventually became her girlfriend. She definitely hasn't forgotten that I stopped answering her messages and calls when I was expelled almost three months ago.

Never mind... I start to type, then delete it. I have to think of something better than that. Mary is the only person at school I told about my mother being in the hospital. Out of everyone I know, she's the most likely to understand about how messed up my job is. Mary will get it—she'll tell me to quit, and even though I can't, it'll be satisfying to have someone say it to me anyway.

Before I can generate a real answer, Mary texts again.

How are you...

Even though it's Mary and therefore inevitable, someone asking after my well-being for the second time in five minutes makes me light-headed. I become an actual space cadet, floating, flying above the things I don't want to talk about.

I hastily write Fine?, adding a bunch more question marks for emphasis, because even though I'm not okay, Mary doesn't know the half of it. And it should stay that way.

Hows your mom? Mary adds, Is she still in the hospital?

We're at three questions now. Exactly what I was avoiding.

Sure enough, the phone rings. I almost drop it on the pavement. Around me, the summer school crowd has started to thin.

"Finally," Mary says when I answer.

"I'm sorry," I say.

"You already said that," she taunts. "So where've you been?"

There's so much to tell her that it bottlenecks: my horrible job, the robbery, being stuck with Nicole indefinitely when I just wish I could leave.

Now, getting kicked out of school.

"Just working," I say.

"At the Ice Creamery, right? That place is so cute." She trails off, and then I hear other voices behind her. They swell and fade, as if she just walked through a loud room and then out. My stomach sinks.

Again, though, Mary doesn't wait for me to answer. A door clicks shut in the background, and her voice is close and serious. "Why didn't you answer any of my calls?"

I should've known she wouldn't let me off that easy.

"After I got in trouble . . ." The truth feels like picking out a splinter. I leave part of it in. "I didn't know if there was a point."

"What?" Mary scoffs, as if I'm a thrift-store dress that

doesn't fit after all, and right away I wish I hadn't answered the way I did and that I'd said something vague but true like *I've been busy* or *My mother's been dying*.

Mary knows some of it, but the worst I've kept to myself.

"Of course there's a point," she says. "You disappeared on me, though."

"I know."

"You know I need you, right? Here? On planet Earth?"

Astral Kingdom starts playing in the distance, and that voice from before is there. A few of them. Laughter trickles into the space on Mary's end. I wonder if she's going to mention it or act like it's not there. It's the middle of the day, and both her parents are likely working. That used to be me, coming over to an empty house.

"Who's there?" I ask.

"Just Vera and a couple other people." Pause. "You want to come by?"

I look around me. There's nobody watching, of course. The campus has mostly cleared out. "But they all hate me."

I freeze, not quite believing I just said that. Mary better not expect me to explain.

"Nobody hates you," she says, predictably. I'd bet the entire Probable Orphan Fund that she's grimacing, her mouth all wavy from trying to contain a lie. She's terrible at it.

Which means they *do* hate me, my old friends and their friends. The entire fucking world.

When everything went down, Mary and Vera were just fooling around. I've gotten along with all the other girls Mary's dated, but Vera was the only one who didn't like me. She's also the richest.

There was a rumor going around—so suddenly it had to be true—that Vera called me weird. Not good weird like Mary, with her gothy cottage-core aesthetic and goal to be the first queer neurosurgeon-fashion designer on the cover of *TIME* magazine.

She meant crazy weird. Off. Psycho.

So I went psychotic on her. I found her and punched until my shoulder gave out, which was somewhere between two and three punches. By the third one, Vera got enough leverage to pivot around and grab a chunk of my hair, and then someone broke it up (not Mary, who wasn't there).

Mary told Vera I was dealing with my mom being in the hospital again, asked her to tell people it wasn't as bad as it looked. Mary *believed* it wasn't as bad as it looked.

Except—I was there—it *was* that bad. It took Mom making a trip to the school and begging the administration for my reentry, which usually wasn't granted in cases of violence. Just poor grades, absenteeism, and excessive poverty, which luckily were also relevant.

After that meeting with the school, Mom ended up right back in the hospital. The timing made it seem like she'd been discharged for the sole purpose of saving my ass yet again. Which I hated.

The thing is, I don't even remember the moment I lost it. All I remember are the moments after, when I hid in the girls' bathroom, my hands and face burning, the ammonia smell I couldn't tell apart from the panic flooding my lungs. I could barely breathe by the time the school security guard found me.

To top everything off, someone claimed I tried to steal Vera's jewelry, too. Which was a lie, of course, but by then

I didn't care anymore. What I *did* do was bad enough on its own.

"Min?"

"I have to go. I can't come by."

"Oh—" She interrupts herself to call out to the voice in the background, which has shown up again. The door shuts loudly. Mary says to me, "You have to work?"

I make a pathetic noise of agreement in the back of my throat. I think maybe it's my missing tears, but it's a false alarm.

"What's going on with you?" she asks, her voice low with meaning.

"Nothing. Honestly. Just tired. And working a lot."

"Ugh. You sound like my mother."

"Yeah, me and your mom. Two peas in a pod." I almost say *your rich mom*, but we just got on speaking terms again.

Mary's quiet on the other end. "So when will you come over?"

"I'm sorry."

"You already said that," she whispers.

I promise to be around soon. We hang up, and I sink back down to earth. Real earth.

Things are probably better this way. But Mary doesn't understand—not this time or any other time I've attempted to explain. It's the same as dealing with customers at the ice cream stand when they don't want to pay in cash. The same as the teachers. The same as the school psychologist, who I only saw once.

Whom I only saw once. Mom's voice. *Whom.*

That day with the school psychologist, I tried to say how hard it was to find control, how the anger would drag me down until I forgot everything outside of it. I tried to describe the chaos in my head, first loud and explosive, then quiet, the noise seeping out little by little. Until there was nothing left. Kind of like an illness.

I tried to explain. But nothing I said felt like enough. In fact, it usually made things worse.

So I stopped trying.

CHAPTER NINE

Duke's Ice Creamery reopens on a weekday morning, the slowest possible time. True to his word, Eli texts my schedule for the next two weeks early Friday morning.

See you soon, he adds. It's a new entry to our growing lexicon of awkwardness.

I stare at the screen, confused by the sudden density in my chest. I can't tell if it's excitement at hearing from Eli, dread at the idea of going back to work, or both.

Anthony is in the worst mood I've ever seen. He manages to count the register money and give me the evil eye at the same time. Like it's my fault he doesn't trust me with simple math.

"Would you wipe that look off your face?" he finally blurts. He places the last bills into the register. "A thousand people would kill just to have a job."

I clench my teeth and fight the urge to react. Why do adults always say that, So-and-So would *kill* to have whatever shitty thing I have? I'm supposed to be grateful. Grateful to show up and count ice cream cones, measure and distribute toppings into bins without spilling. To wipe down all the melted ice cream somebody missed during the last shift, a job made more difficult than usual because of the unexpected three-day closing. I'm supposed to thank the heavens I get to mix the buckets of water and powder that become the base for Duke's milkshakes—famous throughout the region, though almost no one knows of their disgusting, gelatinous origin—a task that now reminds me of that one pervert cop every time I have to do it.

To make matters worse, Jordan shows up early to catch up on cleaning and inventory.

She calls from the mouth of the walk-in freezer, "That's just her usual face, Tony. You're glad to be back, aren't you, Min?"

They both stare, and I realize they're expecting me to answer.

"Of course," I mutter.

This shift is supposed to be just me and Eli, but he's not here yet, a rare occurrence that worsens Anthony's foul mood about the robbery. He sets his dagger eyes on my first few orders to make sure the scoops aren't oversized. He checks my math as I count out the change, then hands it to the customers himself, all fake smiles.

In between customers, my task of the moment is to transfer the vanilla—scraping the last of the ice cream from one tub and adding it to the top of the next. As I smash and smear the ice cream, I fantasize about doing the same to Anthony's face. I imagine taking the blunt handle of the metal spatula and jabbing him in his cold blue eyes, punching his sunburnt nose.

"Watch this one at the register." Anthony's talking to Jordan but looking at me. "Don't let it happen again."

Jordan waits until he leaves the room to speak. "He's right. After what happened the other day, we can't afford to be careless." She pulls out a fresh box of cake cones from a lower shelf along the wall.

I roll my eyes. I can't help it. "How does Anthony getting robbed mean *we* have to be more careful?"

Jordan gapes at me as if I'd screamed all of this directly into her face. "Don't you care about your job?"

"I care about getting paid." I shut up, lest I further incriminate myself with Jordan, who actually aspires to be the boss's favorite. It's sick how badly she wants to take Eli's job when he leaves for college in the fall. Although nobody here tells me anything, it's clear she's gunning for it. So far, Anthony hasn't indicated whether it'll be her or Jamira, who's worked here even longer.

Not that it makes any difference—Anthony will probably just hire another boy to make sure we all know our place.

Watching Jordan, I feel like there should be more to life than counting cones until it's time to stop.

DURING MY SHIFT, every single customer asks about the robbery and alleged fire. I've figured out by now that the fire is a complete fabrication, likely kept alive by that nosy ramen-haired woman.

"Is it true it was an inside job?" asks a guy with blond dreadlocks and a picked-red face. A regular who only orders coffee ice cream milkshakes.

I let the change fall into his hand.

"Guess what." I point to Jordan at the other end of the counter, who's unwrapping a roll of quarters into the register. "She knows exactly what's going on. You should wait a few minutes and then definitely ask her."

"For real?" he squeaks. "Okay."

The next customers, a brother and sister who always share an order, ask soon after that.

"Did they find it?" the brother blurts. I hand him their usual order of two different-flavored scoops in a medium cup. The boy, whose T-shirt says *it's not that serious*, is draped over the bike they seem to share.

"What are you talking about?" I say, playing space cadet. It's become my go-to response after several hours of people asking the same questions.

"The treasure," he says, waving his plastic spoon and relishing every second of my interest. "It's, like, money or gold or something."

I fold my arms over the counter and watch the two of them, unsure if this is just another fabrication.

The sister tugs on the back of his shirt and speaks in a flat, bored voice as if I'm not there. "I bet she doesn't know. Told you you shouldn't have said nothing."

"I guess," he says.

My face gets warm. "Don't know what?"

The urge to storm off strikes again. But they're kids and don't know any better. They're not someone who's trying to teach me a lesson. Keeping this in mind, I try again. "I've never heard about treasure being hidden here."

"Grown-ups hate talking about it." The sister angles for a perfect spoonful of ice cream. "It's not nice to keep secrets like that, though."

"I agree," I tell her. "It's probably just a rumor, though, right?"

"A rumor?"

"Like a story someone made up."

"I know what a rumor is," she answers heavily. "And no, it's not just a story. It's real."

At this point, my pretend confusion turns genuine. They're regulars, but I can't remember if I've ever served them myself. Kids this age will stick around Duke's for hours on a nice day, with its too-big lot and free ice cream samples. Anthony says we have to tell them to leave if they're not spending money, but nobody follows that rule.

I check over my shoulder for Jordan. It turns out she isn't in the room at all. Habit makes me move on to the cameras. Counter, freezer, toppings station.

If Anthony cares, I'll find a way to deal.

"Wait here," I tell them, then fix a duplicate order: one scoop of peanut-butter-chocolate and one of marshmallow fluff. I hand the second cup to the sister, whose eyes widen.

"The treasure," I say. "How do you know about it?"

She snatches the cup from me. "We already told you."

"Huh?"

"Grown-ups hate talking about it. That's how I know."

They wobble off with the bike and their ice cream. I stare after them. What did they mean by "treasure"? What are adults telling, or not telling, these kids?

"Wow," Jordan calls from the back, where she's arranged a handful of premade cakes to be decorated. "You figured out how to get them to leave. Good job."

Unsure if she's referring to the free ice cream or speculation on treasure, I wave her off. "I used up my complimentary order of the day. Got a bunch saved up." Which I haven't taken advantage of in at least a month, around the time I fully realized I was sick of ice cream.

She materializes from behind the cake freezer. "You know they don't roll over, right?"

The conversation is cut short when a family with a double stroller hurtles toward the wrong end of the counter. I take a deep breath. Jordan pats my shoulder, charm bracelet jingling. "You're up. I'm just here to decorate cakes."

"I thought that was Jamira's job."

She shrugs, but there's a tiny smile on her face when she walks away.

WHEN ANTHONY'S AROUND, the only real escape is the employee bathroom, where I have a specific routine. First I check the closet-sized bathroom from top to bottom for cameras, which takes about thirty seconds. Then I read over the multiple signs on the bathroom wall.

IF YOU SPRINKLE WHEN YOU TINKLE, PLEASE BE NEAT AND WIPE THE SEAT.

ONLY NUMBER 1 ALLOWED.

!!!!DO NOT FLUSH YOUR GIRL STUFF!!!!

All in green marker, slanted, boxy handwriting on loose leaf and fixed to the pocked wall with electric tape. All signed, *Thank you, Management :)*

I sit on the closed toilet seat lid and try to ground myself in the moment. Unfortunately, the moment is insufferable and unworthy of my effort. It's a shame I can't stay in here forever avoiding the others.

Avoiding *him.*

At some point, I gather the strength to dive back into the mess. When I leave the bathroom, I run into Eli slipping in through the side door. He's setting down a massive leather bag.

"Sorry I'm late," he says.

I think he's talking to me until Anthony appears from behind the cake freezer and says, "Don't let it happen again."

Anthony stalks away, his keys crunching in his hand. Which means he's heading out to his car and—ideally— away from here. The air in the room decompresses.

Eli wipes off his neck with a paper towel. He's not wearing his glasses and seems to be missing his visor. Part of me enjoys witnessing him in this scattered state, even though he's been nice to me the last few days.

He breaks the silence—"The schedule's up; did you see?"—and I realize I've been staring at him.

I scramble to check the dry-erase board Anthony mounts in the back near the big sink. There, I discover that every single shift of mine for the next two weeks is opening. More late mornings with Anthony. On top of that, I have even fewer hours than last week. First I lose several days of hours and tips, and now this. I go back to wishing I stole the envelope myself and started my life over.

The only silver lining is that most of my upcoming shifts are with Eli.

When I get back to the front, he's already arranged frozen waffles for an ice cream sandwich. I kind of hate him: he's been here fewer than five minutes and has already started an order.

"Did you get screwed on hours, too?" I ask.

"He's all messed up about the robbery," Eli answers without looking away from the waffle iron.

"Sure. It's *just* the robbery."

"You've got a point." He removes the sandwich from the iron and wraps it in wax paper. A small line is already forming outside. "No, I asked for this shift."

My cheeks light up. There's no way Eli's implying that I'm the reason for his own dramatic schedule change, but the fact that it crosses my mind anyway—that I'm even noticing how many shifts we have together over the next two weeks—is equal parts invigorating and embarrassing.

I pretend to notice something disgusting on one of the

freezers, despite the customer already waiting behind whoever ordered the sandwich. They don't need to catch me
blushing, either.

I expect Eli to be annoyed with me for slacking off, but
toward the end of the shift, he says, "I want to give you
something."

My stomach flips, like I'm driving too fast on an unpaved
road. "Really?"

He hands me a glossy postcard from his back pocket. The
photo on the front is of a graffitied water tower beneath a
cloudy sky. In plain white font, it lists a bunch of names I
don't know the meanings of. *Breaker 7. William Flowers.
The Qutt.* The address at the bottom is in Brooklyn.

"I'm doing the sound for this show," he says. "It's going
to pay next to nothing, but it looks good. I know hip-hop's
not really your thing—"

"How do you know?" I don't hate some of what CeCe
plays, which is entirely rap except for a few random songs
by the band Queen.

His eyes dart over to my bag hanging in the employee
closet, dotted with Astral Kingdom pins. "Yeah," he says. "I
shouldn't assume. It's just that the more people I get to come
to the show, the more likely they are to ask me back. I've
been kind of stressed there won't be enough people."

"Oh. I had no idea you had another job."

"It's more like an . . . internship."

"You must really like doing it, then."

"I do." He gestures at the schedule. "It does mean more
random nights, so more openings."

I fold the postcard into my back pocket, snug beside
my outdated poverty phone. The embarrassment of what
I thought he'd wanted compared to what it turned out to

be—a favor for his internship—stings. More opening shifts so he'll have nights off. Maybe that's why he was talking to me out of nowhere, even the part about asking if I was okay.

"So you think you can make it?" he asks. "I might be able to get you in for free."

"Don't worry about it." I jump off the freezer. "Maybe. I'll see."

CHAPTER TEN

More than a week after the robbery, two detectives from the county show up at the Beach Blossom. Nicole has to give up on cleaning for the moment, but she's too embarrassed by the mess I left, so she tells the detectives we've been spraying for ants. We stand on the walkway.

"You're her mother?" they ask Nicole, like a confirmation.

"I'm her aunt."

I give her a dirty look. "Cousin."

The detectives nod, not caring about this information. "Did you notice any suspicious activities the day of the robery?"

I tell them no. According to CeCe, though, suspicious activity is all over if you're just paying attention.

"What about in general?" one of them prompts. "You know. In the area."

Duke's, the unofficial gateway between Nautilus Point and civilization, both geographically and spiritually. Because everybody's a sucker for ice cream when it's 95 degrees in the shade. If you ask me, there's no end to the suspicious activity: the creepy single rich guys, the construction workers on uppers (another tidbit from CeCe), the condo squatters, and basically anyone over the age of five who orders birthday cake–flavored ice cream.

The detectives are still waiting. *As a matter of fact, yes,* I want to say. *My boss is a creep, and so are most of his friends, who just happen to be your coworkers.*

"No," I say. "Nothing different than usual."

"After the robbery happened. Did you call the police?"

Nicole raps her pale pink nails on the door. "Can't you look that up?" For a second, I almost like her. Then I remember she's wearing Mom's dress—black with red poppies, something I'd never have the guts to wear but don't want anyone else wearing, either—and the positive feeling toward her fizzles back into nonexistence.

"I just assumed someone else called," I tell the detectives, hoping to move things along. "I don't—"

"She was obviously traumatized," Nicole interrupts, irritable and distracted by the warped apartment door, which won't stop flying open in the wind. "She's a victim, too, in case you couldn't tell."

I turn and squint at her, surprised. Is she actually on my side?

But even Nicole can't delay the inevitable. I have to describe what happened. By now, the moment I held the envelope has played approximately one thousand times in my head. I tell my version of the story as quickly as I can. Carefully. Like crossing the street. But I leave out the part about me holding the envelope.

When one of the detectives asks what I was busy doing beforehand, the word *cleaning* materializes from my vocal cords. Nicole side-eyes this answer but doesn't comment.

"Right," says the other detective. They finish up their notes. "You call if you see or remember anything funny, all right?"

"Anything?" I repeat, thinking again about the gross cop and Anthony's closed-door meetings, which I'm guessing don't count.

After the detectives leave, Nicole goes back to dusting all the surfaces throughout the front of the apartment as if she completely forgot about the interrogation. Which makes sense, since she wasn't the one being interrogated.

"Hey." I approach her as she rubs cobwebs off of the wall behind the TV. She's humming a tune I don't recognize, maybe something from church, if she still goes. I don't ask.

She doesn't turn from what she's doing. "What's up?"

"Thanks for being there while I talked to them."

"I work at a law firm. Force of habit." She continues scrubbing.

Is this her backward way of calling me a criminal? "Right. Anyway, thanks."

"You're welcome."

I watch as a spider narrowly escapes Nicole's wreckage. "You've been sleeping here every night, right?"

"Yes. I told Sunny I'd watch you. You clearly need watching."

I give Nicole the finger, even though she isn't looking at me. All her cleaning has been out in the living room and kitchen area. She hasn't really touched Mom's room, with the obvious exception of stealing clothes.

Mom would understand how I feel about the robbery. Scared one minute, envious the next. Full of hate for my boss.

She didn't really want me to take the job in the first place—that push came straight from Nicole—but it didn't stop her from asking for rent money soon after I started getting paid. She asked when she saw my off-the-books pay, plus tips. She was watching TV and eating sunflower seeds. At first I thought I'd misheard her. There was a lurching in my chest I didn't understand as I told her, *Yes, sure, I guess.*

Later that night, I found CeCe and got higher than I'd ever been before—or tried to, until that feeling in my chest was small enough for me to rip out and leave on the ground.

AFTER MY SHIFT, I come home to find Nicole on the couch, painting her toenails. The color is soft gold and belongs to Mom. It's one of hundreds of bottles. Nail polish became a hobby of hers after being hospitalized so often—something about feeling exposed in front of strangers.

"Don't you have a life of your own?" I ask Nicole. I mean to say a *house*, but I don't correct it. I know it sounds cruel, and I don't care. First the dress and now the nail polish.

She closes the bottle. "You really shouldn't talk to me that way. I'm not *your* cousin. I'm your *mother's* cousin. So you should consider—"

"Okay." I continue toward the hall.

"Wait," she calls. She sets down the bottle and plucks another from the shoebox of colors. Clear for the top coat, the realistic image of a single diamond on the label. "I'm staying."

"Staying where? On the couch?"

She unscrews the next bottle. "No, here at this apartment. I just applied to take over the lease."

I turn and stare. A memory punches me in the face, hits my cheekbone especially hard. I'm a little kid, picking up those nail polish bottles one by one and shaking them to hear the secret *click* of the ball bearings. Back when there weren't so many bottles and Mom didn't care what her feet looked like. She is laughing and kissing the top of my head. Still letting me mess with her stuff.

"Min? Are you going to say something?" Nicole's actually still painting her nails. I could knock the bottle out of her hands. I could throw it all the way to the ocean from here.

She keeps talking, painting. "I'm going to visit her again soon. Thought you'd want to come."

I keep my voice level, though my chest feels tighter and the air in my lungs is thin, like I've been climbing a mountain. "Why didn't you tell me any of this?"

"Which part? About visiting Sunny?"

"No." I step toward the coffee table and snatch the gold polish—it really is one of Mom's best shades—and tuck it into my pocket. "*No.* About moving in."

"I just told you now." She shakes her head. "I thought you knew this was coming. It just makes sense."

"But you didn't *say*—"

"I don't have time for head games, Min."

She blows air in the direction of her feet, looking again like Mom, and I truly hate her for it.

WHEN I WALK into Mom's room, I half expect it to be visibly stripped. But it's the same as last time: dark and cool and still, no matter the temperature outside, with a relentless moisture in the air like bad breath. There's a thick rug she placed on top of the ancient Beach Blossom carpet the color of marigolds—her favorite—and several blankets folded at the end of her bed with its thick red comforter. The fabric smells more like detergent and less like Mom, a scent I can't describe but nonetheless makes me angry with its three-month absence.

The last time I was in here with her, I'd just been expelled. I remember waiting for her to talk about the expulsion, how I'd ruined her lifelong plans for my success, how hard she worked. *She* worked.

But she didn't yell or even say she was disappointed. For the first time, she was silent.

When I finally got the nerve to bring it up myself, she said, "I can't afford to be mad."

She was referring to the stress. The kind the doctors and nurses kept bringing up and sending home information about in pamphlets. *Stress: The Silent Killer.* It sounded like one of CeCe's Thai kickboxing movies (a brief obsession of hers).

We never got back to it. Mom dealt with my expulsion in her new, stress-free way, and then she was admitted to the hospital again. The timing was like a confirmation that my expulsion had broken her.

I probably put my mother in the hospital.

Now I slide open the closet door to the sound of hangers clicking together. The wardrobe has been utterly pillaged by Nicole, as I expected, but the remaining clothes include some of Mom's favorites—a few jackets, some with matching skirts; jewel-toned sweaters. There's also a stretchy, yellow-striped embroidered dress—definitely for work. She wore it on a date once, when I was super little. Nicole babysat.

The fact that Nicole left everything good when she cleaned this place out like an imperialist is just proof of her terrible taste.

I leave the clothes where they are and transition to searching for pills, specifically one called Lumata, which I first took months ago on the night Mary bleached my hair. I came home to find Mom passed out to public access TV. I tried waking her up to show her my hair, but she wouldn't budge or even crack open an eyelid. She was a light sleeper before getting really sick, and swore to only take the pills if she needed them. She must have really needed Lumata, and it must have really worked.

I wanted to hate Lumata when Mom was too unconscious to look at my hair, and again when she was too groggy to notice the next morning. Instead, I found the little orange bottle among all the other medications, plucked one pill for myself, and fell in love.

Tonight, I hit the jackpot in Mom's dresser. Digging behind some holey black stockings, I find a Lumata bottle with four and a half remaining capsules.

Satisfied, I slip out to grab my headphones—there are certain Astral Kingdom songs that go especially well with a gradual loss of consciousness—and cover up with the only clean hoodie I can find.

I'm settling down to take my pill on the walkway outside the apartment, legs dangling over the railing, when CeCe appears on the stairs. "Mini-Mart."

I stare at her, the pill so present in the center of my palm it already irritates my skin.

"I need your help," she says.

I tumble the pill around in my pocket, then leave it alone so my sweat doesn't turn it to paste. "Yes?"

"I need a ride."

"No."

"Please? It's not even that far. Just over by Neptune Heights." I wait for CeCe to use her old standby, *there and back*, but she just waits, looking as if she asked for a ride to the hospital instead of some random house on the other side of Nautilus to buy drugs.

"I'm only supposed to use the Boat for emergencies."

"I'll give you fifty bucks. Plus gas. Full tank."

I stand up. "Call me Mini-Mart again, and the offer is void."

"Sure." She pauses, giving me and my hoodie a once-over. "Aren't you kinda warm in that?"

I shrug, not wanting to explain how I prefer to be sweaty and covered and holding my pill, untouched in my pocket. If I'm being honest, I know CeCe won't stop with the nickname. The gas and money are what make me walk down to my mother's car. Already I can feel the unmistakable texture of bills between my fingers. Money always wins out.

Anyone who says otherwise is lying.

CHAPTER ELEVEN

Neptune Heights is ugly and beautiful at the same time. It has what is the technically oldest marina in Nautilus and old bungalows on narrow, bumpy streets. The seagulls are plentiful, and the sound of the tide carries on the wind. There isn't a beach, but the ground is still damp and gray, like a T-shirt you can't wash the sweat stains out of. It's one of Mom's favorite spots.

The house we come to is on a run-down but slightly more suburban-looking street where the houses are the same except for their different, faded colors. Only a couple are still boarded up and spray-painted from the last big storm—first with warnings, then graffiti. A long-dead wreath hangs on the doorway.

CeCe tells me not to park in front of the house but down the street instead. She cracks open the passenger door, Large Marge springs out from the backseat, and out the door first.

"I'll be back," she says.

I sit there in the darkness, thinking of all the reasons she might leave me stranded, intentionally or unintentionally.

I should've asked for more money.

After a few minutes, there's a knock on the window, and

CeCe is peering into the car urgently. She chin-points up the street. "He wants you to come inside."

"Who?"

"My contact," she mumbles.

"I'm fine out here."

"No, it's . . . can you just come inside?" She winces and shuts her eyes at her own begging. "We're just going to sit around for a bit, smoke, do our thing, and be on our merry way."

When I still don't move, she says, "You being out here makes me look bad."

Without waiting for an answer, she stalks back down the sidewalk. I follow her onto a porch covered in dust and red paint chips. A tired-looking woman is waiting at the door. She wears a shaggy blonde ponytail and a tank dress that hangs off her thin frame like a spiderweb about to break.

"Sweater," she says to me with a flat sigh and no hint of a question. There's a whining sound coming from upstairs, a kid or a dog, that she tilts her head up to once, then chooses to ignore.

I glance over at CeCe for an explanation as to why *she* doesn't have to take off any of her clothes. She looks away.

Biting the inside of my mouth, I take off my hoodie and hand it to the woman. This leaves me in a T-shirt I cut the sleeves off at some point earlier in the summer, because it was donated by a church Mom and I don't even attend—we're both agnostic—and I needed to deform it before accepting.

The woman still doesn't move.

CeCe gestures that I should lift my shirt.

"What?" I ask, too loudly.

Wire, she mouths.

At least she has the decency not to watch. The woman nods and drifts upstairs, still holding my hoodie, which I just now realize still contains my pill. I think about running after her, but in the end I don't do anything. She doesn't look like somebody I'd want to randomly fight.

CeCe and I walk down a hallway lit only by a TV at the end. We enter a living room containing a giant L-shaped couch and several huge mirrors. On the opposite wall, a big-screen TV plays cartoons.

An older guy and a boy of maybe fourteen are sitting on the couch, watching TV. Neither of them looks up when we walk in.

"This is my girl, Mini-Mart," CeCe says. Her voice sounds different. Heavier.

The old guy takes his time tearing his eyes off the massive TV screen before he smiles up at us, and the kid keeps watching. The colors blink and change all over the walls every time a different character shows up.

"Mini-Mart . . . ," the old guy coos, as if it's the most exotic name he's ever heard. He gazes at me with eyes that are almost entirely pupil. Then he takes one of my hands and kisses it.

I sit as far from him as possible, at the end of the couch, where I cross my arms and do my normal routine of trying not to pay attention to what's happening beside me. CeCe sits in the corner of the couch, a buffer in her too-loose tee that she's still allowed to wear. Large Marge trots in belatedly and attempts to climb onto the couch between us. CeCe guides her down and scolds her more firmly than usual.

"I told you not to bring that dog around next time," the old guy complains.

"She doesn't like being left alone," CeCe says just over her breath. I've never seen her talk to anyone in this specific way, like she doesn't want any trouble.

"If she scratches my furniture, you're buying it brand-new."

"I know."

The old guy opens a gigantic Tupperware, and the room instantly smells like the time Mom ran over a skunk. The air shifts from the sheer weight of the weed.

The kid lights a blunt, and CeCe passes it over to me. I say no, but she gives me a look that says, *Don't be weird*, so I take the smallest drag I can. It still kicks me in the chest.

She's going to sell it fast.

"Aren't you Sunny's kid?" the old guy asks all of a sudden. The cartoon switches colors, temporarily shining a spotlight on all of us. "She wasn't doing so great, last I heard."

"How do you know my mother?" I ask, against CeCe widening her eyes at me to stop. Even though *he* was the one to bring up the subject, CeCe's "contact" or whoever he is.

He chuckles. "I know everybody."

"That's not really an ans—"

"All right, okay," CeCe says. Her voice at this point is low enough to feel in the precious leather couch cushions. Large Marge lifts her head and sets it back down on my foot.

"Did you know," CeCe asks, "Mini-Mart works over at the Ice Creamery?"

The old guy sits forward, intrigued. "Oh, yeah? A Duke's girl?"

I cringe at the familiar title.

"You heard about the robbery the other day, right? She was there." CeCe points at me, like there's anyone else in the room she could mean.

I bite the inside of my cheek. The blunt has baked my tongue into a brick. Why are we still talking about me, anyway?

"They didn't find it, did they?" CeCe asks, more to the old guy than to me.

I remember the kids on the bike and blurt, "The treasure?"

He bursts into laughter. CeCe laughs nervously, and the kid turns away from the TV screen. Everyone looks over at me like I just walked in.

"Treasure," the old guy repeats. "I guess you could call it that."

The blunt dies. The kid walks over to one of the windows and opens it wide, even though the air-conditioning still hums in the background. Once back on the couch, he changes the cartoon to a video game.

CeCe licks her lips furiously, opens her backpack, and moves things around. I think she might be nervous. "Tell her what you told me."

"Well, if she doesn't already know—"

"Come on." Her eyes gleam. "Tell her."

"Tell me what?" I interrupt, but of course they don't answer right away.

"Sweetheart." The old guy reaches into a jar and rolls a joint this time. My lungs ache just watching this. His hands move sloppily in the dark, like he doesn't care who has to clean the mess in the morning. Like how I started acting when I was alone during Mom's hospital visits, before Nicole wormed her way in. "Your little boss has a lot of friends."

"Yeah," I say, thinking of the cops. "So?"

"When you have a lot of friends, you end up doing a lot of favors. And vice versa." He takes a puff and leans back into the couch, the smoke hitting the ceiling. I'm thankful when he doesn't pass it over. "You think everything he's got—the cars, the boats, the big houses—you think that's all from ice cream?"

"Yeah, I mean, I guess not."

CeCe puffs out her cheeks at the ceiling. The old guy smiles and says, "You *guess*? Don't you care where you work?"

"Hey," she says to him. "Get to the good part."

"It's all there," he says shortly, puffing longer on the joint. "All in that little ice cream stand."

"What is?"

He smiles. "Treasure."

"Cash," CeCe adds. "Money and shit getting moved around. That's what he does. And he uses the ice cream stand to cover it up."

"Are you sure?"

The old guy clears his throat. "What's that supposed to mean, Duke's Girl?" His tone is light, but he measures me with his eyes. "You think I just go around saying things?"

CeCe clears her throat and stands up. "We should go. Mini-Mart, a *child*, has summer school in the morning. Don't you, Min?"

I don't, and I'm pretty sure CeCe knows that, but I follow her lead and stand up to go.

When we're nearly at the door, the old guy calls out behind us, "If you don't believe me, wait there after they close. You'll see what I mean."

CeCe practically lifts me by the collar. She has somehow procured my hoodie, which I am now too high to have remembered. I don't thank her, though.

The block is absolutely still, a silence broken only by a lone seagull who doesn't realize how late it is. We've been inside this weird house longer than I thought.

Halfway to the car, CeCe murmurs, "Duke's is probably closed now."

A groan escapes me. Mostly I'm thinking about the pill, which is miraculously still intact, and how long this night has been. "Are you actually saying we should see if it's true? And then what?"

CeCe kicks a torn pacifier across the sidewalk and into the road. "You know what."

"No, I don't." But I do—whenever I remember handing back that envelope of money, and how if I had just waited a minute longer, it would be unaccounted for and mine. But that was circumstance, a missed opportunity.

CeCe's suggesting something different.

I shake from the clinging, wet air. "Who was that guy, anyway?"

"My ex-stepfather," CeCe says. "He and Bonnie were together for a few years when I was a kid. I usually just call him my stepdad."

The way she lets the information sit about her stepdad implies that it was another lifetime, like me and Mom and the entrance exams. Before.

I remember that her stepdad knew Mom and slow down on the sidewalk. CeCe makes it about ten feet ahead before she notices. "What?"

"Why did you bring all that up? The robbery and that I work at Duke's?"

CeCe scoffs. Keeps walking.

I catch up with her. "Did you even need a ride? You still owe me a full tank."

She whirls around to face me. "As a matter of fucking fact, I brought up Duke's because he was talking about your mom, which you hate."

"Oh."

"Anyway," CeCe says, all business again. "At any given moment, your boss has tons of cash just *sitting* in his office. All hidden away."

"It might not be cash," I remind her. "Then what?"

"We sell it for cash."

"What if it's drugs?" I demand.

"It's not drugs."

"How do you know?"

She raises her eyebrows, rearing back on the concrete. "*I would know.*" She sucks her teeth. "It has to be cash, though. That's what those robbers were looking for."

I force a laugh. "This is ridiculous. And if it's true . . ."

I picture those cops in and around Duke's the night of the robbery and all the free ice cream I've had to scoop over the last few months. Now I understand it's not just about free ice cream; he's bought their protection. "It's dangerous."

"So what? It's worth it." CeCe walks backward to the Boat. Large Marge whines at her feet, which she ignores. "You have a perfectly good opportunity to make shit happen *and* get revenge. You're telling me you have no interest in finding out what he's hiding? None?"

My face burns when she says the word *revenge*. That never seemed like an option. "I'm not going out of my way to steal from my criminal boss."

"What else are you going to do? Keep working a job you hate, waiting for the next hurricane to swallow you up?" She yells this, then draws back, taking in the row of houses beside us. "Fuck. They probably heard that."

I take a sharp, briny breath as the imaginary flood comes around the nearest corner, rising over me, CeCe, Large Marge, and the Boat. The water deep gray in the night and swirling fast, like something out of a news story. I blink, and the water is gone, the street still bare except for us.

"Come on, Min. We can do this." CeCe looks me in the eye for the first time in a while. "At least think about it. Write a pros and cons list. Make a spreadsheet. You know we can."

I circle around to the driver's side and unlock the door. "We're going to the gas station now."

She slumps against the passenger door in disappointment.

"Hey." I clutch the door handle, which is wet with condensation, and call over the roof of the car. "Hey. I'll think about it."

CHAPTER TWELVE

It's the hottest day of summer so far, and a weekend morning, and the line has formed right away. All hands are on deck—except for Anthony's, of course. Jamira, who's only supposed to be decorating cakes, mutters about hiring more people. Jordan, who wishes she got to decorate cakes more often, is short with the customers. Eli and I are stuck handling most of the orders.

The thought of the money, or something else, hidden nearby distracts me all through the beginning of my shift. As if the next time I open the freezer for the vanilla fudge or mint chocolate chip, the treasure will be right there. But I know it's not that simple.

"You thought about it?"

Eli's question startles me out of my vision—stacks of cash from the night of the robbery, multiplied many times over—and for a whole second I think that's what he's asking about. We've reached our first lull of the shift, and since Jordan and Jamira are on a self-imposed break, it's just me and him.

He means the show he "invited" me to (via postcard) a few days ago.

"Min?"

"Oh," I hedge, my stomach twisting because I'm still not used to him saying my name when he's not talking about switching tubs of ice cream or taking out the garbage. "I didn't really get a chance to think about it."

Actually, I decided last night that I wouldn't go to the show. Too many variables—what if I show up and three other girls have done the same? Or worse, all my coworkers? He probably invited every single warm body he knows.

"Probably not," I conclude.

"Oh. That sucks."

"It does?"

He gives me a funny look, a quick smile followed by a frown. "What? Of course it does."

"Well." I shrug. The words appear, and I push them out before I can change my mind. "Maybe I still could. I'm not sure."

Aside from not fitting the typical Duke's girl profile, there's another reason I can't believe Eli would want me at his show. The same reason I've been smothering my crush on him all this time, lest the embarrassment kill me.

While training, in between learning about sundaes and proper scoop-cleaning hygiene, I asked him why he was assistant manager.

"Is it because you're a guy?"

It just sort of came out, meant as a joke. My theory is that because it was probably true, it sounded rude. I didn't even know his last name yet (Ronan) or what kind of car he drove (Dodge) or his favorite flavor (strawberry, and he doesn't get sick of it).

He didn't answer, and we didn't speak for the rest of the shift. Before leaving, I tried to make amends, having noticed the headphones peeking out of his bag, and asked what kind of music he liked. He answered, "All of it," and left. My guess is he just wanted to get away from me—if not forever, then for the moment.

After that, everything was about ice cream.

Each and every thing.

I'm not like my mother. I can't just say whatever I want and make people fall in love with my bluntness. With me, the words tumble down from space, and instead of falling in love, people just look at me like they aren't sure what I am.

I've still thought about kissing him. A lot. In fact, my attraction to Eli is directly proportionate to my inclination to avoid him. I admitted this to Mary before things got weird between us.

You know, she said, *you're allowed to find someone attractive and not really like them at all.*

I asked her if that was like her and Vera. They had just started talking. Soon after that, they'd get more serious and I'd have to share my best friend, the last normal thing about me, with somebody else.

Wanting Eli, thinking he might want me, makes me feel normal. The way we've suddenly started talking like it's the easiest thing in the world. As if we haven't said fewer than ten collective words to each other for six months.

It makes my pulse quicken almost as much as the idea of the money.

Almost.

I touch the counter, familiar with the plastic bubbling at the edges. Years upon years of ice cream and money. Millions of dollars. I'm not the kind of person who thinks in magic like Mary (or, technically, Nicole), but I swear I can feel the invisible weight of it rising in a slow, thick heat.

Should I ask him if he knows about the treasure?

"Eli? Have you ever . . ."

He touches his visor, wiping away the sweat with his fore-arm. That little move we all do. "Have I ever what?"

"Nothing."

"What?" he prompts, oddly intense. "Say it."

The pop-rock on the radio grumbles between us. We both like to keep the volume low, since we don't have much of a say in the station. Anything we choose, Anthony will change it back—if any of the others don't get to it first. He'll say it's about what makes the customer "comfortable."

I remember how Eli and I looked at each other that day outside of school and how much I liked it. What pops out of my mouth is even more chaotic. "Do you ever feel kind of glad that it happened?"

Eli adjusts his visor, his face out of view, and I recognize the moment for what it is, one of those times I shared a concept that only made sense inside my head. Like the time I asked Eli why he was assistant manager: of course it's because he's a guy. But, as everybody in my life *except* Mom has said to me at one point or another, not everything needs to be pointed out.

At the window, a new line forms. Everyone has decided on their orders at the same time.

Eli looks down at his rag, then out the window, as if he suddenly has no idea why he's holding it. "Actually, yeah. It feels different here now."

Gripping the mop I'm supposed to drag around the floor, I want to yell at him, at everyone. *It's the money.*

MY SINGLE SHIFT becomes a double. When I text CeCe during my five-minute break to make sure she'll still be around later, she replies, Stay there, and stops answering.

I spot her near the end of the night while taking out the trash. She's talking to someone on her phone, her hands knifing the air passionately. No Large Marge. I walk over and toss CeCe the keys to the Boat so she can wait inside.

She nods at me and yells to the person on the phone, "And I *told* you about Blastoise, didn't I? Exactly."

By the time I crack open the door to the Boat and sink into the driver's seat, my legs sticking to the leather, it feels like sitting on a cloud after being on my feet all day. I close my eyes and tilt the seat back. The heat's not bad tonight—the breeze even hints at fall.

"God, I could sleep in here," I whisper.

CeCe sneers, now playing a game on her phone that she doesn't look up from. "Your low standards continue to amaze me."

Mock-glaring, I lean forward and shove the key in the ignition. I don't turn it yet, still conserving the full tank CeCe made good on. "I'm just tired. Where are we going?"

She clears her throat. "I was thinking we could stay right here."

"Right here . . . at Duke's?" I watch my coworkers leave one by one. Eli exits last, keys jangling as he nods to the music on his giant headphones. I smile and we meet eyes—as in, he catches me staring—and he salutes before getting into his car. My smile burns out in embarrassment.

"You going to dude's show?" CeCe asks in a distant but not quite uninterested voice. She taps at her phone screen.

"I don't know. I can't tell . . ." I don't have the guts to finish the sentence—*if he likes me*—so I switch topics. "You never gave me a destination."

"I told you. Here."

"Very funny." My muscles throb, as if irritated by CeCe's

flair for mystery. I feel like I've swum the entire length of the bay.

"I want to see what happens after closing. Don't you?"

Of course I do. But. "I think you mean, *if* something happens. What if it's nothing?"

"Then at least we'll know." She sounds let down by this possibility.

"Fine," I say at last. "We can't stay parked here, though. Somebody will notice."

"Obviously," CeCe says, grinning.

The other cars leave the lot. When mine is the only one left, I turn on the engine. At the very least, I have plans to turn a portion of my tips into something fried with cheese.

We drive to the busier part of Nautilus and kill time in the parking lot of Carnival Jack's, where CeCe runs into five people she knows, all of whom stop to talk to her and ignore me.

I don't mind, too distracted by what we may or may not see at Duke's.

"Ready?" CeCe asks, balling up the aluminum foil from her cheeseburger. Even though I wanted two of everything on the (admittedly short) menu at Carnival Jack's, I kept it simple and ordered a chili-cheese dog and onion rings. In the name of conservation.

CeCe has me park the car slightly down the road from Duke's, under a drooping tree that takes over the sidewalk. We have a partial view of the lot, but a clear one of the side door, which is the part that matters.

"Nothing's happening," I say after a few minutes.

"Wait."

I finish my cold onion rings and prepare to wait even more. The dark and stillness blend together. There's a swishing above us like wind through leaves, but when I look up, the trees don't seem to be moving.

At 1:38 A.M., Boat-time (some two to eight minutes ahead), a white pickup truck crawls into the lot. CeCe slinks down in the seat. I do the same.

My heart beats in my throat. Why am I so nervous? Nothing has happened yet.

A slim figure jumps out of the truck. We're parked too far away to see their face, which is obscured by a baseball cap anyway.

We watch the figure unlock the side door and walk inside the stand. I zero in on the only visible window, in Anthony's office, my breath trapped and waiting with the rest of me. A weak yellow light switches on.

What exactly am I expecting to see?

They come back out holding several shopping bags, bulky and rectangular from their contents. The figure makes the trip two more times, each time holding more bags.

CeCe actually hisses. "You see?"

"See what? That could've been anything. Inventory."

"Taking boxes *out*? Of ice cream? In the middle of the night?"

She has a point. I happen to know we're fully stocked. Jordan took the lead on inventory and has been extra insufferable about it, clipboard and all.

"Maybe that's Jordan." I accidentally mumble this out loud. Jordan, doing inventory in the middle of the night. But that isn't her car—a gleaming blue Volkswagen Jetta. Even more importantly, based on body shape and movements alone, it can't be Anthony or anyone else from Duke's.

"Who?"

"This girl I work with." I shake my head, picturing

Jordan's long reddish-blonde hair fitting under that baseball cap. Not to mention that she's even shorter than I am. "No, it can't be."

The figure makes three more trips in and out of the stand, then climbs back into the truck and leaves. Before we can follow suit, a police car glides past on our street, unexpected enough to feel like a mirage. CeCe sucks in her breath and yanks me deeper into the seat. Gasoline-scented terror fills my lungs. I forgot about the cops until now.

By the time it seems safe enough to sit up, both the cop car and the white pickup are gone. We start back toward the Beach Blossom. CeCe keeps sticking her head out the window and checking behind us for the truck.

After her third big look, she says, "Let's go back tomorrow."

"To do what? Intercept the boxes?"

"No," she admits, though she scowls like she wants to say yes. "To gather more information. Maybe see something new. Something that tells us where the money is."

"Might not be money," I remind her, like a song lyric.

"Ugh," she growls. "Listen. Can you just check the place to see if anything's gone missing?"

"CeCe, I've been there almost six months. There's nothing there. It's way too small."

"What do you call what we just watched?" she cries. When I don't answer—can't answer—she grits her teeth and says, "Just check."

"Yeah, yeah," I mumble every time, though it's mainly to appease her. Another part of me thinks about the money. Wants it to be the money.

All of me is terrified.

Coincidentally, I get my new schedule tomorrow. Two

new girls are starting, which likely means yet another reduction of hours. Maybe it's the chili dog, but the idea of having to keep fighting for decent hours makes me shut my eyes at the next red light.

When we pass the faded Beach Blossom entrance sign, I think of Mom. If the treasure has been a rumor for years, has she known this whole time?

If I'd told Mom about the hiring process and the cameras back when I first started at Duke's and she was still home, she would've stormed Anthony's office and dragged him into the street. She and Nicole always swore the women in our family have a secret brute strength in times of great distress.

But I never told her how messed up my job or Anthony truly is. I was too relieved to have found a job at all—and even though she never said it out loud, Mom was relieved, too.

It was baffling that so many people had lined up to be ogled, but at the end of the day, so was I. Still am.

Mom must not have known, because she'd have made me quit. I'm sure of it. What's more: if it was her driving the Boat, she would've followed that pickup truck. She'd want to see inside those boxes.

Just to be sure.

CHAPTER THIRTEEN

Eli's postcard stays with me from pocket to pocket until I decide for sure to go. Since I refuse to drive the Boat into the city, I convince CeCe to take the train, offering to pay for both the LIRR and subway fare.

She's only interested in talking about Duke's, though.

"It's a dead end," I tell her, watching the houses and buildings turn denser the farther we get from home. I checked all the storage at Duke's the following day and found everything the same as we left it while closing up the night before. Nothing was missing, including a dozen mystery boxes.

CeCe and I take a series of trains to get to the venue, deep on the map of Brooklyn on my phone. Every station involves wading through a flash flood of people. We end up in a neighborhood lined with brick walls and looming truck-sized gates. I make out the address from an outline of numbers on an old restaurant supply store, where the same postcard Eli gave me is taped to the metal door. A yawning guy on a stool waves us closer until I realize he's asking for money.

I'm too self-conscious to mention Eli at the door, which brings down the Probable Orphan Fund another thirty dollars.

The show is on the basement level and seems like it's just getting started. It's dark, aside from the deep yellow spotlight pointed at the stage, and a couple of white fluorescents like the ones at Duke's in the back of the room, where the bathrooms are. Although it hogs most of the light, the stage is empty. Songs with catchy beats play over the space.

CeCe seems into the music, but she also gets to drink because of her fake ID. I, on the literal other hand, am wearing a neon wristband that reads *UNDER 21* in bright orange. I have to scratch the insides of my hands to keep from begging her to buy me a beer to calm my nerves. The embarrassment of getting thrown out wouldn't be worth it.

I spot Eli in a raised booth near the back. He watches an older guy tending to a set of turntables. I try to catch his eye, make one feeble attempt at waving, but he's completely absorbed in what the other guy is doing. There's a crowd in front of the stage about four bodies deep, and more people keep filtering in from outside, still almost all guys.

"So that one's your boss?" CeCe asks, pointing her sweaty beer bottle. "The one who isn't doing anything?"

"He's not my boss." I shudder, picturing Anthony up there. The ache for alcohol in my fingers switches to bloodthirst.

"Does he know you like him?" When I shoot her a look, she cries, "Come on! Nothing wrong with trying to get some."

I harden the look.

"Why the hell you even here, then?" She shoves one of my shoulders and almost sends me flying into some stranger's backpack.

CeCe's right, but it's hard to admit it to her. She just isn't that kind of friend. Mary's the one I'd talk with about crushes and my (extremely limited) experience hooking up, and I still haven't texted or called her since that day I did it on impulse, let alone fulfilled my promise to come over.

CeCe nudges me. "Hey, look."

Eli, now alone in the booth, places a new record onto the turntable. At first it doesn't sound like anything, until a loud crackling fills the room like faraway lightning, followed by a man's voice. The clip is familiar, spooky all by itself.

Me, I want what's coming to me.

"Did he just sample *Scarface*?" CeCe shouts in my face. "I love that movie!" The beer must be making her forget how many times she's recited entire scenes or quizzed me on its death count (forty-two).

The beat drops, explodes into pounding bass and organ. A few people around us nod along, while the ones closer to the stage cheer.

But then the other, older guy in a knit cap reappears in the booth beside Eli and subtly pushes him away from the turntables. Eli's music plays for a couple more seconds before switching back to a more upbeat song that everybody seems to know the words to.

It seems like Eli's going to protest, but he doesn't. He stands there for a moment longer, then steps down from the booth. The crowd is thick enough now that he disappears from sight.

"What was that about?" CeCe says. "I thought he was pretty good. For the twenty-something seconds he played, at least."

"No idea." I'm trying to find him in the crowd, but it's growing thicker by the second, and the lights have shifted from bright yellow to soft and multicolored and kind of useless for seeing. I look for him without letting myself think about it too much. CeCe and her beer follow; she keeps one eye on the stage, where some people are setting up an assortment of drums under the colored lights.

We find Eli near another wall. He's rifling through the same large, boxy-looking bag he was carrying the other day. I force myself to speak. "Hey."

He looks up, adjusting the bag. "Whoa. You came! Nice."

"This is my neighbor CeCe," I say.

"What up." She leans in and slaps his hand effortlessly.

"Hey, yeah, you looked kind of familiar." He smiles back, but his eyes are someplace else.

"That was good, what you played," CeCe says. "What the hell happened with the other guy?"

I widen my eyes at her to shut up. Eli shakes his head, amused, and puts a finger to his lips, even though the music has gotten so loud we have to yell to hear one another.

"Well, anyway, I'm out," CeCe says.

I try not to sound panicked. "Already?"

"I got some unfinished business." She's referencing her plan to meet an ex-girlfriend at a bar that won't even ask for her fake ID. She squeezes my arm and whispers, "You got this." Then she slips into the wall of backpacks behind us and is gone. The crowd is shoulder to shoulder now, still mostly guys.

"You wanna go?" Eli says.

"Don't you have to stay longer?"

"I've been relieved of my duties," he says with more sarcasm than usual. "At least I got paid up front this time."

I follow him through the crowd toward the exit, pulled in the wake created by his gigantic record bag. We make it to the relatively empty entryway, where the music fades at our heels.

Outside the venue, people are smoking cigarettes and talking under the lights. Most of the building walls here are covered in graffiti.

"Aren't you upset?" I ask when we're farther down the block, away from the crowd. A dark body of water glitters just up ahead.

"Kind of, if I'm being honest, but I can't really afford to show it." Eli's walking slows, then mine. The wind blows across us and over the water, a canal of some kind. The grass on the other side flutters in the breeze.

He stops at a car I recognize as his. "I had to park kind of far away," he explains. He opens the trunk and gently places the record bag into a box. Then we climb into the front.

Eli turns on the engine and plugs in his phone. The lights on the console shine like a Christmas tree. His parents probably bought him this car on his sixteenth birthday. I try not to resent him for it, instead studying how his eyes crinkle behind his glasses as he scrolls through his music, the olive-purple of his skin in the dark. It's so quiet I can hear his breathing above the engine, slow and deep, part of him not here, possibly still inside the venue. He's singing to himself, replaying something.

A song comes on the car stereo like a raucous party, a woman's voice grinding over the music.

"What's this?" I ask.

"It's the rest of my mix. This sample right here is Tina Turner."

"I like it."

"I know." Eli glances over, smiling. "I mean, I do, too."

"How come you never play this stuff at Duke's?"

He dips his head at me. "You know why."

"Yeah, but you're assistant manager. You could just do it anyway." I widen my eyes at him in the dark, and he laughs. I like the sound of him laughing and want to make him do it more.

I decide it's the right time for my real conversation piece: the joint I've been keeping in an old orange prescription bottle. I smooth it out and hold it up for him to see.

"Oh," he says. "Shit."

We pass it back and forth through a slightly more comfortable silence until he says, "It's been a while since I did this."

"Me, too," I lie. "My neighbor gave this to me."

"That girl who was with you? Yeah, a few of my friends bought from her before."

Sometimes I forget how small a place Nautilus really is. I sigh and look out the window at the anonymous brick wall beside us.

"I can't believe you came," he says all of a sudden.

"Why? I said I might."

"So did everybody else, and they didn't." I wonder if he's disappointed by this. Eli clears his throat and adds, "It's just, I thought you kind of hated me."

"Huh—why?"

"Because I'm the only guy?"

I cringe at Eli using my own past words so suddenly and without warning. But when I glance back over, he's grinning, teasing. He looks frankly beautiful in the orange lights of the canal. Like a stone sculpture.

"You're right, though," he says, his smile gone. "I am assistant manager because I'm a guy. I'm qualified, whatever that means, but so is Jamira. It's Anthony. He does it to make a point. I think you might be the first person to say it out loud."

"Oh." I never realized I was that obvious. "I thought *you* hated *me*. For asking you that."

"I couldn't." He sneaks up the volume.

I try to swallow the knot in my throat that's only there because I know what's about to happen or just because it's what I want. I want Eli, and it scares me. It was there before when I gossiped with Mary, and tried to with CeCe. But the way it's grown in just a couple of hours, and yet more in the last few minutes, is frightening. The thought of fleeing occurs to me. Just like that night Duke's was robbed.

But I have a choice to make right now. And it's to stay.

I lean over and kiss him.

His hand brushes the back of my neck, and the knot in my throat disappears. The fear melts away. Or maybe it's grown so giant I can't feel the shape of it anymore.

CHAPTER FOURTEEN

Nicole has a mission.

"Do you have any plans today?" she asks in a subdued tone while stirring milk into her coffee. Around us, the kitchen and dining areas are finally to her satisfaction, the surfaces clear for the first time in my entire childhood. I don't ask about the *Weekly Waves*, or the coupons that Mom said she was going to use and didn't, or the books we gave up slowly.

It happens to be the Fourth of July, one of those holidays I forget about until everybody else appears to be excited about it. Mom has always preferred to stay at home, as it was one of her few days off from work, and the streets were flooded with people looking to be entertained. Sometimes we ended up at the beach, eating chips and sandwiches.

I don't have plans, and I don't have work, either. The Ice Creamery is open—early, in fact—and everyone else on staff is working. Anthony is having Jordan and Jamira train a couple of new girls—Jordan took the initiative on letting me know in a text littered with smiley emojis. I wanted to ask what she was so fucking happy about.

I try not to panic at how I seem to be getting punished on

the biggest day of the year for tips. Did Anthony find out I was giving away ice cream and asking questions? Is he phasing me out for that reason? Am I going to be like the last girl who tried to say something and only ended up seeming to disappear off the face of the earth?

Lastly, related and unrelated, I try not to think about how I haven't seen or heard from Eli since the night of the show. After losing an undisclosed amount of time making out in his car, listening to music, talking about music, and finally additional making out, he admitted he was sober enough to drive back to Nautilus. I foresaw Eli offering to walk me across the balding Beach Blossom lawn, so I made him drop me off down the road.

"Hello, Min?" Nicole presses.

"No." I've been puttering around the clean space, looking for any remnants of my mother's belongings from before Nicole's massacre. "I don't have plans."

She brightens. "Great."

"I'm not going with you to visit Mom."

"I already knew that. I went yesterday." She clears her throat, and we both look away. "I'm going to a barbecue."

The air returns to my lungs. "That's nice."

"You should come. It's at Winnie's house. You remember Winnie?"

"Name rings a bell." Still standing, I turn on the TV, the most basic of "complimentary" options at the Beach Blossom. The channel it's already on plays some kind of reality show, a beautiful girl at the wheel of a beautiful car, chattering illegally on her beautiful phone.

Nicole looks up from her own phone, tilting her head in disappointment. "Minerva. You really don't remember Winnie?"

Clearly, I'm *supposed* to remember this person. I think through everything Nicole and I have in common—again, the only thing I can come up with is Mom. But the people who care about Mom, most of whom never appeared until recently, have nothing to do with me. And I plan to keep things that way.

"Mom . . . ?" I ask, not able to finish. My head swirls, and I find the opposite end of the couch from Nicole. With her dark-honey hair, like a normal version of my spur-of-the-moment bleach, she could pass for Mom before sickness took away her colors.

And then Nicole opens her mouth, and she's not Mom at all.

"You really don't know Winnie?" she asks.

"We're still on this?"

"She got you the job at the Ice Creamery." Nicole gulps her coffee and slams it down on a glass coaster I've never seen before. There are times when it turns out grown-ups aren't mad about the thing they claimed to be mad about originally, and this seems like one of those times. "If you aren't working or doing anything else, I want you to come with me to the barbecue."

"Fine."

She opens, closes, and reopens her mouth. "Really?"

"Yes, really. I could use a burger." And maybe sneak in an adult beverage or two. Bonus: soaking in some human normalcy, getting my mind off how penniless and stranded I am.

Nicole sits up straight and pats her cotton headband. "Okay. Well, I'm gonna wash my hair. Then you can do yours—"

"Hey!"

"We leave in two hours and—" She makes a show of

holding up her watch so I can see the display. "Eighteen minutes."

I KNOW I'VE made a terrible mistake today the moment Nicole's silver Nissan Altima touches past the gates. The name of this neighborhood is Sandy Acres. There isn't any sand or open space anywhere, but blue-and-white townhouses that line up ominously under the matching puffy-clouded sky. Across the landscape, an extra layer of red-white-and-blue paraphernalia dots the lawns, hangs on doors, and off the eaves of many of the houses. Along with a generous dusting of Thin Blue Line flags in between.

You're doing a real *good job with that*, I think.

"Wait," I tell Nicole as she pulls into the visitor parking spot and turns off the car.

"What is it?" she asks in a toneless, patient voice. She's still riding high from my agreeing to be here in the first place.

I have a bad feeling, is what it is. But I can't tell Nicole that. She'll brush it off faster than any insult I could come up with.

"Mom wouldn't want to be here," I offer at last, a kind of Hail Mary. I'm not wrong. Mom would see the cutesy lookalike houses and flags and turn right around. I imagine her behind us in the backseat, her hand on Nicole's shoulder to steer us back to the beach, any beach. But, in my imagination, she's wearing the dreaded hospital gown and pulling plastic tubes from her nose. I cringe and shut my eyes to make it go away.

Nicole takes a deep breath and turns off the car. "Sunny definitely has a lot of opinions on things."

"Oh, *does* she?" I shoot back. It's so hot today that the air-conditioning in Nicole's car is already fading. The dread of being in this new place tricks me into worrying I might never get home again.

"Listen," she says evenly, "I know a regular old Fourth of July barbecue isn't exactly Sunny's *favorite* thing. You two have that in common." She reaches for my hand across the empty cup holders, but I'm too terrified to take it. I wipe my hands on my shorts instead. It's a good time to lack the ability to cry. Tears are too inconvenient.

"But," Nicole continues, "I just . . . I thought it'd be nice. Some music, a few drinks too early in the day, socializing with other people. Sunny isn't right about everything. Sometimes the rest of us are right, too."

"Fine," I say. "Just stop talking about her, okay?"

"Min, you can't just act like—"

I open the door and step out into the frying pan of the day. A few seconds later, Nicole follows, locking up the car. As we start past the townhouses, she nudges and hands me something plastic. A pair of sunglasses.

"Hey, thanks."

"I always have an extra pair," she says, actually patting my arm. "For her. Plus, your eyes are as red as Satan's—"

"Nikki!"

A woman calls out to us from a nearby porch. She's white, wearing an off-the-shoulder cotton dress with an American flag on the front, the word *freedom* in painted cursive. Her blonde hair is tied back in a pretty, casual-looking French braid. Winnie.

"Oh my God!" Nicole and Winnie scream at each other, before leaning into a loose hug that keeps their hair and outfits and nails intact.

"Is this your baby cousin?" Winnie demands after they've finished air-kissing. She smiles hugely at us both, tipsy even though it's just past noon. (I'll bet nobody is taking *her* aside and giving lectures about her ruined life).

"Not really a baby anymore," Nicole says, to her credit and mine. "But yeah. She's the one you helped with the Ice Creamery." Nicole doesn't face me, but I know I'm supposed to use this as an opportunity to thank Winnie.

"Oh, yeah." Winnie sips something red and cold from a flowery cozy. "How is it? Isn't it great?"

They both stare—Nicole with ever-widening eyes. I can practically hear her thoughts now. *Say thank you! Now!*

"It's fine," I say. "Where's the bathroom?"

Winnie tells me where the bathroom is, and as I trot off I overhear Nicole rushing to apologize. Swearing she doesn't know what's gotten to me, when she and Winnie and probably everyone else at this sad little barbecue know exactly what's gotten to me.

Do we really have to talk about it?

I gather myself in the downstairs bathroom with its flower soaps and framed inspirational messages—*Live Loud, Laugh Hard* and *Be Yourself Always*. The window above the toilet faces the yard, and things look harmless enough: there's a massive grill, a cooler, a table of food and picnic accoutrements, and different-colored deck chairs along the grassy space. Red, white, and blue balloons are tied to every surface possible with shiny silver ribbon.

Nicole's and Winnie's voices pass through the house to the yard. Their conversation carries like they're next to me in the bathroom.

"If there's anything I can do," Winnie is saying. She sips what sounds like the last of her beverage. Maybe I can offer to get her a refill and snag a little something for myself.

I splash some cold water on my face, even though the

house is so air-conditioned I forgot about how hot it was outside.

Just as I'm about to execute my plan, Nicole says, "I'll go find her."

"Didn't you say she was Puerto Rican?" Winnie interrupts.

"Well, she's Dominican, too. Like me."

"Yeah, but you *really* don't look it. Remember how I kept thinking you were Italian?" Winnie says this like it's a compliment.

Nicole laughs through her nose. The fake sound is like a cheese grater against my ears.

Winnie, though, doesn't seem to notice. "Plus that hair. She got the job like that?"

I wish I could barge out to the yard and say something rude in Spanish that only Nicole and I could understand, but of course I don't speak it. Mom tried to teach me, hers isn't perfect, it never stuck, and so on.

Nicole's answer surprises me. "She's just a kid, Winn. Don't you think you're being a little—" Her voice becomes muffled.

Confused about where this more thoughtful version of Nicole is when it's just the two of us, I finish up in the bathroom and reluctantly return to the party. On my way, I load up a plate of chips and vegetables and offer some to Nicole, who says no and continues past the halfway point of a light beer. I plunk down on the chair next to hers. Aside from the stink of prejudice, it's not so bad out here. There's food, as promised, plus rolling green hills inside the circle of townhouses, punctuated by fountains and gardens and, of course, more flags. There's an unexpected breeze that smells kind of sweet, like fruit, mixed with smoke from the grill.

"Why won't you say it?" Nicole mutters once her friend is out of earshot.

I eat three giant potato chips before answering. "Why do you care?"

"It was a huge favor." Her voice shakes. "You guys needed the money, and it was the only thing I could think of. No one else was hiring."

I point at the fountain a few feet away, in front of which Winnie poses for a photo with some older woman in a white blazer and approximately a dozen necklaces. "Does she look like she's risked anything? Does anybody here?"

"You're so damn stubborn."

"Language."

"Why can't you just do what I'm asking?"

I turn and glare with my whole body. "It really means that much to you that they don't think *our kind* is ungrateful?"

This is the push I need to resume my quest to sneak a beer. I stand up so fast I hit my ankle on the deck chair. Swallowing a scream, I hobble to the cooler.

Here, I almost run into Anthony.

Just a few feet ahead, beer still dripping from the cooler. He's standing with some men who are loudly complaining about traffic on the roads, silently tapping on his phone. He hasn't spotted me, which makes sense as I barely exist to him.

I back up and find a tree to stand behind. The sound of voices and laughter and droning, decades-old pop music soars to unbearable levels. Time stops and starts. My heart gallops like it's trying to catch up (Mom always said her heart condition is super rare and not at all hereditary, but I do wonder).

Remembering the shades Nicole lent me, I slip those on and continue to observe Anthony, mostly to ensure I'm not hallucinating. He has a lot of nerve leaving the stand during the busiest day of the year and, more importantly, after bumping me from the schedule without warning.

I weigh the pros and cons of confronting my evil boss in the middle of the whitest party in existence.

While I'm still deciding, he brings his phone to his ear and walks away.

I curse under my breath. All frozen up yet again. Maybe CeCe's right. I wait too long, play it too safe.

If she were here right now, she'd push me to follow him, or she'd just walk off and do it herself.

So I follow him around the yard to the front of the house. This time, I take cover behind one of the many cars lining the driveway.

Anthony stands in the middle of the lawn and glances up and down the street. He checks his phone again, then pockets it. He takes a couple of steps toward the road, as if he just laid eyes on whatever he was waiting for.

When I see what it is, time stops yet again.

Rolling up to the curb is the white pickup truck from the other night.

At least, I think it is. There's nothing specific that sets it apart from any other white truck on the island. But I stared at that thing for an hour the other night; I know a familiar vehicle when I see it.

The glare of the sun on the windshield makes it impossible to see behind. I watch Anthony step off the curb and go around to the driver's side. I'm not close enough to hear much, and then I catch the sentence that detonates chills down my back because of how many times I've heard it. Because I'm conditioned to fear it.

"Don't let it happen again."

That person *works* for Anthony.

"Mi*nerv*a! What are you doing?"

Nicole stands at the top of the driveway, where the back-yard starts. Her voice is so loud it carries down the length of the driveway and gets Anthony's attention.

I stand up straight, dusting my shorts as if recovering from a fall.

"I . . . well . . ." I steady myself on a taillight, nearly burning my hand on the sun-heated metal. "I just really like this car."

Nicole rolls her eyes, oblivious to Anthony's presence—to her, he's just some guy—but in my periphery, he's openly staring.

I follow Nicole back to the party, mentally patching together an excuse to leave while she keeps scolding me. A head rush, I'll claim, a need to puke. Which wouldn't be far from the truth.

"Space Cadet," I hear behind me.

It's not quite habit that makes me turn around. It's that I don't know what else to do. That he knows who I am, now even knows my name. We meet eyes, and he winks.

"You have yourself a Happy Fourth."

CHAPTER FIFTEEN

CeCe and I have both grown tired of the woods, so we move to the beach near the good boardwalk. I ask her if she wants to go swimming, and she mutters something sideways about the ocean being too mysterious for her, which I've heard before and take to mean she can't swim. Or it's the fact that she has to work; her phone pings every few minutes, and a few people even stop by.

I tell her about the Fourth of July, on a quest not to be the only person to think about running into Anthony in the real world. I leave out the white truck, since I can't prove it means anything. And if I told her, she'd just get mad at me for not taking a picture or writing down the license plate number. My nerves can't handle me being a disappointment again.

In fact, the more time passes, the sillier it feels. I wish I'd taken the envelope the night of the robbery, run away, and never come back. Instead, I'm too scared to beg my sociopath of a boss for more hours.

In the end, it's just one more thing I couldn't do right.

"You gonna quit?" CeCe chuckles. She's tossing a handful of Takis at a seagull. When it goes in to eat, Large Marge lunges on cue. CeCe cracks up, far more into the wildlife than my venting.

"CeCe, it's not that—"

"Easy. I know. It's not easy." She flings a single Taki and smiles at Large Marge like they share a secret. As soon as they ambush another few seagulls, CeCe grows bored and leans back on the sand, using her bag as a pillow. "Quit the job, keep the job. Whatever."

"What's that mean?"

She purses her lips beneath the shadow of her flat-brimmed cap in what could be either a smirk or a wince. "Nothing."

Just then, a shirtless white guy in giant aviators jogs up and nods at us. Large Marge leaps up to sniff his leg, her tail wagging frantically.

"You still have that stuff we talked about?" he asks CeCe, taking a wary step back from Large Marge.

"For sure." CeCe takes her time digging through her backpack. He scans the beach several times, refusing to look at any of us.

CeCe produces a tiny baggie. This time, the contents are white pills I've never seen before. Something likely more serious than weed. I know better than to ask in front of a customer—but *what the hell?*

The guy pockets the bag, then looks around the beach again, smiling now. He points to Large Marge, who has progressed to licking his jeans. "How come you don't use a leash or whatever? For him?"

"*Her,*" CeCe corrects, slipping the money into her bag. "And I was just about to ask you the same thing."

He frowns. "But I don't have a dog."

She stares back until he gets uncomfortable and squeaks

goodbye. When he's just a dot approaching the boardwalk, I finally ask about the pills. "What'd you sell him?"

"Molly. Just came in."

"Have you been carrying those around? Did you have them in my mom's car?"

"Mini-Mart . . ."

"No. No 'Mini-Mart.' You know I could go to jail for that, too, right? Why didn't you say anything?"

CeCe balls up the empty Takis bag and shoves it into her pocket. There haven't been garbage cans on the beach in years. "Weed alone isn't doing it. I need more money."

"Maybe if you didn't take your own product."

"Says the girl who's always being smoked up by me."

"I've been driving you at least every other day!" I raise my voice, competing with several Jet Skis as well as the seagulls, who against their better judgment have started skulking around us in higher numbers. "I should know what's in my car!"

CeCe sucks in air through her nose, as if she's about to snap back something even more brutal than suggesting I've been using her.

What comes out instead is, "You ever been under the boardwalk?"

I heave a sigh at yet another of CeCe's mysteries. It's not an answer, not really. But we gather our small amount of belongings—I brought an old psychology book of Mom's that I couldn't focus on, CeCe brought her phone, and neither of us brought a blanket because we each expected the other to bring it—and head over to the boardwalk. There, we trudge alongside it toward the Point until it becomes as decrepit as the corresponding bungalows and buildings.

CeCe stops at an opening in the sand under the boardwalk.

Large Marge bounds in first and disappears. Then CeCe starts crawling and I follow, through what feels like the underside of the filthiest kitchen table in the universe. The space narrows, appears to lead to nowhere, then opens dramatically on an alcove about the size of a Beach Blossom living room. The space is littered with bottles; a couple of beach chairs; and a pile of charred, unidentifiable bits that look like someone tried to start a fire many weeks ago.

"This is so weird, CeCe," I say.

"I know, right?"

Large Marge does her typical walking the perimeter, bobbing in and out of view behind the dunes. I drop my backpack near one of the beach chairs and sit, nearly sinking into the sand. "Do you come down here a lot?"

"I'm everywhere a lot." CeCe takes the other good chair. There's a third that, on closer inspection, turns out to be a heap of broken parts. She lights her one-hitter and passes it to me.

"No, thanks. I start work pretty soon."

"Evening shift?" She raises her eyebrows. "You got back on the schedule?"

"I knew you weren't paying attention before!"

"I *was*." She broods. "You think Lover Boy's gonna be there?"

I shrug, moving one of my feet in a circle in the sand. Large Marge is curled up on the damp sand like a doodlebug. I reach down and scratch Large Marge's gray-brown fur, which is softer than it looks. She opens her eyes, serious. "He thought I didn't like him."

"Well," CeCe says after a silence, "I used to think that about you."

"What?"

Large Marge's ears perk up the way mine would if they could.

"You always seemed like you thought you were too good for this place." The smoke from CeCe's one-hitter drifts through the spaces in the boardwalk above our heads where the sky is showing.

"This place?"

"The Beach Blossom. Nautilus. Like you don't want to be bothered."

I don't want to be bothered, I think. *But still.*

"It was before I knew you."

"You still don't know me," I say. The words hang cold in the air, and I want to apologize until I remember the Molly.

I wonder if CeCe even brought up Eli for her own purposes. My mouth feels parched as I think about Neptune Heights and how she claimed she brought up Duke's to distract her stepdad from talking about Mom. This feels the same.

"Actually, no." CeCe sits up straight and wipes sand off her boots harder than necessary. "But you know what? All you want to do is complain and act like you're beneath everything. You heard what my stepdad told us. You've seen with your own eyes there's shady shit going on. And you still don't even care."

She's found and pressed my button. One more person saying I'm not doing enough. "Why do *you* care, huh?"

CeCe laughs so hard I worry people might hear us on the boardwalk above. "Don't be dumb, Minerva. You're not a dumb person."

"Can't you just answer the question?"

She grows serious. "You think I *want* to keep doing this? You think I don't want to change *my* life the way you want to change *yours?* I hate this shit." Her voice falters, and she sucks her teeth, seemingly at herself. She stares up at the planks. The lines of shadow and light make it difficult to read her expression.

Moments like this I feel a lot younger than CeCe, more than just the actual year and a half or so.

"Look," I say, "I'm sorry."

"Why? It's not your fault." But the way she says it, it almost sounds like a lie.

CHAPTER SIXTEEN

When I get to work, Eli's car isn't in the lot even though he's on the schedule. Jordan's car is. Inside the stand, she's blasting her favorite music—a genre I call inspirational pop—and setting up the register. I nod at her and check the schedule on the dry-erase board, hop onto the closest freezer, and continue to stare. It still reads, *Eli/Min*.

"Where's Eli?" I ask.

Jordan shrugs. "Couldn't make it."

"Why not?"

"How should I know?"

I step down and kick the back corner of the sherbet freezer. Eli must regret kissing me and can't face me during our first shift together since it happened.

Well, fuck him.

CeCe's idea slides back into focus, reminding me of what's important. Money. Revenge at Anthony for being a sleazy motherfucker. Not being broke. Leaving Nautilus as soon as humanly possible.

I repeat it all, grab a napkin, and trace the words onto the surface with my finger until it's filled my entire body with purpose again.

• • •

CECE SHOWS UP near the end of the shift and orders two scoops of strawberry in a cup. "Not on the house?" she cries when I tell her the price. "Not even a discount?"

She's in a better mood than before. But now mine is even worse, clinging to my skin like wax. I scrape at a praline stuck to the counter in a congealed dollop of ice cream that's been bothering me all shift. At least it's served as a distraction from the barbecue and Eli not coming to work after ignoring me a whole week.

CeCe slaps the money onto the counter and slides the ice cream close. "You around later?"

I skim the room. Jordan's doing inventory in the walk-in freezer, and Jamira, who's arrived early for the evening shift, is counting out the register. I realize dully that they've probably been blaming every single register shortage on me. "I don't know. I guess."

"You don't know." CeCe backs away from the counter, lowering her head in suspicion. It's that thing she does when she wants me to think she can see right through me, something she learned from an audiobook on power moves and the art of intimidation in business, her favorite—and only—genre of books.

She wags a threatening finger. "This place is getting to you again."

"Do you mind? I have to finish up." The praline budges at last, skids across the counter, and hits the dusty ground outside. I stare after it, feeling defeated.

"Okay, fine," she says, her hands in the air. There's a streak of ice cream along one of her forearms. I don't tell her. She walks off.

Jamira appears beside me, watching CeCe leave. "You friends with that girl?"

"She's my neighbor."

Jamira mutters something in Spanish.

"What?"

She rolls her eyes. "Don't tell me you don't know Spanish, either."

I almost start to explain about how I never learned, but I want to know what she said about CeCe.

"I said that girl, your neighbor, is a fucking trouble-maker." Jamira hands me a supposed half of the tips for the shift I just worked. "Always getting into some shit or another. I wouldn't trust her for anything."

LATE THAT NIGHT, CeCe directs me to the highway, where we drive for all of five minutes and two exits before she tells me to turn off. I've never gotten off at this exit before. Never had to.

"Where are we going?" I ask for the umpteenth time, and for the umpteenth time CeCe doesn't answer. She doesn't smirk or sneer or give any sign whatsoever that it's a good surprise instead of a terrible one. My nerves start to light up, my fingertips almost numb from the anticipation.

She tells me to park on a street with almost nothing on it, just trees on either side for the equivalent of blocks and blocks. Except there's no sidewalk, no side streets. Just trees and road. On our right, just barely visible behind the trees, is a tall metal fence.

When we're out of the car and walking, I glimpse water behind the trees and fence, a sliver of moon shining above it. I think I hear gentle splashing in the distance, but it could just be my mind filling in the sound, the rush of activity and traffic I'm used to hearing all the time. The familiar sound of the entire world passing me over and over.

The road slopes down, curves, becomes gravel. The brush is dense and sharp to the touch. In between the trees are snippets of another world: a parking lot for visitors, benches, trees, and flowers. A pool glows neon blue behind an actual white picket fence. Next to it, a little white clubhouse.

The gravel turns into sand, and the path suddenly opens onto a beach. It's empty, of course, because of the time. The view goes on maybe a few hundred feet until it's blocked by more brush, then a jetty. Above us on a cliff, overlooking the beach, is a chain of giant houses. Every house has a deck and long, winding steps that lead down here to the beach.

"Are we allowed to be here?" I ask.

"No."

"CeCe, come on—"

She pokes the middle of my back and quickens her pace. "Just shut up, and nobody will notice. They're all on painkillers anyway, from what I heard."

"That sounds great right about now," I mutter, rolling my eyes extra hard since she can't see. I want to crouch and hide in the presence of the houses on the cliff with their huge glass windows and tiny porch lights *(imagine having a real porch!)*.

CeCe stares at the water as if she wants to make out with it, then carefully removes her boots and socks and proceeds to walk the entire length of the dock, the wood dipping under her weight. I take off my own sneakers and follow as soundlessly as I can.

By the time I reach the platform at the end of the dock, past a couple of bobbing wave runners, CeCe is sitting on the edge, looking out over the water. I run my eyes across the houses behind us. There's no movement or anything, but fear continues to eat away at my stomach lining. All along the other docks belonging to the other houses, boats are tied and waiting for their passengers. Some of them look bigger than my apartment. This must be the other side of the bay, past where Mary and Vera live and probably Eli, too. Except that by the looks of this place, whoever lives here might be even wealthier than all of them.

"CeCe," I whisper, "what are you *doing*? Whose house is this? Is this one of your"—I search for a word and come up with the one she uses most—"your contacts?"

She takes a deep breath. "One day, I'm going to learn how to swim," she says to the water, as if I'm not even here.

Despite my better judgment and the terror of being found by whoever lives here, I kneel next to her. The water, pitch-black and with a few scraps of weak moonlight, is the same temperature as the air. Like a soft sweater at the exact time that you need one. Perfect for swimming.

"Put your feet in," CeCe says. The water laps and gurgles. I bet if I lived here, I could fall asleep to that noise instead of the sound of other people's TVs through the walls. But I definitely don't live here.

"No!" I check the shore again.

"Ugh. You're no fun, Gutiérrez." She lifts herself onto the platform. "Whatever. There was something else I wanted to show you."

We trudge back down the dock, which bobs with the weight and movement of our sneaking around. Slipping her shoes back on, CeCe stares into the dark sand. "We should look for crabs." The casualness of this suggestion sounds insane, since she still hasn't yet explained where we are. She starts climbing the wooden steps leading to the house on the cliff. "Now for real this time, you need to be as quiet as you've ever been in your life."

"Oh, we're being careful now?" I retort.

When we get to the top of the steps, she stops abruptly and draws back.

"What is it?" I whisper.

She doesn't answer, her shoulders tensing. I push past her and step onto the deck, where the furniture is way more comfortable than mine, even though it's meant to be outside. This place is paradise, there's no way around it. The house attached to the deck is sprawling, wood and glass. A huge tree trunk grows in the center of the deck, towering up to a canopy of leaves.

That is when I see Anthony.

The glass wall on the same level as where we stand separates us. He's passed out in a recliner, no more than twenty feet away.

I feel a yank on the hem of my shirt from behind, CeCe pulling me backward. "Pay attention," she hisses.

"Why the fuck did you bring me here?"

I start backing away slowly, then steadily, until we're both on the wooden steps again and out of Anthony's direct line of sight, should he wake up at this exact moment.

"Because." She directs my gaze to the water and the houses lining the bay that stretches back toward Nautilus. "I want you to see what he has. And what we don't have."

"Really?" I say, trying and failing to keep my voice down. "You brought me all the way here to tell me we're poor? I already knew that."

CeCe does something I've never seen before. She grabs my face with one hand, squeezes, and says, "Look again. And *listen*."

I don't know what she means. I dig my nails into the railing, the wood smooth from the weather, and close my eyes. I listen for the lapping water and boats knocking against the docks. Somewhere below, the frogs sing and interrupt one another.

"It's nice, isn't it?" CeCe says.

I sink into the quiet, waiting for the peace to shape-shift into something else, something chaotic, since that's what would happen at the Beach Blossom. A group of kids giggling in one place becomes a sad, screaming baby in another. But that doesn't happen here, because of course it doesn't. Everything here will be the same as always, which is comforting for them and terrifying for us.

"It's nice," I admit, opening my eyes.

"Don't you think it's time to take some of it away?"

I do.

CHAPTER SEVENTEEN

The first step is what CeCe refers to as recon and I think of as treasure hunting.

"No more stakeouts," she says. "We already got an inside person."

"Who?"

We're driving around for her drop-offs; CeCe promised nothing too illegal was afoot and pointedly left it at that.

"Is that a real question, Min?" Her face sours in the light from her phone screen. "You. *You're* the inside person."

My first step is to gather information without raising suspicion. Ask anyone at work if they've seen anything. Under no circumstances am I to specifically mention the money.

"Make it sound like gossip," she says. "Make it about the cat-mask robbery."

"Gossip," I repeat, pumping the Boat's stubborn breaks for a sharp turn onto the street of our destination, a party near the big marina. This part of town is all twinkling lights and signs for food and beer. The air smells like French fries.

My hands grip the wheel. I'm so hungry.

I find us on a cobblestone dead end and put the Boat in

park. CeCe gets out abruptly, leaving me alone with Large Marge and our plan.

The first thing to do is ask around, but now that I'm alone, it just reminds me that I haven't spoken to Eli in over a week. My neck heats up as I think about the lost cause of my one and only night with Eli Ronan, and then I realize Large Marge has climbed onto the center console, panting, right next to me.

When CeCe quipped that the phone works both ways, I pointed out that he hasn't been working the same shifts, either. That I suspect that he asked to switch hours on purpose, having decided he didn't like kissing me—or being around me—after all.

I gently shove Large Marge out of the way, my neck at least ten degrees cooler, and take out my phone. I could take CeCe's advice and just talk. Break the dam. And while I'm at it, use him for information.

After all, he used me to get more people at his show.

I could ask him about that girl Jamira mentioned months ago—*besides, some girl already tried that*—and then clammed up about. The girl whose very existence makes me feel less insane.

I find his name and start a text. Hey.

What do I even say? *Hey. I know we kissed and are back to not existing to each other, but do you remember this girl who used to work at Duke's?*

I erase the text and glance at the alley behind the building CeCe just entered. There's no reason she should take this long for a drop-off. Unless she's having a drink. But when I check the time, it's only been a couple minutes.

A watched pot doesn't boil, et cetera. I tear my eyes away from the door. That's when I notice a familiar figure, tall and curvy and dark-haired, leaning against the wall between bars.

Mary.

I turn on the hazard lights and get out of the car. Mary is alone, tapping her foot on the concrete as if she's waiting for someone.

"Mary?"

She lifts her head, her eyes widening. "Min! Minerva!" Before I can step back, she throws her arms around me in a bear hug. She smells like sugary alcohol that might or might not have been regurgitated. Beneath that is her normal scent: lavender and pencil shavings. When she pulls away, there's a white streak in her hair dark brown bob that wasn't there before I was expelled. She's wearing her lucky black sundress and the peep-toe heels that obviously belonged to her the moment we discovered them at the Goodwill.

"You here alone?" I look around for whoever was laughing in the background the last time we spoke on the phone.

"I was here with Vera," she says, pointing vaguely behind her, "but I don't know where she went. You know how that goes."

As a matter of fact, I don't know how that goes.

"How long have you been here?" Mary asks. Before I answer, she pouts and says, "You never came over."

She's very drunk.

"You want a ride home?" I ask loudly, steadying her shoulders in the hopes that her eyes will stop rolling all over the place.

"I'd love to—" Her head snaps forward on the last word, something between a shrug and a dry heave. I gently detach her from the brick wall and steer her toward the car.

"What are you doing?" CeCe, back from the house party,

appears on the sidewalk just as I'm helping Mary into the back seat of the Boat.

"This is my friend Mary. I'm giving her a ride home."

I expect CeCe to balk at this, but she doesn't. Instead, she goes into some kind of sober first-responder mode, forcing Mary to eat a slice of cold pizza and take some ibuprofen while I turn the car around and maneuver past the few busy streets of Nautilus toward her house. Large Marge contributes by licking Mary's elbows.

"Your parents home?" I ask her. I can't see her very well in the rearview mirror because of her hair and all the black she's wearing.

"I don't know," she says. "Maybe. I have to puke."

I start driving five miles over the limit. Mary gags near the window, tapping at the button to lower the glass all the way, which for some ridiculous reason it refuses to do. Stupid Boat.

CeCe reaches into the back seat, producing a plastic bag just in time. Mary grabs it but keeps gagging, which is somehow worse than if she were to actually throw up.

She still hasn't puked by the time we reach her tiny street, which is located at the end of a chain of a half dozen tiny streets. I'm secretly proud of remembering the directions but also guilty about how long it's been.

Mary's house is set farther back from the road than the other houses. It's white and modern, lit up from below, which makes it look even fancier.

"You live here?" CeCe asks Mary, then shoots me a look like, *You didn't mention we'd have to be around rich people.*

I leave the Boat parked at the end of the Dicksons' marathon-length driveway, and we help Mary up the driveway to the house. I try to open the front door, but it's locked.

Before, I've only entered Mary's house through the garage or side door, which would be impossible to access with her in this slumping, barely conscious condition. Not to mention, her parents never seemed to like me and will assume this is my doing despite my own obvious—and unfortunate—sobriety.

"Where's the key?" I ask. CeCe stands a few feet behind us, eyeing an abstract sculpture in the center of the rock garden.

Mary fumbles with her purse, but her fingers seem to be moving on their own. I reach over and search the bag myself. There are no keys.

I suck in my breath and ring the doorbell.

A brown woman I don't recognize answers. She closes her eyes when she sees Mary.

"We ran into each other," I explain to the woman, who I'm guessing works here, running the Dicksons' entire lives for them. My words sound childish in the quiet, cool-aired hallway, but not in a way that helps me. "I gave her a ride home."

Another woman's voice calls from deeper inside. "Glenda, who is it? Who's there?"

Glenda pulls Mary inside. "You're in it now," she says in a West Indian accent. Mary stumbles toward her, leaning into her shoulder. It's like CeCe and I aren't even there.

"We should go," CeCe says.

"Glenda?" the voice repeats, drifting closer to the door. Mary's mom appears in the vestibule. She has the same dark hair and cheekbones, but the rest of her is a thinner, less happy version of her daughter. "Oh. Hi, Minerva."

Mary's mom looks completely unsurprised.

"Hi, Mrs.—" I start.

"I think we'll take it from here. Glenda, the door."

Glenda closes the door in our faces.

A moment passes before CeCe whispers, "Damn," which seems to encompass everything else that can be said for now.

CHAPTER EIGHTEEN

The next day, new information about Duke's comes without me having to gather anything—from Nicole, of all people.

We're in the Beach Blossom laundry room, a small, freestanding structure off to the side of the main building. Today, like most days, only two-thirds of the washers are in working order. Nicole stations me to stand guard over the next available dryer, putting us at odds with a woman who brought her cat with her to do laundry. Both of them glare at us from their seat by the window.

I'm thinking about Eli. I'm sure he's back to disliking me, but that doesn't stop me from picturing his arm muscles straining to scoop a whole pint of vanilla, the hardest flavor.

Nicole jabs my arm. "Look at this." She holds up her tablet, typically used for social media, Candy Crush, and romance novels she thinks I don't know about. It's currently on a news page.

"What now—" I start, but she shoves the tablet into my hands.

"They found the guy who robbed the Ice Creamery."

"*The* guy?" The headline on the screen says, PLANS MELT

FOR SUSPECT IN ICE CREAM ROBBERY, which to me is surprisingly poetic.

Nicole starts reading aloud over my shoulder, as if I can't read on my own. "'Twenty-one-year-old Tristan Maynard of North Babylon has been identified as a key suspect in the robbery of the beloved Nautilus institution.'"

Institution? The giant bowl of cereal I had earlier churns in my stomach.

One of the dryers beeps loudly, and both Nicole and the cat lady stand up. "Don't even try it, you witch," Nicole says loud enough that the cat lady would've heard without the roar of the machines.

Just then, a small-framed older man strolls in, smiles at everyone, and empties the dryer.

Nicole walks over and offers to help him, ensuring our use of the dryer next. I have to give her credit for initiative.

I go back to the news and start the video at the end of the short article, a local news clip about the arrest. At louder-than-necessary volume, it repeats what the article says, along with shots of the ice cream stand wrapped in caution tape and finally the mug shot of a guy with brown skin and facial hair.

"Such a relief," one of the anchors says to the other. "It's good to know our area is now just that much safer."

Nicole comes back from the dryers. "Didn't you say there were *two* guys?"

I manage a nod, my thoughts racing faster than I can catch them. Two guys, two knives, two masks. *Get the fuck down.* Then running and running and running.

"Yeah." I hand her back the tablet. "They were white, too. Which I definitely mentioned to the detectives."

"Huh," Nicole says with a shrug. "Weird."

And yet the guy they caught *did* look familiar. Where have I seen him before?

The article and video didn't say he was armed or wore a mask. They didn't say much of anything. All of it feels like complete and total bullshit. The people who did this—the *two of them*—are still out there.

I reach for my phone, about to text CeCe, when I see the text from Eli.

Did you hear they arrested someone?

I should ignore it. But as much as sheer spite drives me to, I can't ignore him forever. Even though that's exactly what he's been doing to me.

I know, I write back. So wild. There it is. Noncommittal. How things should be.

I start to text CeCe again when Eli sends two more messages in rapid succession.

Want to do something later? I'm getting out of work early.

Assistant manager perks haha

He didn't change his mind about me, after all. CeCe's dumb saying about the phone working both ways was actually relevant. Then I remember, too, what Mary once suggested with all the sweetness in the world. Maybe I was pushing him away before I even tried to know him.

Maybe this whole time he thought *I* was ignoring *him*. Again.

I look back down at the messages, rereading them character by character, before typing out an answer.

Sure. I'm around.

ELI MEETS ME at the picnic tables outside Duke's. He comes out for a five-minute break and gives me a quick kiss on the cheek, as if Jordan and the new girls don't have a decent view from behind the counter, or as if he doesn't care.

We don't touch after that, which is fine, because half my face and neck are on fire. We perch side by side on the farthest available table and pull up more articles and videos on his phone. There aren't a lot, and the information is the same. Along with the conspicuous lack of detail about what really went down.

Jordan keeps peering over at us from the serving window. I try not to pay her any attention and listen to Eli talk about how he got extra projects at the studio where he works for even less money than here—how he had to shuffle his Duke's hours last minute, and it luckily coincided with the new hires. I nod and smile at his excitement like I haven't been theorizing about Eli changing his mind and going out of his way to avoid me.

Except for the fact that we haven't resumed making out, it's like no time has passed since the night in Brooklyn.

"I can't believe it," he says. When we don't find anything more, he clicks the screen black. Jordan eyes us again, but Eli doesn't seem to notice.

"What," I ask, "that they arrested one guy who doesn't even match the descriptions we all gave?"

"That, *and* that it's—" He puts away his phone. "Wait. Don't you know who that guy is?"

I shake my head.

"That's Jamira's boyfriend. Anthony fired her this morning. This must've been why."

"Well, that doesn't seem fair." Jamira barely acknowledges my existence, but I still feel bad for her. "Do you think she had anything to do with the robbery?"

"No idea."

I think back to that day. While I don't have the exact picture in my mind, I'm sure I recall Jamira was as shocked and
terrified as the rest of us. Not that someone couldn't fake
that kind of thing.

Eli jumps down from the table and puts his visor back on,
even though he technically doesn't have to, because Anthony
isn't around.

He touches my knee as he passes, causing shock waves.
"See you in a few minutes?"

I nod and watch him go back inside.

Jordan leans out the big window and refills one of the
napkin dispensers. "So you two are a thing now?"

"No," I say. I train my eyes on the street, looking out for
Anthony, in case he comes back from whatever mysterious
place he's gone.

"I thought you hated Eli."

This breaks my facade. "Why does everybody think
that?" The sentiment is like a horde of mosquitoes at twilight. I didn't even know it existed until after I'd been stung
by it several times.

"Come on, Min." Jordan wipes down the counter. I can
smell the mildew rag from six feet away. "You're not exactly
thrilled to be around any of us."

I wish I could just leave, but I took the bus here again,
and running to the bus stop isn't very dramatic. I go back to
watching the road.

A minute later, Eli comes back out. He's switched out his
Duke's visor for a Yankees cap. "Ready?"

"Yeah." I hop down from the tabletop. "For what,
though?"

"Some people from the studio are setting off fireworks by
the old fort. I was thinking maybe we could go there."

My first thought is that fireworks sound positively whole-some compared to some of the shit I've been up to lately.

"Or we could do whatever," he adds.

"No, I like it. Fireworks with the studio people."

"Nice." He smiles, and I look for his slightly chipped tooth in the dark. I find it at the same time he takes my hand, and we walk to his car.

The old decommissioned fort, last used for a suspiciously brief time during the Cold War and rumored to go all the way back to the Revolutionary War, is a half hour away. So I settle in, lowering the window and letting my hand ride on the wind, which tonight is thick and damp. Eli takes all back roads, which makes me like him even more. He puts on jazzy hip-hop—drums and trumpets and saxophone and a guy shouting behind it all like he's trying to catch up.

Eli tells me more about what he's been working on in the studio. The closest he comes to mentioning school is a pass-ing reference to a "portfolio" he worked on for months to get into college.

Then he asks me what I've been up to.

"Just the usual shenanigans."

"Is that right?" He glances over. "Tell me about these shenanigans."

My heart pounds at his flirting. "Seriously, nothing except ice cream and driving." And losing brain cells in between.

"What about school?" He keeps his eyes on the darkened road, a glare coming off his glasses. "Didn't we see each other there a while back?"

I'm annoyed he doesn't remember the moment for sure—I can still see the freckles at the nape of his neck—on top of suddenly feeling exposed at the mere mention of school. Just as it was settling nicely into the past, along with Mom's

surgery and starting a fight with Mary's girlfriend and everything else I hate talking about.

I force a change of subject. "Hey, Jamira said something
funny the other day."

Eli makes an interested sound, distracted from the conversation by the road disappearing in and out of view. The
street narrows, barely wide enough for his car despite being
a two-way road. A wisp of a deer tail waves just ahead, and
he slows down even more.

"Yeah." I'm lying about it being the other day but otherwise lean on the truth. "She said some girl tried to get
Anthony in trouble once."

Eli winces. "Do we have to talk about that place?"

"I just wonder what happened to her." The trees almost
swallow the road, most of them unnaturally bent from one
storm or another. "I think we would've liked each other."

He considers what I said. "Well . . . I wasn't working
there yet. I think her name was Sierra."

"Sierra what?"

He half smiles. "No idea. And nobody told me what happened, either. Or if they did, I don't remember. Any other
questions?"

"Yes. Is Duke real?"

His smile shrinks to confusion. "What?"

"The Duke of Duke's Ice Creamery. Mr. Duke or whatever. Is he real?"

"Where's this coming from?"

"Just something I've always wondered."

"You wonder a lot about Duke's." He grins. "I'm just
teasing. No work stuff, though. Is that okay?"

I nod and lean into my seat and stare at him. He's serious
now, smooth-faced in the light from the dashboard, his eyes

focused on the winding street ahead. I think about laying my head on his arm but chicken out and rest it on my own arm, against the open window, instead. Another song comes on, and he skips it, then skips the one after that. When he settles on a song, he nudges the volume until the sound fills the space inside the car.

He switches hands on the steering wheel so our hands touch, his thumb against mine. It gets a little easier for us to keep finding each other.

CHAPTER NINETEEN

Eli parks at the end of a long, leafy street with one working light. The sidewalk is lined with wild, sharp grass, most of it taller than both of us and dense enough to block the beach on the other side. He locates a skinny, boarded path that branches off from the sidewalk, and we follow it to the sand.

By now, we're holding hands as if it's something we do every day.

We get to the beach, where the last of the sun is slipping into the bay. The beach narrows as we walk, and the tide comes in closer. The sand widens again, this time dramatically all the way to a perfect wide-open peninsula. A campfire burns at the base of it. Farther out, a few more people set off fireworks, which arch into the sky and break into stars over the beach. Laughter rolls out over the sand and water.

My first thought is how this seems almost as enjoyable as being high.

The next is that I wish I were high to enjoy it more.

Eli introduces me as Minerva to the people at the campfire. The sound of his voice holding my entire first name has me too distracted to remember anyone else's.

One of the firework-setters wanders back from the shore. "What you been up to, DJ Quandary?" I recognize him as the guy from the show who pushed Eli offstage. His curly blond hair is tucked into a knit cap, same as last time. Even up close, it's hard to tell how old he is.

"Man, you know I don't go by that name," Eli says. Our hands aren't touching anymore because Eli and the guy are slapping theirs in greeting.

"You thought of a new name yet?" somebody else asks.

"Nah. Not yet."

The guy from the show turns to me, his gaze lingering on mine. "You look familiar. You ever go to the Barn?"

The Barn is a decrepit Victorian house where CeCe used to do a lot of her pickups.

I shrug. "I don't remember."

"Yeah, you were with that broad."

"Broad?" I repeat.

"What's the Barn?" Eli asks.

"The Barn is basically a trap house," the guy answers, tearing his eyes from mine.

"I ended up there with CeCe a couple times," I explain to Eli, hoping to steer the conversation away from trap houses. "Just tagging along."

"The neighbor who gave you that joint that night?" Eli says. "That thing was strong." I can't tell from his voice if this is good, if it's my imagination that makes him sound just the slightest bit more distant. The firelight that hits his face is too harsh.

Someone offers me a beer from a cooler, and I take it easy drinking at first, letting the taste gather on my tongue and the familiar loose sensation disperse into my body.

Eli's making patterns on my palm as he talks to his friends

about sound layering and different brands of record players and the next shows coming up around the city. He's holding a beer but barely taking any sips, which kind of bugs me, because I've been trying not to give in to how much, how soon I want another beer, to keep this happy feeling afloat.

I squeeze his hand. He squeezes back and smiles.

When the others start setting up another round of fireworks, Eli goes with them. I hang back and wander to where the tide is coming in. The water threatens to soak my sneakers, but I don't care.

A girl who may or may not be somebody's girlfriend comes up next to me smoking a cigarette. She looks like Snow White in short-shorts, with dark, wavy hair spilling over pale shoulders and pink-red lips. She sits down close enough to the water line to have my full attention.

"You with Eli?" Snow White asks in a sweet voice that's hard not to like. She's probably who Nicole wishes she were taking care of as a favor to her sick cousin. Not the bleached, stoned animal she ended up getting stuck with.

"I guess."

"Sorry. I thought 'cause of the way you two were sitting just now." Snow White shrugs. "I know how it is, though. Nothing wrong with having some fun. Especially if he's leaving soon, right?"

"Right."

"He's going to some kind of fruit school," she mumbles, leaning in for a drag off her cigarette.

"Carnegie Mellon?"

"Yeah." She giggles. "Anyway, Eli's a good one." She presses her beer bottle into the sand and lights another cigarette. "Want one?"

"Nah. My lipstick." But it's not about my lipstick. It's

that cigarettes remind me of Mom and all the times she swore she'd stop. How it seems like one of the only things she couldn't achieve, aside from good health and leaving Nautilus, of course. But I can't tell Snow White about that.

She coughs. "You okay?" Her sweetness falters; she doesn't particularly sound as if she wants to know the answer.

"Oh. Sure. I mean, with Eli and me . . . it's not like that with us."

"Me, neither," she says, though I have no idea who she means.

We drink our beers in the silence outside the yelling and one-upping around the fireworks. Then the yelling turns frantic, something about pigs, and there's a rush to put out the fire.

Multicolored police lights illuminate the grass behind us. I gradually recognize the sound of police sirens, on a slight delay because of the beer now swirling around my empty stomach.

Eli appears and pulls me up off the sand. We run back along the beach the way we came.

He calls out, "This was a safe spot forever . . . They must've found out about it at some point."

Out of nowhere, he parts the grass and dips in. There's a faint path here.

"Careful," he says, referring to the greenery slapping at us as we make our way down the path. He goes first, holding back as much of it as he can. A lot of it feels prickly. My heart feels like it's hanging from a bungee cord.

We reach the sidewalk and run some more. The sirens sound much farther away. But as we're hustling along the street in the direction of his car, another cop car comes flying down the street.

Eli stops and pulls me into a deep kiss, and the cop car swishes past.

The cover actually, stupidly, works.

We're still kissing long after the cop passes.

Eli pulls away. "We should get to the car." But I can't stop watching his mouth, the adorable tiny chip in his front tooth. He leans back in, this time making his way down my neck.

"I know." I'm laughing at his breath on my skin and because we just ran from the cops over some fireworks and underage drinking.

I probably could've tried harder to get information from him earlier, but what was I supposed to do? Keep talking about work when he asked to stop?

Besides, everything in my life is about the plan, the only chance left at catching up. My real Second Start: better than having to depend on my mother's cousin, who doesn't even like me, or deal with that fake, holier-than-thou guidance counselor again.

Eli's the only thing that makes me forget why the plan exists in the first place. For now, at least. While he's still here.

"You okay?" he asks.

I nod.

"Sorry we had to leave like that."

I kiss him again. I swear he smells like some kind of spice. Cinnamon or nutmeg. Something turned sweet in a fire. We both probably smell like sweat from sprinting through foliage.

I don't want to care that he's leaving. I don't want to worry about what it means to hold his hand or not hold his hand.

"No," I say. "It was perfect."

CHAPTER TWENTY

Later that week, CeCe is in a frenzy. When I let myself into her apartment, she's got several lamps in a cluster on the floor, all plugged in and shining aggressively. Everywhere else in the apartment is dark. She's holding tweezers above Large Marge, who looks like she's about to bolt any second.

"Ticks again," CeCe says. "This time, like, four or five of them."

"Stop letting her loose in the woods," I reply.

"I don't know where else to take her. It's not like I can drive anywhere. I just need some flea and tick medicine."

"So get some."

"It's more expensive than I thought it was."

"What happened?"

My question to her is shorthand for, *What happened to all your money? From dealing?* Although she's not coming right out and admitting it, she's broke.

She purses her lips. "My mom moved out," she says. "Guess who's stuck paying rent?"

That's when I notice the apartment is emptier. A lot emptier—most of the furniture has been removed, leaving big ghostly rectangles in the carpet where the sofa and love seat used to be. How long has it been since CeCe mentioned her mother?

"Hold her down while I try to get the rest of these fuckers out?"

Large Marge directs her wet, begging eyes at me as I hold her collar straight.

"So where'd your mom go?" I ask.

"With her boyfriend in Laurel Harbor." CeCe grunts, leaning in with the tweezers. "Living out her wildest gated community dreams."

After a few painstaking minutes, she locates and removes each tick, dropping it onto a plastic shopping bag on the floor. I try my hardest not to dry heave.

Large Marge skitters away as soon as we let her go. CeCe ties the bag shut and slumps against the wall. "We have to do something," she says.

"What else can we do?"

"I'm talking about the money. I can't wait anymore. We have to make a move now, or I need to figure something else out."

"Now?" I repeat. "How soon you thinking?"

"Like tomorrow." CeCe wipes down the tweezers with rubbing alcohol from a bottle she had lying there. "You still hooking up with that dude Eli?"

"We're not hooking up," I say, even though I'm not sure what objectively counts as hooking up.

"Whatever. You still *involved*? Did you get anything we can use?"

"He doesn't know anything." My face crumples; I might be blushing. "I asked him about Sierra."

"Yeah, and he didn't even know her last name. You already told me, remember?" CeCe grimaces. "It's a dead end."

Large Marge lays her head in my lap and whines. I scratch the back of her ears. I'm not sure which one of us feels sorrier for herself.

CeCe packs her bag, clearly thinking. "What about that girl whose boyfriend got arrested?"

"Jamira?"

"Yeah. She's gotta be pissed at Anthony for firing her, right? Maybe she knows something about where he keeps it."

"She'd at least know if her boyfriend actually committed the robbery. Which he didn't." My mouth tightens at the news report again, at the nagging feeling that the cops didn't care at all what I told them about that night. Why did they even want to talk to me? Was it just to *look* like they were working on it? Didn't it matter to them to find the person— *people*—who actually committed the crime?

"If she's got anything, great. In the meantime, we need to find a way to search your boss's office." CeCe leaves the room and comes back chewing on a cold slice of pizza. "You ready to go?"

"Where now?"

"Hello? Large Marge's meds aren't gonna pay for themselves." She crams the last of the pizza crust into her mouth and picks up her backpack.

There's a knock on the apartment door.

CeCe stiffens, pizza crust sticking partway out of her mouth. "Who in the fuck could that be?"

"How should I know?" I demand.

"You locked it behind you, right?"

"Of course I did."

She stomps to the door and checks the peephole, then turns to make a face at me. "It's that girl."

I have no idea who she means, so I just shrug. She unlocks

the door to reveal Mary, her face a multicolored mess of tears and makeup. Mary freezes on seeing us, as if she's just as surprised to find herself here as we are.

On instinct, I position myself between the two of them, an attempt to keep the different parts of my life from colliding.

"Can I help you?" CeCe asks in the voice I've heard her use with white people, older men, and anyone who's given her a hard time in general. Like last time, Mary looks like she's going to puke, but this time from fear.

"What's going on?" I ask Mary, observing the red eyes underneath old makeup probably worth more than a week of groceries. She wears a formless tie-dye shirt from the Hot Topic clearance rack—I remember because she swore me to secrecy—matched with black joggers and ballet flats. No lipstick, no lace, no earrings in her multipierced ears. "Are you okay? Did something happen?"

What I really want to ask is, *What in the world are you doing here?* In all the time we've been friends, she's never come to the Beach Blossom. I never offered, and she stopped asking. I don't even know how she got the building address.

"Your cousin said you'd be here," she starts.

"Nicole?" I ask. She nods. I'm so shocked that Nicole even knew where to find me that I don't bother to correct Mary on the whole second-cousin thing.

Mary crosses her arms, clutching the cursed tie-dyed fabric of her shirt as if she's freezing. "I just wanted to say sorry. About the other night." She glances at CeCe, whose eyes are twitching in frustration. "To both of you."

"That's nice," CeCe hollers, and I almost jab her in the side.

"It's okay," I say. "Really. You didn't have to come all the way here."

"Yes, I did. Look, I don't remember everything that happened that night, but the things Mom said the next day . . ." The lower half of Mary's face buckles, and she looks like she's going to cry. "I have some idea of how it went down."

CeCe rolls her eyes. "Yeah, well. Your mom was rude as hell, is what happened. Now, do you mind? We have somewhere to be."

Mary's face falls even more. She takes a single step back. "Sorry, I didn't—"

My heart thumps, a muted feeling in my chest caused by months of disuse. Something occurs to me. "Hang on. CeCe, can I talk to you for a second?"

CeCe growls with impatience and stalks back to her bedroom. I follow her in, noticing that it's partly bare now like the rest of the apartment. It appears her mom also took the bed frame, dresser, and a coffee table that had previously been covered with lighters and roach clips. It looks like the furniture popped out of existence and everything on top and inside of it fell to the floor: clothes bunched in the corners, candy wrappers and blunt leaves and random cords snaking around the room.

"Well?" CeCe says.

"Mary might be able to help us."

"No. Are you serious? We already decided not to tell anyone." She unties and reties her ponytail. "She'll throw off the whole balance. It's too random. I don't like it."

"You're so stubborn." The more I think about it, though, the more it makes sense. I can already feel the pressure lightening, redirected just a little. "She's smart. You should see her grades."

"How wonderful for her."

I bring out the big guns. "Her dad works with celebrities

and rich people." When CeCe just stares back at me, I add, "Maybe it could come in handy."

She raises her eyebrows. "How exactly is her rich dad knowing other rich people supposed to help us?"

"It's not, I just—"

I can't tell CeCe about my lingering guilt for having ghosted my friend. Or about how having Mary around will make this all less terrifying. But CeCe claims to be good at reading people. I'm sure my guilt and fear creep in under my words.

"Hold up. Is that what you think? That she'd use her 'connections' to help us?" CeCe bobs her head, using air quotes.

"I think she'd help us however she could." This I know isn't just a byproduct of my guilt. It's true. Mary tried to be there every time Mom was hospitalized, and the past few months I simply didn't let her. And now here we both are. "I promise we can trust her. And she feels bad for what happened the other night."

"Oh, you mean when we tried to save her ass and got a door slammed on us?"

"Yeah, that."

To my surprise, CeCe nods.

"You promise, huh?" she says. "Fine. We could use a lookout or something."

She turns on her heel and storms back to the eerily, vacant living room. Mary's sitting in the middle of the floor with Large Marge, who's correctly assumed she can snag extra belly rubs out of the situation and has fully recovered from her tick removal.

"See?" I try to sound light and hopeful. "Large Marge likes her."

"Large Marge likes everyone."

It's true.

CeCe whistles sharply, and Large Marge runs over and dances circles around us. "All right, Amy—"

"My name's Mary."

"Whatever." CeCe juts her chin at me, as if to prove a point. Whether it's mine or hers is still to be determined. "You want to help find some laundered money and get back at Min's awful fucking boss?"

Mary hiccups at me. "Is she joking?"

"I'm afraid not," I say.

Frowning behind dark overgrown bangs, she looks like a character from one of her manga books, so many of them in her room she had to start stacking them under her bed (which, for some reason, really stressed her mother out).

"Well?" CeCe urges. "Do you want to help or not?"

Mary stands slowly, wiping her nose with the back of her hand. Her head shakes in disbelief, first at the floor, then back up at us. "Hell, yeah."

CHAPTER TWENTY-ONE

The plan is pretty simple. I get a copy of the keys to Duke's, and CeCe—who already has a basic understanding of how to pick a lock—is in charge of opening the safe in Anthony's office, which, if I remember correctly, is about as big as a printer and located in the back corner behind his head.

The safe is a last resort, though. "We're looking for stacks upon stacks," CeCe says. "A tiny little office safe isn't gonna be it."

I have a day off before my next chance to steal keys for Mary to have copied. When Jamira's boyfriend comes up again—this time a longer-than-necessary article in the *Weekly Wave* that rambles about local crime—I take it as a sign to ask Jamira about it.

Jamira doesn't answer any texts or calls, so I show up at her house, which sits in a dead-end street in a neighborhood where there are more than a couple of houses with boards for windows. Which doesn't necessarily mean they're empty. The lot containing her house is filled with shiny plants and a few trees. Behind the house, cars are parked in a rough line.

Jamira answers the door holding a squirming toddler.

"He's not mine," she greets me. "What do you want?"

"Sorry to show up like this." I poke at the screen door. "Can you talk a minute?"

She doesn't move behind the screen. "About what?"

"Duke's."

"Well, duh. Of course about Duke's."

"I heard what happened with your boyfriend."

She breathes in long and sharp through her nose and finally lets me in. She sets down the baby, who totters ahead into a carpeted room with kids of various ages. Jamira yells in Spanglish at a younger girl wearing headphones. The girl rolls her eyes but scoots over to mind the baby on the floor.

"I guess this was a bad time," I say.

Jamira shrugs and starts out of the room. "Name a good one."

"True."

We walk through a kitchen where the remnants of breakfast are spread out across the stove and counter, a mess of eggs and bread and butter melting in the lack of air-conditioning. Jamira's kitchen isn't nearly as bad as mine, though—at least the food is recently cooked and not spoiling.

She opens a door to a deck overlooking a yard with a big rectangular in-ground pool covered by a dirty, hole-filled tarp. At certain angles, the holes hint at a full swamp just beneath. Part of the fence is sprayed with dried mud, like from car wheels spinning nearby.

Jamira hits from a vape pen, her head wrapped in a pale mist for a second. She sees me eyeing the pen and says, "Relax. It's tobacco, not the other shit."

"Okay, okay."

She leans against the rail and shakes her head. "Tristan didn't do anything, you know."

"Your boyfriend?"

"Somebody said he was there. I mean, that's gotta be what it is. Except Tristan thinks *I* was the one who told the cops." She takes another, longer drag. "Sometimes I thought he might be messing with other girls, but I wouldn't bring the cops into it. I mean, for what?"

"I believe you," I say. "We saw who did it. It was someone else."

She squints at me and pushes away from the railing, standing up straight. She's much taller than I realized. "Okay. You believe me. Now what? You came all the way to my house to tell me that?"

"Not exactly." I shift my feet on the deck. "I'm trying to figure out what happened."

She exhales slowly, giving me a sideways look. "Because you care *so much* about Duke's. Okay, well, that it? I still have to make lunch for all these kids."

My head lightens. I want to bolt, but I've gotten this far. This is my best chance to find out more about the last Duke's girl who tried to mess with Anthony. "There is one more thing, as a matter of fact. Sierra."

Jamira groans at the sky. "What about her?"

"I'm just curious."

"Sure you are. What do you want to know?"

"Why did she leave? What exactly did she say?"

After a silence in which Jamira considers her vape pen and impressive bejeweled fingernails, she proceeds to tell the story, or what she knows of it.

About a year ago, there was this girl named Sierra who, upon finding out about the cameras, went twice as apeshit as I did. At first, she tried to catch Anthony. Tried to record him doing or saying something sexist, racist, homophobic, transphobic—take your pick. Everyone told her to stop wasting her time because of all his cop friends.

The same thing Jamira told me when I first started working there, I want to point out, but don't.

"But then she stopped talking about it. Stopped saying much of anything." Jamira stares as if watching the memory playing over the yard. "You could tell she was still thinking about it, though. She had a notebook she'd open throughout the shift, write stuff down. A couple times they caught her looking around in places she shouldn't have.

"The few times she did talk, she'd say something about how one day Anthony was going to get what he deserved. How we would all get what we deserve." Jamira pauses. "She was a piece of work, that one. For real."

"And he fired her?"

Jamira takes out her vape again and then seems to change her mind, her hand clinging to the air around her pocket. "No. She just stopped showing up for work. Pissed Anthony right the hell off. He hates firing people, even the annoying ones. Says it's worse to have to train them."

"Why?" I say. "It's not like he does any of the training himself."

"I know, right? That's what Jordan said, too. She didn't like Sierra much, either." Jamira winces. "Fuck, I'm sorry. I didn't mean to make it sound like—"

My face hurts a little, a mixture of embarrassment and my chronically absent tears, but I say, "It's okay. Jordan not liking me's not much of a surprise."

Jamira swivels around, sliding the vape pen back into her pocket. "We gotta be done here. I still have to figure out what to feed these little monsters." Despite her talk, she blows a kiss to a couple of kids watching us through the window.

"Okay." I have an idea and come right out with it, because there's something about starting any line of conversation with Jamira that feels like standing before a pit of spikes. "You want some help?"

"Yeah," she says without missing a beat.

A minute later, she has me slathering peanut butter on an infinite number of white bread slices while she searches the cupboards for jelly and anything else that can feed what turns out to be seven kids in total, a mix of family and neighbors. Jamira makes me eat with them.

"Trade-off is cleaning duty," she adds with a smirk. She taps her manicured nails on the table, avoiding a rogue blob of peanut butter. Kids swarm the table like ants on a sidewalk, yelling and chanting for me to stay. I don't leave for another three hours.

CHAPTER TWENTY-TWO

Catching up with Mary is less painful than I imagined. It might be the screwdrivers she furtively prepared in the kitchen while Glenda's out visiting her sister. We're also sitting on her balcony, which overlooks the harbor. Boats of different sizes crawl by, far enough away to look like toys.

It might also be that Mary barely mentions Vera or anything that happened a few months ago. I don't want to ruin the moment by asking.

When I fill her in about Eli, she cries, "I *knew* something was going to happen with the two of you. That boy is muy caliente."

"Don't say 'muy caliente.' Also, you've never even met him."

"Yeah, but I feel like I have." She takes a careful sip of her drink. I've been eyeing her glass to make sure I don't drink too much faster than her. "I just don't understand. Why didn't you tell me about what happened at the Ice Creamery?"

I'm reminded how everyone in the general community calls it *the Ice Creamery*, or the name in its entirety, *Duke's Ice Creamery*. With a kind of reverence. It's hardly ever just *Duke's*. Even Mary does this.

"I can't believe I didn't even know it was robbed." Her voice is small, barely loud enough for me to hear just a foot away. She dabs at the corner of her eye, getting shimmery orange eye shadow on her fingers. "I feel like if I had been around, or even not hanging out with Vera and those people, I would've known."

"Mary—"

"I'm serious. You're my best friend. You've had all this stuff going on with the robbery. Plus your mom. I wanted to ask—"

"Mary, please." My heart beats fast. I need her to stop talking about these things. I take a giant gulp, mostly melted ice. I need this moment to be an escape.

"I just— I can't believe you were robbed." This may be the hundredth time she's said this since I told her the other day. "And how horrible it is to work there."

I rub the goosebumps rising along my arms despite the heat of the day. Out of everything, what comes to mind is the cop who harassed me months ago and Anthony's laughter. Sometimes it blends with the moment of the robbery. "It's . . . Anthony . . . he's . . ."

"He's a fucking monster, is what he is." She sets down her glass a little too fast. "He shouldn't be allowed to have a business."

"He shouldn't be allowed to have a dick." That one was from Mom's arsenal, something I heard her say on the phone once.

Mary shuts her eyes and laughs. "God, I missed you."

"I missed *you*," I say.

"It's just not the same anymore," she says. "Haven't you noticed?" She reaches over and squeezes my hand. She's always been a hand holder, a hugger, a talker of feelings. I think she's convinced that if she keeps pointing out how weird it's been between us that it'll break up and clear the awkwardness. Before this, our longest fight lasted a single school day; it was that way ever since we met in homeroom freshman year.

"School's not the same," I say. "As in, I'm not going."

I don't know why I said that, except that Mary has a quality that makes people blurt out their shame. It takes a certain amount of skill and practice to hide from her.

Mary shifts in her chair, and I wait for the usual pep talk about how I can just focus and use all my resources to make my mark on the world. Saying a lot of the things Mom's said before, in fact, except a lot nicer. But Mary doesn't say it. In fact, she changes subjects altogether. "Actually, I was wondering what's going on with CeCe," she says.

I finally lean over and steal a gulp of her drink. Mine is all orange-flavored ice with the memory of vodka. "What do you mean, what's going on with her?" There's so much Mary could be referring to: the army surplus wear, the squinting, the spoiled pit bull, the drug-selling.

"She's gay, right?"

"Oh." My focus is off from remembering Mom and her lectures about applying myself. "Yeah."

"I thought maybe . . ."

"What happened to Vera?" I wince at the irony of being the one to bring her up.

She scrunches her face, her half-glass of mixed drink doing way more work than mine. "Vera's kind of . . . small-minded. She has no curiosity about the world."

"And you think CeCe does?"

Mary reaches for her glass. She doesn't drink from it, which drives me nuts all over again. "You don't think so? What are you saying, exactly?"

"She's my neighbor." I don't know what this is supposed to mean. Explaining this feels like that figure of speech about building a plane while flying it. "She just gets into some pretty stupid situations. This whole thing about stealing from Duke's was her idea."

"I know," Mary says, sipping. "I think it's kind of brilliant. It's *something*. Nobody tries anything different in this place."

I look out over the water, all white caps today. My favorite kind of ocean.

Mary tucks an extra-bleached strand behind my ear. "You'll leave one day, you know. It's going to happen." And then she says, "How's your mom?"

The balcony tilts closer to the ocean. The drink resurfaces—how fast I drank it.

"She was in the hospital again a while back, wasn't she? Did she get any better?"

I stand up, accidentally knocking over the glass on the balcony floor. Ice tumbles and slides off the edge under the railing and down to the grass below.

"You okay?" Mary asks, louder than she needs to. So much louder. "Have you taken anything?"

Did I? I can't remember. Maybe I did take something, maybe I didn't. Maybe it was the night before or a few nights ago. All of time sputters, a slowed heartbeat.

"Vertigo?" Mary says into my face. Either she's not speaking in complete sentences, or the blood in my ears stifles the sound of her voice. She pulls me out of the chair and suddenly I'm lying down on something soft, as if the surface came to me instead of me to it.

I wake up in Mary's bed, which is at least twice as big as mine, under a comforter that goes on forever. The white sea

of fabric reflects the white ceiling. There's a pleasant noth-
ingness I haven't felt in a while.

Sitting up, I take a sip of water from a glass on the night-
stand. It's not the first time I've woken up like this here.
When I first started stealing Mom's pills and didn't yet
understand what they could do, I fell asleep in Mary's bed a
few times. She would do her homework, draw, mess around
online, play Astral Kingdom. After enough time, food would
appear—grilled cheese, fruit salad, crackers—like a miracle
on a plate beside me.

She never judged me.

But I kept feeling guilty, ever more aware of how I must've
been coming off to Mary's parents, who were always on the
way to or coming back from somewhere. Never just hanging
around like Mom and I seemed to do whenever we weren't
at school or work. Asking about how the day was going,
demanding the most obscure details just to have them.

Whenever I did encounter Mr. and Mrs. Dickson, they
would say hello, their smiles flat with whatever real greeting
they were keeping in.

I realized one day that they'd never asked me anything
about myself, never called me by my name, either Min
or Minerva. Like they couldn't wait for me to go away. I
didn't have to ask what they thought of me: someone who'd
wormed her way into their kid's school just by virtue of
being poor. And then into their home.

I don't belong here. I force myself out of Mary's bed and
into her bathroom. I'm assaulted by my reflection in the full-
length mirror just past the door. I'm a complete mess in my
donated clothes and sun-chapped lips. My hair is thick and
snarled, like the discarded fishing wire you find sometimes
on the boardwalk. I pick up a pair of scissors Mary left near

her toothbrush. While her bedroom is immaculate, her bathroom is full of items she hasn't cared to put away.

I start cutting off my split ends in the sink. The alcohol turns in my stomach.

"What are you doing?" Mary screeches behind me. "Oh, Min, no."

She takes the scissors and says she can fix the damage. Astral Kingdom plays on the other side of the door, a more experimental album called *When the Days and Nights*. There's an instrumental song on harp and some other string instrument I don't recognize. The scissors *click* away near my ear. My throat tightens and my eyes ache, but again, there aren't any tears to hide. Just a vacant, hurting space.

"This stuff with Eli doesn't feel real," I say. "After liking him so long. Was it like that with Vera?"

The scissors hover before Mary follows through on a slow and tentative cut. "I don't know."

"Do you love her?"

"There are different kinds of love," she answers. "There's love and there's lust and then there's some kind of in-between or combination of the two. I think that last one is what I have with Vera. It's just so different from anything else I've ever felt. Or it was." She cuts some more.

I have a suspicion that I can't love anything. It's too embarrassing to say out loud, like admitting that I never got around to learning how to ride a bike or tie my shoes.

Maybe there's an advantage in being unable to love. I think of my parents. What good was love back then?

One of the many times I asked Mom about my father, earlier on, she said one thing that stuck out. "Love is just chemicals. It makes you feel good and want to procreate. That's all it does."

That was the closest she ever got to admitting she was ever in love. Men didn't seem to concern her very much. There'd usually be something about the guy she decided she didn't like, and then he didn't exist anymore. None of them became part of our lives.

I remember hoping Mom was wrong. Who'd want to believe a thing like that? Who'd want to give up on love that quick?

"Fuck love," I say without thinking. "It's useless."

I expect Mary to disagree, protest, convince me otherwise. We've had this debate before. But she just sighs and rubs serum into my hair. "You're right. Love is useless."

We exchange glances in the mirror. She's done something to my hair to make it appear as if it's been played with by the wind, in a good way.

Her fingertips rest on the very top of my head. "It sure is pretty, though."

CHAPTER TWENTY-THREE

It's the dead hour, midweek opening. It feels like forever since it's been just Eli and me at Duke's. There's no Anthony, Jamira (still fired), Jordan, or new girls. We manage a few strategic kisses between orders.

I still don't know what we mean to each other. We've been texting between shifts, and a few times he's asked to pick me up and go to the beach, and every time I've constructed a different excuse so he wouldn't see where I live. Or me in a bathing suit.

We race through the routine of stocking cones and toppings and popular flavors. He counts out the register while I pretend to sweep. Then we settle at the counter and take turns playing a paint-themed game on his cell phone.

After about ten minutes of this, my back pocket buzzes. I pretend to lose the game and, turning out of sight, open the group text. CeCe has written, You got his keys yet?

Even though I agreed to this beforehand, now all I want is to keep playing games on Eli's phone and sneaking into the corner to make out.

I put away my phone without answering CeCe's text. Absentmindedly, I pat the front pocket of the mechanic's shirt I found at the Goodwill and remove the joint I was going to use in the event I can't relax.

"What's that?"

Too late.

"Oh." I slip it back into my pocket. "I've been getting these headaches. But I wasn't going to—"

Eli tilts his head and reaches over. I think he's going to snatch it up, but he touches my hand instead. "A normal joint?" he says, like it's a genuine question, brushing the inside of my wrist with his thumb, "or one of those monster joints from your neighbor?"

I can't tell if he likes this or not.

"Normal." I close my eyes, relishing his hand on my wrist. He leans down and kisses me, and I've officially lost count of how many times we've kissed. The fact of this hits me like a bus (or a white pickup truck).

When I pull back, he's staring over my shoulder, still absently squeezing my wrist. I turn and follow his gaze to the nearest camera stationed behind the cake freezer.

"What? He's not here right now, and they don't record. Right?" I think back to the last time we made out, about fifteen minutes ago, right here in the cake station. "If not, we probably got bigger problems."

"No, you're right. They're just for show."

I can't help myself. "Seems like Anthony's gotten plenty out of having them."

"I try not to think about that."

"Lucky you."

"Why?" Eli frowns a little, and for a moment I can't quite read him. "I work here, too. I'm on those cameras, too. I get to hear the shit he—" He falters.

"What?" I can feel the earlier perfection of the moment

slipping away, like a smile interrupted by bad news. "Did he say something about me and you?"

"Nothing." Eli jumps onto the stool in the cake station, making us closer to eye level. "Let's not think about people who aren't here."

We kiss again for a good thirty seconds before my phone buzzes yet again.

Eli pulls away, asks drowsily, "You going to get that?"

I might as well.

This time it's Mary. How about now?

I scramble to type out a no and put my phone away.

"Who was that?" Eli asks.

"Nobody."

When he raises his eyebrows, I add, "It's just my friend Mary. We have plans later." *Yes*, I think. *We're robbing this place once and for all.*

A smaller voice in the back of my head says, *Why does he want to know?*

Others join in. The alternate-universe Minervas, perhaps. *Why? Why? Why? He's leaving.*

I need to keep my head on straight.

Eli tugs on me the same time I lean into him, and it feels so comfortable and right that I forget about the joint in my pocket. Right now, he smells like the cold, sweet inside of the ice cream freezers. Every second he keeps touching me, I'm shocked to be this Minerva, in this universe, here with him.

And then I remember the money, and how much I want that, too. My envelope.

It's an exhausting, never-ending loop.

He lifts my face for a kiss. It's the perfect moment. I almost don't do it, but I have to.

I reach down and unhook the small key ring from his side

belt loop, because now his hands are roaming everywhere on me. I kiss his neck, and we both sort of collapse.

It's the perfect distraction for both of us.

WHEN MARY SHOWS up, it's that point in the day when the sun is still going strong. Duke's becomes a little busier, the customers restless from all the heat and light. I'm at the window, wearing an old pair of Mom's sunglasses I found in the Boat even though it's definitely not allowed. Their main purpose is to hide the terror in my eyes, which otherwise would be visible from the gas station across the street.

"Butter pecan milkshake," Mary says when she reaches the counter.

I lean in, lowering my voice. "What the hell took you so long?"

"I was held up," she says with a sunny, unaffected grin. She slides partway over the counter to get a look into the store. "Is Eli in there? Are you in love yet?"

"He's on break, and no, we're not." As soon as I say it, I realize I don't quite know if it's true, which jump-starts my pulse. "Also, Jordan's coming soon, and you need to get out of here. Now."

"CeCe thinks you're in love," Mary teases. She sets down a twenty and winks. "I'll take that milkshake now."

I leave her money and turn around to start the shake. I've already told her about the base and how gross it is, but Mary's sweet tooth is even worse than mine. I place the finished milkshake, with whipped cream and three cherries, onto the counter.

Along with Eli's keys for her to have copied at the locksmith as quickly as possible.

"Goddess," she whispers as she reaches for a straw. "I'm on it."

Eli comes back from break, and we start the phone games over again, but I'm more nervous about the keys with every passing second. It hasn't hit me until now that this plan technically involves stealing from him. This whole time, I've been reassuring myself that it'll only complicate things if I tell him, and that pulling off the plan without anybody noticing, including Eli, would make it like it didn't really happen, technically—but my nerves prove me wrong.

We ditch the phone games and talk about movies in the calm before the evening rush. I'm in the middle of describing one of my favorites, *Taxi Driver*, when I realize Eli has grown quiet. "You okay?"

He looks down. "Yeah, I was just up late working on some stuff."

"Hey." I point in the direction of the tables outside, which are filled with regular customers: a guy who always insists his two vanilla scoops are smaller than the last time he was here, and a married couple who yells on their respective cell phones for the entire duration of their order. "You should take a longer break."

My voice is light and casual, but he has to say yes, or else I'll have to try extra hard to hide the keys when Mary brings them back.

Luckily, he doesn't need convincing. "You sure? There was a piece I actually wanted to make some notes on."

"Of course I'm sure."

He gives me a light kiss on the cheek and heads out back. The pressure valve that's been sitting on top of my rib cage loosens just a little.

Fifteen minutes pass. Mary should have reached the

locksmith by now, and requested the keys copied. We decided to copy all of them, since it's impossible to test them out now.

"Where's Eli?"

I turn to find Jordan walking in, earlier than expected yet again. "What are you doing here?"

She feigns shock. "So rude. I'm here to do the cakes since Jamira went and got herself fired. Where's Eli?"

"On break."

She checks the time on her phone and makes a sound of curiosity in her throat before moving on to the cake station in the back. But not before twisting up the volume dial on whatever Ariana Grande song is playing on the radio.

Back at the counter, I check again to see if Mary texted any sort of update on her progress. Nothing, nothing, nothing.

After checking three times, with several eternities between each, I see Jordan coming back to the counter. She's wearing the plastic gloves and holding a spatula. "Is Eli still on break?"

Before I can figure out how to lie on Eli's behalf, he walks back in. He's rubbing his neck and adjusting his visor.

Jordan wrinkles her cute square nose, annoyed that he's not worried about looking bad in front of her. She levels her gaze at him. My anxiety cranks ever higher as I watch silently from the sidelines. "Are you going to count the register?"

"Sure," I butt in, as a joke.

Jordan shoots me an annoyed, fake smile and turns back to Eli. "The register?"

"Yeah, I'll do it now." He reaches for his belt loop, then grasps at the unexpected emptiness there. "My keys. They're gone."

Jordan shuts her eyes in disbelief. "How do you lose keys you're supposed to keep on you at all times?"

I sort of gravitate to the back corner, near the sherbet freezers. I wish I hadn't just shoved Eli into the middle of our stupid plan. Or at least, I wish I'd taken a second or two to reconsider. Because right now, I feel like a monster. If Jordan mentions this to Anthony, maybe not realizing the true extent of the implications, Eli will catch a mouthful.

And then I remember: if everything goes right and we find the money, they could still figure us out. Eli getting a mouthful would be the least of my worries.

It's too late to stop, though. It's way too late.

I text Mary. Where in the fuck are you?

The phone buzzes back right away. On my way back. There's a funeral procession or something!!!!

I cough into my closed fist.

In front, Eli's patting the whole area around the register, rubbing the back of his neck. "I have no idea what happened . . ."

"You should check out back," I say when I reach the counter. I take an order of multiple chocolate waffle cones as seriously as if I'm collecting data for a trip to Mars.

"Oh. Yeah," he says, shaking his head. "I'll be right back." I squash the urge to run over and rub the worry lines from his forehead.

Jordan retreats to the cake station. She's turned up the music volume even higher and seems to be channeling her annoyance into crafting a series of pink flowers along the cake edges, which actually come out looking quite nice, though not as masterful as Jamira's.

At last, Mary's car passes and turns the corner into the lot.

"Have you seen the sugar pearls?"

Jordan is directly behind me. She smells clean and sweet and plastic, whatever lip gloss smells like. I've been so focused I didn't even notice her approach.

Mary reappears a few feet away from behind a huge family with several howling kids who must have come from the beach. I pretend like she's just another customer.

"What? No." I edge away from Jordan. "Why would I even know that?"

"I just thought you might've seen them."

"Well, I haven't."

What Jordan says under her breath sounds like *such a bitch*, but I have to let it go. Anything to get her as far away from me as the stand allows. I breathe again as she moves on to the cupboard above the toppings station and starts moving containers around.

I wave Mary closer, and she circumnavigates the family, who's still deciding on their order. In the time it takes for her to reach the counter, I check again for Jordan, who's removed several surplus-sized containers of sprinkles in order to see better inside the cupboard.

I reach forward and take the keys. The second they leave her hand, Mary is gone, disappeared behind the family. I shove them into my jeans pocket as soundlessly as I can.

On my way to the bathroom, I pass Eli, who looks as if he just pulled an all-nighter looking for his keys.

"Hey," I say, "watch the counter?"

I dart into the bathroom, check my eyes for redness (minimal), and walk back out, holding the keys in the air. "Found them on the bathroom floor."

Eli lets out a huge sigh of relief as I drop the keys into his hand. Jordan just shakes her head. A small line of customers has started to form outside.

"I don't understand how this could've happened." He opens the register and starts picking through it in a daze.

"Well, figure it out," Jordan says. "If something else happens around here, Anthony could literally murder someone."

The hairs on the back of my neck stand up. I become laser-focused on serving the next customer, a young dad with twins clutching his shoulders and legs like toy monkeys. I bury the usual involuntary jealousy of parents spending quality time with their kids, glad for the excuse to keep busy.

CHAPTER TWENTY-FOUR

The night we plan to break into Duke's, CeCe throws a party at the Beach Blossom. She insists it's the perfect cover. When I walk in, the lights are off everywhere except one wall in the living room, where a movie plays from a brand-new projector she must have purchased recently.

In the movie, mute underneath the music, thick columns of fire and smoke rise up and surround a pagoda. It's a revenge fire, a warning fire.

The presence of other people somewhat hides the cavelike emptiness of the place since CeCe's mom left and took most of the furniture. I recognize some faces from the neighborhood, kids I grew up around but didn't play with—not that I wasn't allowed to, but no one ever asked, and Mom hated dealing with other parents. I remember hearing at school about the fun, normal activities everyone but me had been doing. Handball, basketball, manhunt, beach expeditions. To my mother, being around the other kids was inconsequential, secondary to my life plan of being smart and getting out (like her) and staying out (unlike her).

The rest of the dark is filled with darting lights from people's phones. Forty-ounces and various cups are scattered across the limited surfaces, including the floor. Smoke layers the air across the room and moves with the bodies, the source an orange pinpoint of a blunt.

I'm not even tempted this time, knowing it'll make the dread about our plan worse.

Someone grabs me by the waist. I immediately make a fist.

"Easy, babe." Mary pops out from my periphery, and for a second my confusion grows like a wildfire before dying down. She's wearing a long-sleeved black shirt and pants, per our plan. "That's not the kind of action we need right now. Save it for the target."

She pulls me down the hall to CeCe's room. It's still a shock seeing her in the Beach Blossom, and more so in CeCe's place. Still, I hope and pray she doesn't ask to come over, and so far she hasn't mentioned me getting a head rush at her house and needing to nap like a toddler.

When we reach the bedroom, CeCe's sitting in a new leather recliner I've never seen before. She's glued to her phone.

"Are you ready—" I begin.

"Yes, *got* it!" Practically ignoring me, CeCe shoves her phone into her pocket, stands from the recliner, and bounds across the room to an overturned milk crate with a fitted board on top—a makeshift nightstand/desk with an assortment of items. Beside a miniature pink bong we call Strawberry Shortcake sit a half dozen tiny knives and a gray metal box about the size of a pack of cards.

When I look closer, I realize they have ridges on the ends in different formations—more like skinny keys.

"What are you doing?" I ask, standing over CeCe. "You ready to go?" A part of me wishes she'd say no, that the whole plan is a huge mistake, and we should stay and get trashed at this party.

"Hold up," CeCe breathes, picking up one of the metal pieces and the box, which I notice contains a lock on one side. She slides in one of the pieces—first easily, then with some resistance.

After a moment, the lock makes a clicking sound. Mary claps unironically. I have to admit, it's pretty impressive.

"What's that?" I ask, picking up one of the pieces.

"I've been researching safes," CeCe says. "There's, like, a hundred thousand ways to open one. None of them are even that hard. This was the one I couldn't figure out."

Mary basically swoons in the corner. I roll my eyes and turn back to CeCe. "But if you could do all this, why'd I have to steal Eli's keys? That sucked." I shudder, remembering his cluelessness that day.

"I mean, I just figured this one thing out." She clears her throat and sets the weird lock and key back on the milk crate. "Anyway, it's a last resort, in case the keys aren't enough. Hopefully they're all we need."

Will she use any of these fancy techniques when we get to Duke's, or is it all for show?

I almost ask how much this kit set her back, along with the projector in the living room and the recliner in this one. There's also a black-and-white patterned rug taking up what used to be a vast, empty floor. Large Marge is curled up in the center of the rug, snoring.

"Where'd this come from?" I nod at the chair, then the rug.

"Central Islip."

I purse my lips. CeCe knows that's not what I meant. One second she's broke, the next she's got new decor. One second she's selling plain old weed, the next it's also Molly.

"And the projector?"

"Traded it," she says, tucking the lock-picking gear into her bag. The sound of the dog snoring is loud in the still mostly empty room. There's a tiny smile on CeCe's lips. "Top-of-the-line quality."

"You sound like a commercial."

"You sound like your mom." CeCe looks up for my reaction. "Oh, don't get weird because I brought up your mom."

"You, too?" Mary cries, petting Large Marge while she twitches in deep sleep. "You can't just not talk about things, Min. It's bad for your spirit."

I stifle the urge to tell them both to shut it, which would only prove them right, and sit down on the floor, next to a mound of clothes big enough to be a person. "I just thought you didn't have any money."

CeCe squints, lacing up huge black boots, while sitting in her new chair. "Are you *judging* me for furnishing my home?"

Mary clears her throat. "If you two are done bickering like my freshman mentees when they talk about guys, can we actually do this?"

WE LEAVE ONE by one. As CeCe predicted, everyone is too drunk to notice. I wonder if she really paid for all that alcohol from her own pocket, along with the furniture, audiovisual equipment, a spun-gold collar for Large Marge, *whatever*.

Mary drives. I ride shotgun, which means I get to watch the small waves curling under the moon, the barren strips of sand. CeCe rides in the back seat. She hasn't said anything since we left the Beach Blossom.

There's a sweetness to the air that thickens to fog in places when we drive away from the water and onto the avenue, the long stretches of lit-up cement, the quiet houses and stores. We take the route along the boardwalk even though it's somewhat out of the way. I think Mary's trying to keep us all calm. When Astral Kingdom comes on the stereo at low volume, Mary winks at me in the dark. Aside from driving, her job tonight is to serve as lookout from a safe distance and text if anyone comes near the stand—specifically, a cop or the white pickup truck.

"Turn the headlights off," CeCe says when we're a couple of blocks away from Duke's.

"What?" Mary says, frowning.

"Turn them off. That's what they do in movies."

Mary gestures at the lit-up dashboard. "I don't even know how to do that. They're automatic."

"Let's just park up here." I direct her to the same spot we used the night of the white truck. "We'll walk the rest of it."

"You sure that's a good idea?" Mary asks, eyeing the football field–sized distance from the car to the back of the stand, along with the corner wrapping around it. "What if you need to leave fast?"

"More important to stay out of sight." CeCe cracks open the back door. "Let's go."

"Wait." Mary hands each of us a mask. She volunteered to buy them—cat masks, as close to the originals as possible. An attempt to make it look like the same people have come back for more, or even just copycats, in the event that I'm right and the cameras have been recording. Or that someone is watching.

I hold my mask up to the light. I can't believe what I'm seeing. "Mary, these are Hello Kitty masks."

"You said to get a cat mask. You didn't specify what kind of cat."

"They're completely different things!" I hiss.

"I heard Hello Kitty isn't even really a cat," CeCe says.

"So, what, I was supposed to go to every store in the area in the hopes that I'd *happen* to find three of the same masks that I've never even seen before?"

"I gave you a desc—" I breathe into my closed hand. "Whatever," I say, and put my own mask on. The entire world becomes ten degrees warmer.

Outside, the air is thick and flat. It's partly the heat of early hurricane season and partly that it's the middle of the night and feels just wrong to be outside like this in the streets, as Nicole would say. Even dressed in black and carrying a backpack of sharp objects.

By the time we've unlocked the door to Duke's with the copied keys, I'm boiling inside from the mask and clothes, like a pot of water with the lid on. It's not a totally unfamiliar feeling, but this time it has nothing to do with weed or beer or pills. It has to do with me wanting to get this over with—and possibly solve all (well, most) of my problems.

The air inside the stand is cool and still. The cake freezer shines like a jeweled centerpiece in the middle of the room, sitting and waiting.

It reminds me of the robbery, but I can't let myself daydream now, of all times. I push that other robbery far away from me.

CeCe shines her phone flashlight into the back and motions for me to lead the way to Anthony's office.

It takes seven tries before we find the right key to his office door. Why does Eli have so many keys? Are there even that many locks here?

It's pitch-black in the office except for a blue light glowing from under Anthony's computer, which I wouldn't dare touch. CeCe sets down her phone so the light from it fills the tiny room.

The walls are lined with shelves, which are crowded with binders and papers, some labeled with whatever month and year they belong to and some blank. There's one small window, in which an air conditioner has been wedged and is running at full blast. The rest of the window glass is blurry with grime.

The only clear wall space is right behind Anthony's desk, and he's cluttered that, too, with framed photos of himself shaking hands with various police officers, several mounted badges, one "certificate of dedication" from the Nautilus Police Department, and a key to the town.

No closet. Not even the suggestion of a closet. Nowhere to hide treasure.

CeCe zeroes in on the cop paraphernalia on the walls. "Yep. Total piece-of-shit vibe in here."

"Should we start with the safe?" My voice comes out much shakier than intended. I clear my throat. It's already taken less than a second for my eyes to survey the small room and conclude there are no huge containers of cash hidden here.

"Not yet," CeCe murmurs, her flashlight sweeping the too-close walls. "That's a last resort, remember?" I wonder if she's just scared to test out her lock-picking skills.

She starts opening Anthony's desk drawers, running her hands inside. I take the shelves on one side of the room, the ones packed with dozens of binders labeled with Anthony's surprisingly neat handwriting.

Then it happens. Both my and CeCe's phones ping in the dark, first one and the other. I check my phone first.

Mary's written in the group text, Someone here leave now!!!!!

"Who?" I ask out loud.

CeCe turns off the flashlight. "Does it matter?" she snaps.

She's cut off by a banging outside Anthony's office door, somewhere inside the stand. I feel it in my sneakers, and CeCe must, too, because we both turn toward the door half a second before the sound itself, something heavy falling onto the floor or ground. Or a door shutting too hard.

Behind this plastic, likely overpriced semi-cat mask, my sweat starts running cold, full of dread. This feels so much worse than the night of the other robbery.

The sound of footsteps is undeniable now to both of us.

I lift up the mask for a second, shocked further by the rush of cool air on my face. "Shit, shit, shit, shit."

"It's going to be fine," CeCe says. "We'll climb out the window."

Except the one window in here looks too small to get through and is full of air conditioner. I know because I've imagined climbing out since the day I interviewed to work here, when Anthony leered at me for the first of many times.

"I'm telling you," CeCe says, moving to the window. "We should at least try."

I strain to make sense of the footsteps on the other side of the door, whether they're getting closer or not. It feels impossible to tell.

We're startled by another banging—this time outside the window. Mary, in a Hello Kitty mask of her own, is waving at us in the dark, the lot shining empty behind her like a promise. She pantomimes opening the window.

CeCe tries the window, which slides open. She steadies the air conditioner while Mary pulls it from behind with surprising strength and sets it down on the ground with a decisive metal thump.

"Gross, it's wet," Mary wails in a stage whisper.

CeCe starts hoisting herself out. I want to shut my eyes at the sight, afraid she won't fit and we'll be stuck in here, caught by whoever it is on the other side of the door. "What in the actual hell, CeCe!"

But she's already halfway through the window. Past her shoulders.

"Hey!" a deep voice says from outside the door. One that could be Anthony's or not. "You notice this?" More than one person.

I don't know what *this* is. *This* is me. But I don't have time to care.

CeCe makes it all the way out the window, with Mary's help.

It's my turn. My heart dives into my stomach. I'm still not so sure about my own shorter and wider body.

I catch the blur of Mary cutting across the lot, painfully out in the open, probably running ahead to start the car. Only CeCe is left, waving for me to follow out the window. "Mini-Mart, *now*!"

I hoist myself through the frame. As expected, the metal scrapes the sides of my shoulders, then my hips, along with dirt from the windowsill that looks like it hasn't been cleaned since the place was built. CeCe loops her arms under mine and yanks.

The doorknob starts to turn.

As CeCe pulls me out of the window completely, I'm offered one last glimpse into Anthony's office. A figure hovers in the doorway. I nearly choke on my spit, struggling to breathe behind the mask, and tumble to the dusty ground outside.

I don't have to tell CeCe. It's like she already knows,

the way she pushes me to running once we're both on the ground. But I say it anyway.

"Someone was there," I call to her, as she's already broken ahead of me. "They saw us."

"Just keep running," CeCe says, and it's the night of the robbery again. Except this time, I know even less about who I'm running from and why.

This time, it's so much worse.

"We're coming back," I spit, using up the last of my air. All three of us are hurtling across the parking lot. Mary's car is back in sight as we approach the side street parallel to Nautilus Avenue. In the light from the streetlamp, it looks like the surface of the moon. Everywhere else is a shadow, a new and different place to hide.

CHAPTER TWENTY-FIVE

There's a memory from Before that I keep to myself. I don't want anyone to think it's why I turned out the way I did.

Or maybe I'm lying to myself, and it's exactly why I turned out the way I did.

I had just turned fifteen and started the second half of freshman year. Mom's illness had come back—a problem she'd had when she was born that showed its face again. Soon she'd have to reduce her hours at the bank. In less than a year, she'd have to stop working altogether.

That morning, she woke me up before my alarm was supposed to go off. It was so early, the sky pitch-dark outside the window, I thought I was still dreaming.

"Get packed and ready." She tossed my book bag on top of the blanket. I knew from its weightlessness that my mother had taken out my textbooks. "We're going on a trip."

"Now?" I had an important biology lab, a social studies exam, and a hinted-at pop quiz in language arts that day.

"Yeah, *now*," she echoed, as if she wasn't ordering me to skip school. The same school she tried to prep me to attend from outside the school zone, that endless process made me hate her and love her and hate her again. She often made me feel like I couldn't keep up with what was supposed to be important.

The sound of traffic reports and weather and breaking news screeched in from the TV in the living room. She was serious.

We drove through the Point, then the center of Nautilus proper, on empty roads. The ground was dark and slick from an early-morning mist that belonged in the spring instead of winter. Mom seemed on edge but happy, more excited than I'd seen her in months. She took quick sips of her coffee and finished it by the time we left the county. She talked about how free she felt driving.

"Everyone should learn, to save their sanity," she declared as we crossed a bridge over the Hudson River. The trees had lost most of their leaves, but they were still beautiful. Downriver, the massive towers of New York City shone even without the sun.

When I asked where we were going, she just answered that I'd see. We had talked about a trip like this for so long—stopping everything and driving off—that it was almost like the answer didn't matter. I didn't ask again.

When Mom crashed a few hours later from all the coffee, she told me to take over for the next hundred or so miles. I'd only known the basics of driving for a few months.

I got used to the road quickly, driving to the sound of low-volume radio and my mother snoring. Like a recent dream, I remembered the lab, test, and possible quiz I was missing, curious if my friends and teachers were wondering where I was.

Then I realized I didn't care about any of it. I felt at peace for the first time since everything started turning for us.

Somewhere upstate, Mom woke up and made me stop

for gas and more coffee. She took the wheel again, in a good mood about how far north we had gotten. It started to snow, tiny snowflakes that turned to enormous clumps. She studied the wet road in front of us, and I knew that wherever we were going would make this all worth it.

We were both exhausted when we arrived in Niagara Falls. We parked and walked into junk gift shops with the same waterfall T-shirts, mugs, and key chains. There were pictures of waterfalls on everything. They were nothing like the actual falls, which were larger and louder than life. They just existed, huge, no line or anything.

I looked across the vast loop of the falls to the Canadian side. The water was shining in the weak sunlight before dropping into mist below.

"You ever been there before?" I asked, meaning Canada.

Mom startled. She seemed to have forgotten me standing beside her. "Once. In college. I had a passport then." She turned back to the waterfalls. "We should get passports."

"You went with my dad?"

"There were a few of us," she said, then added, "Yes, with your father."

I felt years younger, watching the falls with her. She seemed so sure of things everywhere she went. Sometimes I envied her, even hated her, for knowing the whole story about things and never telling it. For making me feel like an outsider in my own life.

When I asked if my father had anything to do with us coming back here, if she ever missed him, she cut me off, irritated. "I just needed this, and so did you. It has nothing to do with him."

Her next words—maybe on purpose—made me forget my father.

"They're going to operate on me soon."

We checked into a hotel. It was the first and only time we ever stayed in one. The lobby was pale pink stone, and in the center was a water fountain two stories tall, a replica of the larger-than-life waterfalls.

Our room had two gigantic beds with cold white sheets that warmed up fast. Mom ordered room service: a cheeseburger for me and a turkey wrap for her, a large order of fries to share, and two milkshakes. Afterward, she lingered in the giant bathtub while I sank into the sheets and watched the local news. The people on the screen didn't seem real—nothing seemed real. I didn't want the day to end.

Mom was called in for her surgery a few weeks later, just like she'd said. I was allowed to stay home alone. Without her there, I bought too much junk food with the EBT card and read books I was too old for. When I couldn't read anymore, I watched TV until the blue light of the screen burned into my eyes. Or I fell asleep too early and woke up in the middle of the night surrounded by too much light, my heart racing and my breath so short I thought I might be dying, too.

Later, when she came home from the surgery, Mom's health got worse. They started talking about a heart transplant instead of just a surgery, but the wait list was long. I felt stupid for thinking our trip to Niagara Falls meant our lives were getting better, when it was merely a break before the opposite. Nothing more.

I asked her: If I died, could they replace her heart with mine? Would that work? I'd read about it in an old copy of *National Geographic* from the hospital waiting room. The article wasn't even about transplants—it was about a family of chickpea farmers in India affected by global trade. Their teenage son had died in a threshing accident. Immediately, doctors implanted the son's heart into the dying father.

When I told Mom about this, she didn't react at first. I wasn't sure she heard the whole thing and was prepared to tell it again. Before I could, she walked across the room and slapped my face. She was crying.

CHAPTER TWENTY-SIX

I can't sleep after the botched attempt to search Anthony's office. Past Minerva has gone through the remainder of the sleeping pills, and because of this, I'm forced to witness the events of the night on a perpetual loop even as the sky brightens into early morning and the birds start singing in the trees.

We parked nearby but hopefully out of sight, using a car nobody will recognize. We opened the side door, then Anthony's office. We searched everything we could get our hands on—every drawer and shelf in that hellhole of a space. Then, before we could search anything else, we just happened to get intercepted—ambushed?—by at least two mystery people.

Not only did we fail to find anything, but we were almost caught.

On the drive back, CeCe insisted we must have set off an alarm.

"But it was only a few minutes, wasn't it?" Mary asked.

How could they have gotten there so fast? The only explanation is that they were watching, waiting. That, or—

"There's no such thing as coincidence," CeCe blurted.

"Not for shit like this. Something we did set off a trigger. Someone told them to go."

We even speculated that one of the figures was Anthony himself, even though I can't picture him hustling anywhere in the middle of the night.

I wake up to texts from Mary. The air conditioner is back in, no emergency vehicles identified. For a second, I have no idea what she means, and then the failed break-in plays one last time like an extra-embarrassing night of partying. The heat of the day filters in through the window screen. It's mid-morning, by the look and feel of the light.

I don't want to ask why Mary knows about the air conditioner, ignoring the growing suspicion that she and CeCe stayed up after I went home, based on how much they were still talking and planning when I went to bed.

That's a good sign, CeCe writes, then adds exactly what I was thinking. Doesn't mean we're clear yet.

We'll be clear when I go to work later today, where I find out whether I'm destined for the Jamira treatment at best—and at worst, all three of us arrested, our lives ruined by different degrees.

Nicole bursts into the room while I'm getting ready to leave for work. I'm warned only by the pounding of her heels on the thin carpet. The bedroom door flies open so fast it turns the air, a mix of hot day and the general mustiness of my room and now Nicole's fruit-based perfume.

She wears an old outfit of Mom's, a denim dress buttoned down the front with a thick belt at her waist. Her nails are a deeper shade of blue than the outfit. "We need to talk."

I drop the deodorant I was in the middle of applying.

The chalky white material explodes when it falls to the floor, breaking into pieces.

Nicole glances at the new mess. "I need the car keys."

I relax slightly. "The what?"

"The keys to your mother's car. Look, I happen to know you're not even supposed to have them."

I bend down and start cleaning up. "I'm not giving you the keys."

"Well, guess what? The law says you have to."

"Mom wouldn't want you to have the Boat. We both know that."

Nicole pauses and sort of smiles. "It's not *for* me. I'm going to sell it."

"Why?"

"To pay the back rent and bills on this apartment."

"It's not your problem."

"Are you kidding me?"

"How much are you selling it for?"

"Minerva—"

"You know what?" My head feels like a lemon that somebody's just squeezed. There are tiny flecks of white all over the carpet in my room. I just need to get to Duke's and find out if I'm in trouble or not. "I'm going to buy the Boat myself."

Now Nicole is laughing, which is worse than any other reaction. "Minerva, I . . ."

"How *much*?"

Her smile disappears, and she holds her forehead as if she has a migraine. "Can you tell me something?"

The question itself is going to be rhetorical. Something along the lines of, *Just where do you get this attitude?* or *Do you ever think about anyone but yourself?* or even simply *What is your problem?*

But she says, "You do know this car isn't the same as Sunny, right?"

"What?"

"You know it's not the same as connecting with her instead of wishing she was here? That it's not going to bring her back home?"

I've entirely had enough of Nicole butting in, of telling me how to feel every time Mom comes up. Waking me up all the time. And now taking my car. The room tilts just like it did at Mary's the other day. "Get out."

She sighs and make her way to the door. "I have too much going on to chase you around. You have three days to give me those keys."

I'm left alone, wishing I could run down the hallway yelling for Mom. The word itches at the very bottom of my throat. But I can't. And I have to stop wishing, for what little it helps.

I ARRIVE FOR work almost an hour early and park the Boat under a dwindling scrap of shade in the lot, engine off and windows open. Mary was right about the air conditioner. Whoever came that night simply replaced the air conditioner and left everything how it was. They know we were here—maybe not us specifically, but someone—and yet this time there are no cops, no fire trucks, no crowds. Almost like they don't want anybody to know.

Why?

Regardless of how many more questions than answers there are now, I take out my phone and text Mary and CeCe. I think we're good.

While they continue congratulating us on not getting arrested yet in the group text, I stay quiet. According to the time on the stereo, it's now ten minutes past opening. Eli still hasn't arrived. Nobody has arrived. Did I speak too soon, like an idiot?

I try to breathe, to refrain from panic-texting my friends so soon after declaring we were in the clear. To wait it out.

At twenty minutes past, Eli finally shows up, parks the car, and slams the door.

I scramble out of the Boat before he even starts walking to the side door of Duke's.

"Oh. Hey." He does a double take and slows down. We're standing between the cars now. His olive cheeks are bright red, like he's been running.

"Eli, what happened?"

He winces and checks the time on his phone, digging through his pockets for the tainted keys. He still won't look me in the eyes.

"Eli?"

"He found out."

My breath stops short. "Anthony?"

"Yeah. He found out I lost my keys the other day."

"Oh. You mean, Jordan told him."

"Maybe. I guess she wants to be assistant manager that bad. Which, fine. I never asked for it anyway." Still, he looks troubled by it.

Then he says, "He also knew about you."

"Me?"

Once again I think he means the plan—my and CeCe's and now Mary's plan to find the money. That plan. Until I understand he's referring to the two of us fooling around. Or whatever you want to call it.

"Oh." My brain glitches keeping track of all there is to worry about. "Do you want to stop?"

"Huh? No." Eli draws close and kisses me. I lean against his car. The warm steel under my spine wakes me up a little. He pulls away, cupping my face. "It doesn't matter what he or anyone thinks."

Anyone. I want to ask him to specify who he means, but he's already trudging to the door. I follow silently, realizing we never locked it behind us last night. But it's locked now.

"Eli?" I call. He's just finished unlocking the counter window, which means we really have to start working now. I puff out my cheeks and call his name again.

He reappears, wiping his glasses with a napkin. "Yeah?"

"Do you know if Anthony installed an alarm system or something?"

Eli slips on his glasses—not his usual wire frames but thick black ones with inexplicable scratches on the sides. He stares at the cameras around us by turns. Maybe out of habit. "I don't think so. Why?"

I should've prepared a reason for asking. Space cadet.

"Just wondering, I guess because of the robbery. I want to know how safe this place is, exactly." I start turning on the tiny faucets in the scoop holders, shrugging in a way I hope looks casual.

He smiles dryly and cracks open the register. "The thing is, he's too cheap for anything like that. I promise you."

"I'll hold you to that."

He drifts closer between the freezers, and I angle the scoop water to hit his leg. I think he's going to spray me back, but he loops his arm around my waist. "Come by tomorrow night."

Please, God, I think. *Please don't mean Duke's Ice Creamery.* "Here?"

"No," he laughs. "My house. Where I live."

"Your house?" I parrot, feeling silly. Mary is the only friend whose house I've visited, at least recently. I feel as if Eli just asked me to "come by" Mars.

"I have studio work tonight, but maybe tomorrow night. Neither of us are on the schedule." He looks at me like he's actually unsure if I want to hang out with him. "There's a beach near me. It sort of belongs to all the neighbors. It's all kids and old people who go there during the day, so at night it's pretty dead. No bad music. No fireworks."

"Well, shit," I joke. "Where is this?" I brace myself for the answer after months of half-assed speculation.

"Crystal Cove." He's embarrassed, but just a little. He even blushes, adding, "Not that part." He means a little up the coast from Mary. Not as rich, but more suburban. Crystal Cove is one of those communities where, at least once every peak season, some kid ODs on whatever drug is the most popular and another has a grisly car accident. "Just the beach," he says, like a reminder. "Music. Sitting."

"Okay," I say.

"Excellent." He kisses me, this time a light one between my mouth and cheekbone. I wonder if there are nerve endings there. If not, my body could have fooled me.

CHAPTER TWENTY-SEVEN

CeCe's apartment is still littered with flotsam and jetsam from the party when I walk in after work. Most of the apartment lights are turned off except, again, for the projector. But this time, there isn't a movie playing on the off-white wall. Instead, the image of Duke's Ice Creamery glares down like a punishment at full brightness and high resolution.

I turn around and accidentally look into the projector light. "Can you turn this off, or at least change it to something else?"

"No!" CeCe's voice calls from elsewhere in the apartment. She appears wearing a dark blazer I've never seen her wear before, along with her camo pants, which I've seen many times. I make my way to a beanbag on the floor and shut my eyes.

"Min," she says, entering the room fully, "what's the one part of the Ice Creamery we haven't seen?"

"Not now, please."

"Answer the question."

"Is Mary here? I thought I saw her car. She's gonna be in huge tr—"

"Mary's asleep on my futon next to Large Marge! Now focus. *Which part of the Ice Creamery have we not checked?*"

I snap a little. "I don't fucking know! It's not like I can search Anthony's office while I'm at work."

CeCe sinks on her haunches, so we're eye to eye. "I know, Minerva. And it just so happens I've made a breakthrough." She reaches into the front pocket of the blazer—Mary's, I realize—and takes out a clicker, which she points at the wall. The image changes from Duke's to another, very similar, storefront. "Hold on, I just need to zoom out a little."

She does, and the full image turns out to include a headline. LOCAL BALLOON BUSINESS RAIDED FOR CASH, GUNS. The store, eerily similar-looking to Duke's Ice Creamery, is a place called Andy's Famous Balloons.

"The article doesn't say, but according to town records, it was owned during that time by a little company called Future Optics, LLC, based out of Ronkonkoma."

I rub my temples and try to look anywhere but the screen. "Okay?"

"Guess who was *co-owner* of this failed business, Future Optics, LLC?"

CeCe clicks and clicks, but nothing happens. By now, she has my attention. Finally, she slams down the clicker and faces me. "Ugh. Whatever. Your boss. Anthony. Is listed as co-owner. Along with some guy who got two years' probation." She squeezes and releases her fists. "Because white guys."

Mary walks in, yawning, with Large Marge tumbling in behind her. "Oh good," she mumbles, "You're showing her the Andy's thing. Are we going now?"

"Going where?" I ask, confused again. "To Andy's?"

"No." CeCe sits on the other beanbag chair. Mary sits directly on the floor with Large Marge. "According to the article, it was in the basement of this . . . balloon store."

"So?"

Now Mary and CeCe are smiling goofy, open-mouthed smiles at each other across the living room.

"The basement?" CeCe prompts, the laser from her clicker flying around the room.

"Duke's doesn't have a basement," I say.

"That you know of," Mary pipes in gleefully, like she's been waiting for this part. She plunks down on my beanbag chair, practically on my lap, and shows me her phone screen. Which I can't read, since she won't keep it still. "This article says it was—quote—*an elaborate storage system concealed by false drainage*—unquote."

"Does Duke's have a random drain?" CeCe asks. Now they're both staring at me.

I shake my head. "I don't think I've noticed. I'm not sure."

CeCe whistles ominously.

"But listen," I say. "How do we even know that's what he's doing?"

CeCe stands and stretches. "We already know it's there somewhere. Those robbers knew it, too. Why not the 'elaborate' basement system? Where else would it be?"

"We don't even know if there *is* a basement!"

"But . . ." CeCe has started walking around the room again. We lock eyes, and I feel like I'm supposed to know something I don't. "Please. We'll just check the place for drains, find the money, and that's it."

"Give me a day," I tell them. "Just a day. To make sure it's safe to go back. Remember what happened last time?"

Eli already told me—promised me—there isn't an alarm system. Technically, we're already in the clear, but I haven't told CeCe and Mary that. Nor do I tell them I already have plans with him a day from now. One thing at a time.

"We're fine, aren't we? You're still employed there, aren't you?" CeCe is aglow with confidence.

"What happened to no such thing as coincidences?"

"There's nobody watching the place!" CeCe says, practically laughing.

"How do you know?" I ask.

She and Mary exchange a look.

"What is it?"

Mary plays with the ever-present row of bracelets on her wrist. "We went back."

"What?!" I almost push her off the beanbag chair, but she instinctively clutches my arm.

"Relax, Mini-Mart." CeCe whirls around to mess with the projector. "We just watched the place from outside. We wanted to see if anybody showed up."

I do relax, but not a ton. "And?"

"And what?" CeCe asks. The screen flickers, becomes a lush rain forest. My heartbeat slows.

"*And* did you see anything?"

Mary clears her throat. "I'm just going to say it. CeCe and I made out the whole time. That's what happened."

She gives me a look like, *Don't make a big deal, please,* so I don't, even though for a second all I can think about is becoming the third wheel again. That, and I'm not entirely sure what's going on with her and Vera. But asking about Vera means thinking about that whole ugly time earlier in the year.

"Okay, *very cool*," CeCe says. "Do you want to talk about your stuff, Eli, or whatever? Since we're sharing?" She's taunting me, rolling a joint that she smokes while watching more safe-cracking videos on her phone with her earbuds in.

Mary whispers, "I have no idea what to do. I haven't talked to Vera in eight and a half days." Her words convey confusion, but she's smiling into her bracelets.

She has two people to choose from, and I just got slightly more sure about one.

CeCe wanders over, her joint smoldering. I turn it down, already tired from work and the looming rain forest and Mary's whispering and the jangling of her bracelets. "One more day," she says. "Check the place out on your own. Then we get back in there ASAP. No more waiting."

THE NEXT DAY at work, I watch one of the new employees counting out the register. I don't want to hate this girl, whose name is either Sarah or Crystal. She's actually been decent to me, if not refreshingly boring. According to Anthony, she gets to count the register because of prior experience handling cash.

I clutch the copied keys in my pocket and focus on my own upcoming experience handling cash. Maybe cash-register envy is exactly what I need right now—a reminder of what I get to escape if we pull this off.

So far, I've checked every inch of the stand outside Anthony's office for anything that might lead to a trap door. All I find are drains placed throughout, each wider than you'd find in a Beach Blossom shower, but nothing even close to door-shaped.

When I've examined and counted the drains for the fourth or fifth time between customers, I know I can't put it off any longer. What I've been avoiding.

"Hey," I say to the new girl. I peer at the schedule on the back wall and confirm her name. "Sarah. Do you know if Anthony's here today?"

Sarah makes a good-natured scrunching expression and closes the register. "You know what, I don't know!"

She's still wondering aloud when I sneak out the side door and check the lot, confirming that his monstrous truck isn't parked outside. I call to Sarah that I suddenly have to go to the bathroom.

Anthony's office door is unlocked, which means he was here earlier and plans on coming back soon. The screen saver on one of the monitors is a bikini-clad model on a beach. The other displays a mosaic of images from the cameras throughout the stand, black and white and gray movements from various angles.

The screen saver flashes onto his main computer screen. More girls in bikinis.

I can't help what I do next, which is marvel at the air conditioner back where it was, grime and everything.

I swallow a combination of nerves and disgust and begin to survey the floor. Instead of large white tiles, like the rest of the stand, Anthony's floor is cheap brown boards, peeling or chipping in some places. There are no drains.

There's only one interruption to this sad, disintegrating floor: the ratty old rug directly under Anthony's desk. I've never noticed it before today. Why would I?

Checking this part of the floor requires actual movement of furniture. I want to make sure one more time that
Anthony isn't here, but part of me knows I might chicken
out if I leave this room. I roll the chair away first and try
to lift the rug, but the massive desk forces it down and
doesn't let me see too much of the floor beneath.

I stand up and lift one side of the desk with both hands
and attempt to move the rug with my foot. It peels back
in awkward flaps, and what I see makes me nearly drop
Anthony's desk on my foot.

There's a line in the floor, a suggestion of a door and
what looks like a lock.

I set down Anthony's desk, considering whether to try
again and get a picture for the group text, when I notice a
giant wrinkle I left in the rug.

I bend back down to fix it. Just as it cooperates and lies
flat once again, a voice behind me makes me freeze.

"Can I help you?"

Anthony.

I stand up and turn to face him. His eyes run over me
as if by habit, from bottom to top and back down. The
screen saver changes again, and this time I don't torture
myself by looking.

I step just a little closer and fight the urge to cover
myself. "I was waiting to talk to you."

He walks around me and takes his place at the desk,
smelling of cigarettes and sweat, with an expression I
can't tell apart from his usual arsenal of glares. It's hard
to say if he suspects me of something or is just making it
clear how much I've inconvenienced him.

"It's my schedule," I add, partly to fill the uncomfortable
silence. "I was hoping for more hours? Even just a few."

"I don't know. Maybe," he mutters. He presses
a button, and the horrible screen saver gives way to a
spreadsheet. "Is that it? Are we done?"

"No." I employ a not-quite-lie. "What about the security system?"

Anthony shifts away from his desk now to squint at
me. "What?"

"Well, with the robbery, I just want to know if I should
feel safe in here."

He doesn't recognize the joke, which is that none of us
feel safe. And even though the robbery was terrible, it's
not the reason.

"It's plenty safe here," he says flatly. "Don't worry."

He's not budging.

In that moment, one of the tiny screens beside him displays a close-up pair of thighs, obviously Sarah's. Though
the camera is so close, it's almost as if the pair of legs
doesn't belong to anybody. Just body parts moving of
their own volition.

Now I just want to run out. The stand seems like it'll
collapse any second, that soon I'll be suffocated in binders
and papers and particle board. Acid shoots up my throat.

"Eli or Jordan will let you know if your schedule
changes," Anthony says.

"I—"

"*Now* are we done?" he says. I can almost hear him
thinking how useless I am for wasting his time.

I nod and leave the office. Instead of returning to the
counter, I step outside and let the heat of the day wrap
around me again. Anything to distance me corporeally
from that man and the moment that just happened.

When I reach the front, I locate and count all the cameras

I know about and become dizzy all over again. I picture myself covering the lenses in salted caramel, emptying the register, and storming back to Anthony's office to punch him in the face. In my mind, I tear him up like a wolf in a children's story.

CHAPTER TWENTY-EIGHT

Eli offers to pick me up after work, but I don't feel like confusing all the girls arriving for the evening shift. The *anyone* Eli mentioned before, whose opinions don't matter. I wish I could stop myself from caring, too.

More importantly, I can't abandon the Boat in the Duke's parking lot, unattended, for hours.

My phone vibrates on the passenger seat. The locked screen shows a text from CeCe. You out yet? Still need more time?

I just know she means that second part facetiously. I could tell her about what I found in Anthony's office, but that's only going to make her start texting more, faster. She might even call.

Instead of answering, I focus on the directions to Crystal Cove, where I've never once in all my seventeen years had a reason to visit. What I do know is that a lot of cops and firefighters live out here.

"Even the nonwhite people are white," CeCe said once. I asked her what the hell that was even supposed to mean, and she just yawned and said, "Not now, Min."

The houses here aren't as large as I expected, but they're

the neatest I might've ever seen. Every lawn is a bright jade green, no bald spots or knotted weeds or plastic bags. Any of those things would stick out like a sore thumb here. Like me.

Closer to Eli's house, the houses are a little older. The lawns are still nice, a lot of gardens and fountains, but they don't seem as uptight. They're more colorful and have porch furniture that looks like people actually use it, voices and TV sounds and general activity behind the windows. The mailboxes are shaped like various animals.

When I recognize the spot from Eli's directions, a basket-ball court, I park and follow a path around the court to the beach. The air is slow moving, warm, smelling of grass. At the end of the short path is a rickety set of stairs down to the beach. At the bottom, I notice a fire maybe fifty feet away. Eli is next to it.

When I get closer, he's adjusting pieces of wood with a larger, forked piece. Sparks fly up near his face, but he doesn't flinch.

"Hey," he says. "You find this place okay?" Still sitting, he closes his free hand around mine. It might be—no, it defi-nitely is—the most normal thing I've done in a while.

"Look at you, with your private beach," I tease.

"It's a community beach." He talks into my hand.

"The other day, at *my* community beach, I found a diaper on the sand."

He groans.

"An adult diaper."

Eli pulls me down beside him. The sand is warm and soft from the fire. "I have to say, this talk is really doing it for me."

"Watch it, DJ Quandary."

We sit by the fire and talk. I find out about his family. He has one sibling, a sister named Caroline a year younger than me who complains a lot. He has a grandmother who's always worried about how much food people are eating. He has parents who run a party venue-slash-restaurant a few towns over and are hardly ever home.

"Nana and my aunt kind of raised me," he says. "To tell the truth, I think my parents like running businesses more than they like being parents."

I can't relate on so many levels I lose count, but it does remind me of the way Mom sometimes acted like she wanted to be elsewhere, a different person, with someone else who wasn't me. Or maybe worse—alone.

When he does what I've been dreading and asks about my family, I give him the Before version: Mom works at a bank, has health problems I can't explain, and is obsessed with getting me out of Nautilus the way she couldn't when she was my age.

When I've successfully warded off questions about home, a comfortable silence falls between us. I rest my head on his shoulder, and he pulls me so close that our heartbeats play against each other as we both watch the fire.

I think he's going to kiss me—anticipating this part every time makes me impatient—and so I'm about to kiss him first, when my phone buzzes. It's CeCe again.

Did you forget about tonight????

Feeling as if I've been shaken violently awake, I peek over at Eli, who's taken the moment to check his own phone. The music coming out of the tiny flat speaker changes from hip-hop to piano instrumental.

I'm with Eli right now.

Then come over after, CeCe answers.

I almost write back, *What if I planned on spending the night?* But that would leave me open to way more ridicule than I could handle right now.

On cue, Mary writes in the group text, Let us know when youre done seducing Eli :D

Eli and I are talking again—and by extension, still not kissing or having sex—when I stop denying that I have to use the bathroom. I ask if there's a public bathroom somewhere nearby. Of course, the answer is no. The only place is his house.

"We can come right back here if you want," Eli says. But ever the law-abiding citizen, he puts out the fire, which seems pretty final to me.

His family lives in a big yellow house a few streets away. Every house on the street has an animal-shaped mailbox. Pig, cow, bird, crocodile. Eli's mailbox is a goose, long neck and everything. We enter through a kitchen that looks like it belongs in a farmhouse and one hundred percent smells like cookies. Almost horrifyingly normal.

In the living room, an old woman and a girl maybe fourteen years old are watching TV. A light ribbon of smoke wraps around the room. My trained nose and eyes follow it to a plate with a stick of herbs I only recognize as not weed. It's that smell I've noticed on Eli sometimes.

Eli hands me a cold water bottle, takes my hand, and introduces me as Minerva. The girl, his sister, is Caroline, and the old woman is just "Nana."

Nana switches glasses and peers at me. She's wearing a T-shirt with a giant rainbow peace sign and dangling glass earrings. She smiles. "You didn't tell me she was Spanish!"

I start to say, "Actually, Spanish isn't—" *An ethnicity. It's a language and the nationality of people from Spain. My* mother's words march along the back of my tongue. "Never mind."

"And what are your intentions with my grandson?"

"Um—"

She bursts out laughing. "I'm just pulling your leg, honey. I know what your intentions are. Look at him. He's a hottie. Do people still say that?" She turns to Caroline. "You made her sound like a hag, but she's a peppermint."

I shake my head. "I don't remember ever meeting—"

"I met you once," Caroline mumbles, not making eye contact. Her hair is wild and curly, and she seems to be hiding behind it. "I came by to get ice cream once. You were super rude."

"Really? I'm sorry—"

Eli interrupts. "Caroline. Come on."

"Don't mind her," Nana says, patting Caroline's leg decisively. "You know kids that age. Life's a bore without the drama. Anyway, it's lovely to meet you."

"Nice to meet you, too," I say. The words are metal scraps falling out of my mouth, even though they sound like the kind of thing people say. Even though I actually mean them. But it doesn't matter, since I was rude enough to leave a bad impression once upon a time.

The shame descends lightning quick, as usual. Was that really how I came off?

"Your house is cute," I manage to offer.

"Thank you, dear." Nana laughs. "But I'm just a loafer."

"You are not," Eli insists, as if it's a conversation they were just having earlier.

His sister leans forward. "The downstairs bathroom is down the hall. If you need to go number two, go upstairs."

"Caroline," he starts again.

"What? I'm just *telling* her!"

"Downstairs is fine," I say to no one in particular, and escape before I disintegrate into their nice clean rugs.

The bathroom is large and drafty, with an antique door that doesn't lock and a blue-and-white nautical theme. I feel like a dangerous bacteria that's contaminated their house. I need to get back to the Boat, where I can let out all my neuroses for air. I pee and wash my hands as fast as I can. When I leave the bathroom, I don't bother looking for Eli and book it straight for the kitchen, the back door, the porch, his car, which will make me feel closer to my car. A thing I recognize.

Okay, sure. I wanted a change of scenery. But this feels wrong—not too fast or too slow, just *wrong*. Like an accident happening too far away to stop. Like riding a kiddie coaster drunk, which admittedly I've done.

Eli appears behind me in the driveway soon after.

"Your family's cute," I say. I kick the gravel and pretend I wasn't about to ditch him. "Why'd your grandmother call me a peppermint?"

"My guess is she finds you sweet and surprising," he says. He takes a tentative step toward me. "I know they're kind of weird, but they don't mean anything by it. Especially my sister. She thinks she's looking out for me. She's been mad I'm leaving for school."

My throat tightens. I've known about this all along, but we haven't talked about it. Him saying it out loud makes it real. I pray it isn't the moment the tears decide to come back. "You think *that's* weird, that someone misses you? That's the most normal thing I've ever heard."

He frowns, unsure how to respond. "You okay?"

"Fine."

"You want to go upstairs?"

"Is that—" I glance toward the house. "Is that okay? For me to be up there?" For *us* to be up there. Alone.

He follows my gaze, amused. "Yeah. It's fine whether they're here or not."

I don't know what to say. More to attribute to the utter normalcy of his family, I guess.

I follow him back into his normal house, up the normal stairs, to his normal bedroom.

Actually, his room is the least normal part. Aside from a bed and dresser, it contains two perpendicular walls of milk crates full of records, forming a vast and colorful corner. The rest of the room is taken up by several computers, a piano keyboard, a long black box with no less than a hundred buttons, and two giant speakers. Black cords curl around the floor. It looks like he tried to contain the mess but gave up halfway to—what else—make and listen to music.

Eli sits down at his desk and starts messing with one of the computers, which has a panel missing and its silver-green insides exposed.

I sit on the carpet. There's a good five feet between us. Shoes aren't allowed upstairs, so I sit with both bare feet curled under me. "Why do they trust you like that?"

"Because I'm trustworthy." Eli pauses over the computer and picks up a small screwdriver. "Huh. It sounds kind of incriminating just saying that."

"What about Caroline? Will she be allowed, when she's your age?"

He tilts his head at his sister's name, leaning down to the computer for a closer look. "All right. Fine. It's because I'm a guy."

"You know that's messed up, right?"

"Of course I do," he says, avoiding my eyes.

"Just checking."

A plain drumbeat fills the silence, eclipsing the distant sound of the TV downstairs. He finally looks up at me after a moment or two. "I like that you point things out, you know."

"Why?"

It's suddenly very real that I'm in Eli's bedroom, listening to the same simple beat, breathing the same air. I get up and walk across the carpet, no longer caring about my hideous bare feet, and he turns to meet me. I lift his glasses off his face and kiss him, even though he hasn't answered my question. He wraps an arm around my waist.

I let myself fall in just a little further before pulling away. "I'm sorry. I can't. Not here, at least."

He nods, his breath tight against my collarbone. "I get it. I wasn't trying to make you think—"

"I want to."

"Yeah," he says. "Me, too."

Does it matter that I want it, too? What if I just accepted that as a possibility and kept moving? Would that be the worst thing? Mom said once that women on TV were always acting like they didn't have sex drives, and that it's one of the worst offenses of modern entertainment.

"It's not sex that's the danger," she said. "It's the falling, the caring. That's the part you don't see coming, and that's the part they get wrong, too."

Being with Eli now, the rush of him so close, being here to feel him at all—it has to be a good thing. It has to be enough.

But it's just going to end anyway.

I untangle my fingers from Eli's and let his hands fall. I run out of his room, but it's not fast enough. Not down the street fast enough. Not back in the Boat fast enough. Not driving away fast enough.

It doesn't hit me until I'm closer to home, waiting for a red light, that I shouldn't have left.

I shouldn't have left.

The traffic light changes in front of me. I pick up the phone to call him and explain everything. It's the first time I've even wanted to try in God knows how long. Something near six months. Maybe more.

The car behind me honks at me to move, but I don't care. I find Eli's number and call it. Then I drive forward.

A voice I wasn't expecting but recognize right away fills the car. *"Your service has been disconnected. For more information, please dial one-eight-hundred . . ."*

I close my eyes and scream in sync with the honks mounting behind me on the road.

CHAPTER TWENTY-NINE

Even though I can't think about or feel anything other than humiliation over ditching Eli in the spur of the moment, I keep my promise to CeCe and come over. My plan is mainly to beg for one more night. I just need to talk to Eli, explain myself. Then we can all start fresh tomorrow.

All of us.

To my relief, the projected image is nothing but a video game. CeCe pauses it as soon as I walk in. Onscreen, a rust-bitten fence in the background rattles with zombies crawling over it. CeCe's character paces back and forth brandishing a machete.

"Finally, you're back," CeCe muses. She looks up at me and frowns. "Is that really what you wore on your date?"

I look down at my usual T-shirt and jean shorts, the most flattering outfit I had available to change into after my shift, in that it was the only clean one.

"*Is* your date finished," CeCe continues wryly, "or are you just stopping by to see if we're still doing all the work?" She's mad I stayed out so long and barely answered her and Mary's messages.

Large Marge trots out from the bedroom. I lean down

and pet her, ignoring CeCe's obvious bait. "Where's Mary? I didn't see her car."

"She had to go home."

"Look. I'm sorry. It's just been a long, weird day." She slow-blinks at me. "I'm tired, Min."

"Then go to bed."

"No. You know what I mean." She turns off the game, leaving us both watching a giant blue rectangle on the wall. "You can want to stay here, or you can want to leave, but one foot in each accomplishes exactly nothing."

I tell her about the door under Anthony's desk. When I'm done explaining everything up until the moment I got caught by Anthony himself, she's quiet for at least a minute.

It's a statement, not a question, when she finally speaks up, incredulous.

"You've known about this thing *all day*."

"I haven't exactly had a ton of chances to discuss the matter at length."

"Bullsh—" She takes a deep breath. "Never mind. What's done is done."

"What's that mean?"

"It means call Mary. Tell her to sneak back out after her nanny or whoever the fuck falls asleep." She starts to roll a joint, but her hands shake with excitement, and she gives up.

I start to leave the room to make the call in private so that I can also gush/vent to Mary about everything that happened with Eli. But CeCe stops me. She's holding one of the Hello Kitty masks from last time, seemingly examining it. "I lied, Mini-Mart."

"Oh? About what?"

"What's done is done also means stop holding out on me. On us." She shakes her head and tosses the mask back on floor next to the projector. Large Marge startles beside me, then walks over and sniffs it. "Not for some guy."

"Fine," I say, thinking about how I already ditched Eli and ended up here. "You don't have to worry about that."

IT'S SO LATE when Mary picks us up that I'm not even sure what time it is. Which seems like a thing you should know when you might have to explain your actions later. Unlike in the Boat, there's no clock on Mary's dashboard at all. I ask both of them as soon as we're on the road, each of us holding our masks.

Mary glances at her phone in the holder beside the wheel. "Just past the witching hour."

"Holy shit, it's three?" CeCe says, her voice echoing from the passenger seat.

"No," Mary says, "midnight."

They begin arguing about whether the witching hour is midnight or three o'clock. I sink into the back seat and try to enjoy my private view of Nautilus sliding past. After a few minutes, I'm already restless and wishing I had something to do. I remember how Anthony found me in his office just hours ago, plus the surprise ambush the first time we tried to do this. Mary and CeCe are sure the coast is clear by now, but I'm nowhere near convinced.

"You know," Mary says, says after we've found the darkest, most obscure parking spot near one of the nonworking streetlights. We're farther away than ever before. "I have a good feeling about this."

"Are you serious?" CeCe says, her booming voice magnified by the mask. "You're really trying to jinx us right now?"

I scratch my arms under the long black sleeves. "You sure you're not just saying that because you get to go inside?"

I can't hear myself think. But the silence doesn't help, either—it's a kind of noise, too. It's the sound of the calm before everything changes. Like still water before somebody throws in the heaviest stone (or piece of garbage) they can find.

The keys still work in the first lock. I don't know why I'm surprised, since we know whoever was here last time didn't tell Anthony anything. Because he's the kind of boss who makes you want to lie about even the smallest mistakes. *Especially* the smallest mistakes.

In the office, Mary shines her flashlight over me and CeCe as we both make our way to the desk. We each take a side and lift it easily, while Mary pulls the rug completely out of the way. There's the line I saw, a gap in the wooden planks. It's not a drain, but a simple hatch.

On one side, where a knob might be, is a metal piece with a hole meant for slipping a padlock through, but no padlock.

Part of me is afraid it was all a hallucination and that my mind, desperate for a way out and maybe also a little too obvious with its metaphors, has imagined this.

But it's real. The door in the floor.

"It's just open like that?" CeCe calls behind me.

I don't answer her. My mind is all crackling white noise. I loop my fingers to pull at the door. It lifts with a groan. Just beneath is a set of dusty stairs that leads down to what appears to be a concrete floor.

For a moment, none of us moves.

Then Mary darts around me and starts down, the light from her phone bouncing all over. As the tallest, she has to duck the deepest the lower we go. "There's nothing here," she says.

"No." I follow her anyway. No offense to Mary or anyone else, but I have to see it with my own eyes.

CeCe steps down, too. The basement area is all gray brick with a layer of white dust. There's a tiny extra room, or closet, where the access to it's just a big gap in the brickwork. Like somebody came and smashed it up. Maybe somebody did—there are bricks here and there on the floor.

The only objects in the room are faded, empty balloons in various colors, like ancient litter. Mary's right. There's nothing down here.

She picks up one of the unfilled balloons like it's an overcooked vegetable she has to eat. "Maybe . . ."

"Maybe *nothing*." CeCe kicks one of the bricks across the room. The flashlight bounces; I can no longer tell who's holding it. The brick thuds against the wall. All of us are breathing too hard for this tiny, lightless room.

"Maybe," CeCe says, slipping off her mask, "maybe we put all our energy into a big, fucking pile of *nothing*. Maybe I'm going to get evicted. I can't afford the rent on my own. It's just me in there."

"I bet there used to be something here," I say, "and they moved it."

"Maybe it doesn't matter." CeCe runs her hand through her hair, wild eyed. Then she lowers her hands and points the look right at me.

"Hold on. You think this is *my* fault?" I take my own mask off. The sweat on my face chills in the stale air.

"You and your half-assed involvement," CeCe says. "So yeah. Kind of."

"Excuse me, but who used her boyfriend to get the keys that got us in here?"

"He's *not* your boyfriend. He's a guy fooling around with a cute girl at work before college. Can't you see that?"

Her words sound gruesome in that small, stifling place. With no place to land besides the dirt and dust around our shoes. Even more heat prickles my neck, my entire face.

Mary doesn't look at either of us but at the floor, her arms folded across her ten or so necklaces, which I now realize she's coordinated with the mask. "You *have* become uncharacteristically infatuated," she murmurs.

Of all people to get on my case for letting a boy distract me, this one—besides Mom, who thankfully isn't here to see any of it—might hurt the most.

"I'm not like the two of you," I shoot back. "I've barely been with anybody. And I had no idea you've been judging me for it all this time."

"It's not about that," CeCe says. She stands up from a hopeless squatting position. "It's like, no matter what's going on, you only care about what you want."

"You think I'd even be down here if *you* didn't want it so bad? More than anybody?"

"Stop it. This was always about you. About *getting out of Nautilus*." CeCe spits out the last four words in a cruel singsong. "Everything is about *getting out of Nautilus*. Maybe some of us are just trying to survive in Nautilus."

"I don't want to be here. So what?"

"Work on what you got first."

My throat is too dry. I have nothing to say. I need to get out of this basement, which I only just found out about. All part of this fucked-up fever dream since the robbery.

"You didn't call me," Mary says. She lets her phone flashlight fall wherever it wants. "You ghosted me."

I step on one of the empty balloons. It squeaks menac-
ingly under my sneaker. "You got a girlfriend—" I start.

"I didn't shut *you* out—"

"Wait," CeCe says to Mary. "You have a girlfriend?"

"Had. I had one," Mary says, veering into panic. "Not
anymore. We broke up."

"'Anymore'?" CeCe echoes. "Since when?" Her voice
actually shakes. "Since *when*, Mary?"

"This morning."

CeCe whistles through her teeth and puts one foot on the
steps. She laughs. "Fuck you both." She puts her mask back
on, bounds all the way up the stairs, and is gone.

"Awesome. Thank you, Min." Mary's next out. But she's
not going to catch CeCe, who could've run track when she
was still in school.

Neither of them turns back. I can't risk walking like the
night of the robbery. It's way too late. I'm going to have to
leave the area, walk somewhere inconspicuous, and splurge
on a taxi home. The bus doesn't run this time of night, not
well past four o'clock in the morning.

I can't ask Eli. I still haven't apologized for ditching him,
and doing so would mean involving him in this mess. I don't
know his number by heart anyway.

I put the mask on, edge out of the cellar, carefully close
the secret door behind me, and replace the floor mat. Mary
left the door ajar on her way out. I shut it firmly behind me.

My gloved hand lingers on the doorknob, and I pause in
front of the camera I know is there, pointing down. I know
it's probably not recording. But just in case.

I give the camera the finger. My voice comes out scratched,
low, as if I haven't used it in a hundred years.

"I hate you."

I'm too angry to think of something smarter to say and do. I mean it too much. It's not just Anthony and Mr. Duke. It's the people at school. Nicole. All the teachers who said that I had an attitude, when by that point I didn't even talk enough for them to know what my voice sounded like. And my old guidance counselor, who didn't ask me what was going on at home. Who just said that me and my grades weren't good enough and expected an answer. As if I was supposed to do a presentation on my fuck-upness.

And the school social worker, who I never even saw. Fuck them, too.

And Mrs. Delgado. And Second Starts.

And Mary and CeCe for leaving. And Eli.

And Mom. And all of Nautilus.

The camera button just stares back silently.

CHAPTER THIRTY

"Butter pecan milkshake," says a shaky voice.

It's midday, the sun at its highest, and Mary still shows up to the counter in black. My first thought is how she must be boiling in that outfit. Then I remember what happened the last time we spoke. Here, a few days ago, in the middle of the night.

I squint down at her. Anthony has gotten stricter about sunglasses. He said—no, *yelled*, in the thirty seconds it took for him to walk in and out from his car—they aren't necessary if I wear the visor like I'm supposed to. I may smell of old sweat from my poor, neglected visor, but at least Anthony doesn't know we broke in again.

I take Mary's money. "You can step aside now and let the other customers come forward."

"Oh, no, we're still looking," calls one of the ladies who've been gawking at the menu, trying to decide for an eternity of five minutes.

I'm about to step away to make the milkshake when Mary says, "I can't believe you didn't tell me."

There are a lot of things that question could mean. Too many of them, big and small, collecting and condensing across time to now. The Before and the After. They gather in force behind her, threatening to crash through the serving window like the masked robbers.

I still ask, "What are you talking about?"

"Your mom—your *mother*—died. And you didn't even tell me."

Mary's words sting, like ice pressed against the skin for too long. Even more because they come from her. Because she's the one who's supposed to forgive my bullshit.

"CeCe told me last night, and that you've been cold and weird ever since. She's still mad about everything."

"Oh."

"She's right, though. About how you've been acting."

There it is, finally, inside the stand with me. The biggest question I've been avoiding, the slow-moving train. The truth. Everything that separates Before from After. I've been jumping off the track, but now I stare into the headlights of it.

"Why did you hide it?" she says.

"It was my news to tell," I say, trying to make it sound simple. But to be honest, my mind has gone blank, and that's all I can come up with.

I glance behind me. Jordan's doing inventory or something. Trying her damnedest to get that assistant manager spot.

"Who does that?" Mary says, looking me in the eye, which I know is hard for her to do when upset. "Who just has someone in their life die and doesn't say anything? Especially not to their best friend."

I thought I'd be ready to apologize for letting her go on for this long without knowing the truth. Which everyone else but Nicole is happy to circumvent like a cluster of traffic cones.

But instead, I'm angry right back. Why is Mary making this about her?

"How could you just pretend like that?" she goes on. "Are you some kind of emotionless robot?"

"Mary." I swallow air. My thoughts thin out even more, spill all over the place. "It's complicated. I wasn't *pretending* anything."

"I don't get it."

I'm about to explain—or try to—when the two women creep over, finally sure of their order, rum raisin.

Jordan gives me the evil eye as she makes a big deal of opening the freezer containing the rum raisin. "I got this one," she hisses. "Do your friend's shake, already. And you better charge her this time. Full price."

I make Mary's order, my mind buzzing and hands shaking, but by the time I've brought it to the counter, she's gone.

I lean out the window and attempt to scan the viewable corner of the parking lot. Her car isn't there. However, a few more cars have arrived, including a van's worth of people with kids.

I squeeze the plastic cup so tightly the milkshake spills over my knuckles. The rum raisin women stare at me, wide-eyed.

"You can take your break now," Jordan says as she reappears at the counter. "And maybe get it together in the meantime."

She must have heard everything Mary said.

I let myself out the side door. I stare at my hands, wishing they'd materialize something to erase the sting. To numb or forget. But I have no weed. No alcohol, which has gotten harder to find, no pills left over from my mother's room.

Talk to them. They can still hear you.

Right before Mom died, the hospital staff would insist on it. The closest they ever came to feel-good, New Age bullshit, as Mom would call it. As if she could come back to us, sit up in the hospital bed, and comment on the whole situation.

She can hear you.

People say that about the dead to make themselves feel better. It's a way of calming down the living.

I'm transported back to the hospital room. Nicole is sitting next to me in the only other chair. Her eyeshadow is smeared up to her forehead. The machines beep in their slow, stupid pattern. Too slow, I realize later on. Too slow.

Nicole's voice is small and scratched. "Her heart. They had to put her in a forced coma."

The air in my lungs has turned solid. Is no longer air.

Nicole says, "You have to talk to her."

"No."

The chair has knots of lint all over it. It's sturdy—perfect for hunching over with your head in your hands. Doesn't knock around or limp like those plastic chairs in the waiting room. And they fold all the way back for people who stay overnight with their loved ones.

Talk to her.

I could've been here when they put her under.

The TV plays on mute in the corner, mounted near the ceiling. I've passed rooms where they kept it blaring, but in Mom's room it's as quiet as time, as air, as all the things we take for granted. I could sit here awhile, and it's like nothing has changed.

No: I'm sitting on the dusty ground in the lot behind Duke's Ice Creamery.

At some point, Eli arrived and finished out my shift. I

don't know this until the shift has ended and he appears in front of me with a bottle of water.

"Hey," he says, tilting the bottle at me.

Yet another person I've stormed away from, I think, picturing Mary.

But he doesn't mention that. "You think you're okay to get out of here?"

"Who asked you to come?"

"Anthony doesn't know, if that's what you're asking."

"Thanks," I say. "Really."

He holds out a hand to help me up. "Come on. I'm not working anymore."

I EXPECT ELI to drive tight loops around the neighborhood, the way I do when I'm behind the wheel at times like this. But he crosses into the main part of Nautilus, past shopping plazas and large stores and normal activity. This is what it looks like to live near actual industry, life. *Civilization,* I think. More than just a few random stores, gas stations, and Duke's.

We pull into the parking lot of a cheesy pink-and-chrome diner—both inside and out, from what I can tell.

"This okay?" Eli asks.

I nod.

We go inside. Eli orders onion rings and, astoundingly, a strawberry milkshake, and I order a pizza burger. I hadn't planned on ordering anything, but it smelled so good when we walked in I could've eaten the air.

I doodle on my place mat, a rectangular paper covered in ads and coupons for other businesses nearby. Really, I'm just blacking out all the letters and numbers. Every time I look up at Eli, he's observing me with a combination of worry and caution, the way people watch those nonprofit ads full of starving and beaten animals.

"You okay?" he asks.

"Fine," I say. "It happened three months ago."

I expect him to be shocked and angry, too, considering he's finding out at the same time as Mary. But he says something I've never thought of myself, let alone expected from him.

"That's, like, no time whatsoever."

I frown. How the fuck does he know? He still has both his parents *and* at least one grandparent.

At that moment, the waitress brings our food, which I use to successfully smother my anger at him for having it better than me. It turns out to be the best burger of my life.

"I'm sorry to say this, but I think the food at this restaurant might be better than sex," I say to break the silence.

Eli chokes on his milkshake and wipes his mouth with the back of his hand. We haven't talked about sex much. I know he's done it, he knows I haven't, and that's about it.

"I used to work here," he says, still laughing a little.

"What? When?"

"First summer I was allowed to work. So, fourteen. Busboy. Everybody thought I was, like, ten."

I'm almost finished with my burger and steak fries, which are also the best I've ever eaten. "Damn. How many jobs have you had?"

"My parents always made me work. My dad especially. He likes to be a hard-ass." Eli dips a small onion ring into the mass of ketchup on his plate. "He refuses to pay for college unless I study law or something useful."

"Really?" I say. Once again, I could never relate. Although, in the multiverse where Mom and I get to have money, I guess I can see how it'd be messed up—especially between a parent and their kid.

"I've been saving," Eli says. "Got some scholarships. Loans, too. It was kind of unavoidable."

I lean forward and dab some ketchup off his top lip with my own napkin. "What's it like to have a plan?"

He lowers his eyes to the napkin in my hand. "Sometimes just as scary as not having one, I guess."

The waitress brings the check when we've been sitting for too long with our empty plates. Eli pays, and we leave. On the walk out, I decide I'm going to kiss him as soon as we're back inside the car. And after that, who knows.

I just can't go home. I can't.

But nothing happens. A few minutes into the drive, he doesn't mention a destination, and I begin to relax, happy to just drive around at last. I still refuse to tell him where I live.

But he drives to his neighborhood, which I don't realize until we're on his street, and now in his driveway. He cuts the engine, and that's when I grab his shirt and pull him in. It's to thank him for lunch, but more than that, it's to feel something, *anything*, else.

But he stops me. And I can't hold on any longer.

The stupid tears come. I collapse into my two cupped hands, there in the passenger seat of Eli Ronan's car. "I have to go," I say.

"Where?" When I shrug, he says, "Like when you had to go the other day?"

"Ouch." I look out my window to the diner parking lot, embarrassed. But he takes my hand.

"You know, Nana would be okay with you staying over if you needed to. If you told her what's going on." He turns on the music, tinny guitar followed by slow drums. *The Rain-coats*, the screen says. *Lola*. "They should be home pretty soon."

"No one's telling your grandmother anything," I snap.

"It sounds like you're in trouble."

"No offense, but you have no fucking idea what you're talking about."

"I just—"

"You know what? None of this even matters." Somewhere in the back of my mind, a tiny voice is pleading for me to stop. But the anger is louder, somehow gaining more strength, too fast to make a sudden stop.

"What's that supposed to mean?" Eli asks. "That it doesn't matter?"

"It means I don't have to listen to your opinion. It means you don't get to have one. It means that there's no point to this conversation."

"Why?"

I've never seen him this upset. I've seen him become distant. But his kind of distance is quieter, probably because he keeps his music there. My distance is full of crying I've never done and yearning for things I'll never have, like my mother alive again.

"Why?" he repeats. "Min, why?"

"Because you're leaving."

The drums in the song pound low, insistent. A pulse. Almost like thunder rolling in closer.

"Wow," he murmurs.

"I have to go," I say again. Or I think I'm saying it again. Maybe the first time was in my head, or in a dream, or months ago. As soon as I leave, everything will make sense again. Everything will be in its place.

He shakes his head and pushes the key into the ignition. But he doesn't turn it. "Seriously, Min? It's like that?"

I look at him.

"I was going to say . . ." He sighs into his fist. "I know how you feel. Kind of."

I don't want to care. I can't care.

"My aunt, the one I've mentioned before who helped raise me," he says, "she died when I was eleven."

I have no room for it. None. Point-blank. But I still find myself asking, "What happened?"

"Leukemia. She found out maybe three months ahead of time." Eli stares at the closed driveway door. "I hated everything and everyone for a long time. Sometimes I still feel like that."

"You don't seem like it."

He shrugs.

"So you've been faking the whole time?"

"Not with you."

I turn up the music. The song is catchy and weird at the same time, like nothing else I've ever heard. He's so talented at finding what sounds good. But it's not enough to take me out of the moment.

I have to say something about his aunt. And it can't be a lie, whatever it is. "I wish we could stay in here."

He lowers the windows and lets his hand fall on the cup holder between us, an invitation. The keys stay dangling from the ignition. "So let's stay in here."

CHAPTER THIRTY-ONE

I wake up in Eli's car under a large blanket that smells like sunscreen. He's asleep in the driver's seat, leaned all the way back with his arms crossed over his chest. The night air wells in through the cracked window, and cicadas chirp all over. It's either the middle of the night or early morning.

It didn't seem right to fool around earlier. Now I want to touch his eyelids and the skin just under his mouth. But then I remember that he knows about my mother, and the air turns colder, wetter.

I let myself out of the car. My abdomen aches with the need to go to the bathroom. It's so urgent that I don't even care about running into one of Eli's family members. At least, not enough to stay outside—although it's not lost on me how cruel the Universe is to force this scenario on me twice.

The house is heavy with sleep. A fan hums somewhere upstairs. I find the bathroom and pee without taking my eyes off the unlocked door. The people who live here seem like they trust one another to function without a working bathroom lock. Mom knew how to fix doors so that they closed and stayed that way. She talked about personal space and said my body was only mine, not even hers, despite the fact that she'd created me. She always had to add that last part.

On the way out, I stop to look at the old photos in a room off the hallway I haven't seen yet. The room has nicer furniture than the other rooms and smells like oil and wood and preserved things. Nicole's parents have a room like this in their house. They only use theirs on holidays.

Above the fireplace is a collection of photos in their matching wooden frames. At least a dozen photos of Eli and Caroline in elementary school, at Christmas, birthdays, and even one of those cheesy studio portraits.

I'm lost in how much I don't understand the experience of having my image requested, printed, hung, and admired this way. Where I live, the photos are kept in a single drawer in the kitchen along with unused scissors and soy sauce packets. Unless Nicole got rid of those, too.

A photo at the very top of the mantle catches my eye. It's in a large frame and contains at least twenty people around a Christmas tree. I find Eli right away; he's all the way to the left beside his sister. Eli smiles for the camera, but Caroline does this sneer that makes me like her more. Nana sits in the center of the photo, her smile tiny and close-lipped. She looks serious, a different person than the one I met the other night.

And then I spot him. I don't believe my eyes at first.

Anthony.

He's in the same sprawling photo, on the other side of the frame from Eli and Caroline and their parents. Anthony isn't smiling at all. Even with the shot so far back to contain all those people, his clear eyes stick out like hidden blades. Two empty points in a room full of color and happiness and love.

And money, I guess.

Eli's related to our boss somehow. Our boss is in his family.

I edge away from the mantel, my thoughts scrambling to rise and run together in a way that makes anything make sense. Eli and Anthony are related. Anthony and Eli.

"Hey."

Eli's sister Caroline stands in the doorway. Her pajama shorts and tank are covered in bunny rabbits wearing skull masks in different colors.

I snap out of my shocked state and point to the photo. "Anthony. Is he your . . ." I don't even want to guess, because I still don't want to believe it's possible.

"Uncle Tony?" She rolls her eyes. "Yeah, he's married to my aunt Jen. He gives the most random gift cards even though they have the most money out of anyone. It's so annoying."

"I have to go."

"Why?" she snaps, which I wasn't expecting. "He got upset when you did that the last time. When you left."

Which of course I'm not expecting, either. She tosses her thick, curly hair and stares back, challenging me to answer.

"I'm sorry," I say.

She frowns and shakes her head as if I'm speaking in a foreign language she can't identify.

So I leave, remembering there's no reason to be in that house and wanting to get as far away from Anthony's face as possible.

Outside, I bypass Eli's car, where he's still asleep in the driver's seat. By the time I reach the curb, I've had ten conversations with him in my head. I keep asking why he never told me, and he keeps saying he felt like he couldn't.

This, of course, is what keeping a secret means in the first place. It's just that I can't think of a reason to make the secret okay.

One time, I dreamed that CeCe stuck me with her cousin's switchblade, which became hers when he went to jail. I shrugged off the dream as the result of her showing it off the night before—that she knew what to do with a knife.

I don't recall much of the dream itself. It was the physical pain as I woke up. The wind knocked out of me and the warm blood in my mouth that wasn't really there. The pain softened into memory, but still just as real. I never forgot.

The pain of learning Eli's secret feels like that moment.

Maybe Eli doesn't owe me that. Maybe none of us owes the other anything.

Or maybe I'm getting what I deserve. My own version of what I caused everybody else who matters.

Maybe I don't matter.

Thoughts cycle as I make my way down Eli's street, which manages to be adorable even in the middle of the night. I bet it's unbearable during the day, with its crystal-green lawns and tick-tocking sprinklers. With its real porch furniture and wind chimes and colorful front doors and stupid fucking animal-shaped mailboxes.

I break into a run.

CHAPTER THIRTY-TWO

The last time I talked to Mom, before that final time in the hospital, I came home to find all the lights in the apartment turned off except for the one peeking out from behind the bathroom door. I nudged it open and found her in the tub with the water still running. She was hunched in the center of the tub like a rock, smoking a cigarette.

I touched the water coming out of the faucet. Cold. Under the smoke, the bathroom smelled like cherry soap and sulfur and puke.

"It's this new medication," she mused. "They said to let them know if this happens."

"And then what?"

She glanced up. "Nothing. My doctor'll just change it back. Sit down, babe."

I sat on the closed toilet and faced her. I wanted to ask if she was going to die. Just wondering filled me with a vast loneliness, as if it had already happened.

Was I old enough to be on my own? Maybe I could live with Mary, if she could stand me. Her parents might not even notice. It just couldn't be Nicole, who for my entire life has been trying to steal my own mother away from me.

Nobody knew my special brand of loathing for Nicole better than Mom.

I said, "Do you ever think about—?"

"I'm not scared of dying, baby."

The smoke from her cigarette rose above the tub until it was pulled out the window.

I believed her. I just wanted to hear her say it. I felt wretched and ugly and warped from everything I'd been doing. From the chemicals swirling in my bloodstream and sweating out, mingling with the salt from the air and ever-present grime all of it created together.

In this moment, I wanted to tell her everything. That I was starting to cut class and drink, and that, worst of all, I was becoming numb.

"Where would you go?" I asked. "If you could go anywhere?" It was a game we played, to see who could come up with the most distant or surprising places. Nowhere in the world was off-limits.

She sucked on her cigarette. The ash glowed and stretched. "Doesn't matter anymore. Wherever I go, I'll still be sick."

I pointed to her cigarette. "How many of those have you had?"

"Just this one."

Without thinking, I knocked it from between her fingers. She stared at it floating in the water. This moment was a weak ghost of an earlier fight. We were both tired, and the only thing left was the anger, strongest of all, fed and cared for better than any one person who had ever set foot in this place.

CHAPTER THIRTY-THREE

I wish she was here.

"You need to eat," Nicole says.

The smell of fried food pushes itself in through the open bedroom door. It reminds me of the times Mom and I had nothing but frozen hot dogs to eat. Or later on, when she didn't seem to have the strength to eat, let alone cook.

"I made you a fried bologna sandwich." Nicole shoves a plate of food at me, the sandwich and potato chips and carrot sticks.

"Gross," I say, but the sandwich looks and smells like heaven. I wolf it down, so hungry I don't even comment on the fact that Nicole has been watching me with an improbable silence.

Then I remember.

"The keys, Minerva."

My limbs freeze, as if preparing for Nicole to lunge for the aforementioned keys as I vulnerably cram food into my face. I wouldn't put it past her.

"I gave you three days," she says. "I believe it's been more than that."

"I know, I know." I start on a carrot. "What if I just pay it off?"

"The person who wants to buy it is willing to pay a lot more than you have. And all at once." Her voice changes, becomes heavier. "Unless there's something I don't know."

"There isn't," I say in a rush, setting down the plate on the bed. My stomach whines for more.

She turns to go. "Some girl called for you."

"CeCe?"

"No."

"Mary?"

"No."

I think of Eli, the only other person who might actually call me. My pulse accelerates but only for a second or two. "You sure it was a girl?"

"Yes." Nicole pulls out her phone on impulse, reminded of its existence.

If none of my friends called, it doesn't matter.

"Hold on. Do we have a landline again?" It was cut sometime after Mom died.

"Yes. We're human beings, after all." Nicole crosses her arms and stares out over the parking lot. "Gosh. What *was* her name? Something with a J. Jamaica? Jamina?"

Oh. "Jamira."

"Yeah. I wrote down the number." Nicole pauses again on her way out. "She said she has something that belongs to you."

NOBODY ANSWERS AT the phone number Jamira left, so I drive to her house. The gas needle quivers toward *Empty* again, and I try not to get distracted waiting for the time bomb of the little red warning light to follow. Maybe the Universe doesn't want me to keep the Boat, either.

I ring the doorbell a few times, but I can already tell by the sounds coming from behind the house that I'll have to walk around to find Jamira and talk to her. And in full sunlight, no less.

This time, there's only one car parked in the backyard. Then the pool comes into view, the bright blue oval of it, and all the kids are inside. Their jumping creates heaving waves that spill over the pool's edge. A couple of orange and gray cats tiptoe around the yard, pouncing to avoid the splashes.

Jamira watches the pool from a deck chair, one hand on her hip and the other holding her vape pen. She's wearing a huge pair of mirrored aviator sunglasses. I can't even tell if she sees me until she nods once, yawning. "You're just in time," she says.

I step onto the deck. "My cousin said you had something of mine?"

She doesn't answer. "Come over here. Watch this."

A girl I remember from last time walks up on the diving board extending from the small wooden deck. All the kids have momentarily paused to watch. She turns around and locates Jamira, who nods at her as if to give permission. In response, the girl turns back and executes a tidy somersault into the pool.

"It took me forty-eight hours," Jamira murmurs, "but I fixed that fucking pool for them. It would've been just another mud puddle around here if it wasn't for me."

"That's great," I say, meaning it.

I'm about to ask again what she has that belongs to me, but a sharp tug in my gut says it's not time yet.

"You going in?" she asks.

I laugh. "Me?"

"You know how to swim, don't you?"

"Of course I do."

"So why not go in? It's hot as hell."

"Why don't *you* go in there?"

"I have snacks to assemble." She does some kind of dancer stretch with her arms. "You want twenty bucks out of it?"

Suddenly, I get it. Jamira doesn't have anything that belongs to me. She just needed the help.

However.

"Hey, Jamira?"

"Yeah?"

When she removes her sunglasses, I see it's fatigue, not exasperation, that's causing her to be short. She peers at me from behind the deck railing. She has a way of moving and looking at the world that I think I want to copy. A way of stripping things bare with her attention. Not like how Anthony does it, which is to humiliate. But how CeCe does, and like how Mom did.

Jamira shoves her sunglasses back on. "You gonna be okay out here?"

And just like that, I'm fine with swimming. More than fine—I take off my shirt, thankful for the sports bra I chose to wear this morning. The world doesn't blow up around me.

I kick off my sandals. "Didn't you say you had something that belonged to me?" At this point, I just want to know what she'll say.

She smiles. "You didn't know I was just saying that?"

So I was right. I stand at the edge of the pool long after she goes inside. It's deeper than I expected, the bottom pristine except for some coins, a few colored rings from a game, and a delicate line of silt unmoved by everything going on at the surface. The splashing is so continuous on the other end of the pool I can barely keep track of a single body, which I suppose is what I'm getting paid to do now.

I'm still not sure if I can execute the move I learned the summer when I was twelve. No, thirteen. When Mom found a private dock at the end of a nondescript field and we sat for hours, most of which I spent swimming as far as she'd let me. The spot turned into McMansions by the following summer.

After I've calculated how, I back up and somersault in, cutting through to the very bottom. The pressure of the water above me is calming, gentle. Like a giant, steadying hand. Nicole would call it God, Mary would say Universe, CeCe wouldn't answer. And I'd just ask for Mom.

I swim almost to the other end of the pool, remaining so close to the bottom I could curl up and go to sleep there. When my lungs can't take it any longer, I push off from the floor.

At the surface, all the kids are cheering.

PEOPLE START SHOWING up to the house from the neighborhood. Some are related to Jamira, and some aren't. One by one, they leave with their kids, usually after some small talk and occasional gossiping. I hang to the side with the kids left in the pool, amazed at how some of them have been swimming for hours.

Amazed, too, at how I used to be one of those kids and have no idea when I stopped.

When just a handful of kids are left—Jamira's siblings and cousins—she wanders back to the deck and collapses into a chair. She's still wearing her giant sunglasses. It's the part of summer when sunset seems to last for hours, refusing to give up. I've been using my arm for shade.

Jamira reaches for a giant bag of potato chips. "I should consider myself lucky."

"Why?" I sit up and make a screw-face that makes her laugh. It sounds like what Anthony said to me the first day back since the robbery.

"I didn't think I'd find a way to make money this fast," she says. "I guess it's not the worst thing."

"You're good at it. Working with kids."

"It's just for now." She hands out what appear to be two twenties. "I can't give you a job, though."

"Thanks. It's okay." I feel bad taking the money, but it'd be worse to give any of it back. "Jamira?"

"What?"

"Remember that girl you told me about, Sierra? You *really* don't know what happened to her?"

"Here we go," she mutters. "No. I told you she just stopped coming. Jordan said she was just too weak to handle Duke's. Imagine that shit: too weak to scoop ice cream. Some people, I guess."

Jordan said.

The words cling to my attention like dandelion fuzz.

"Maybe Sierra wasn't weak," I offer. "Maybe she had a good reason for staying away."

Maybe she was intimidated. Or worse. The pieces drift together, one after the next, like a logic proof. Parts I've picked up and examined, never as a whole. Until now.

There has to be more.

"Did Jordan mention anything else?"

"You *do* know that's my best friend you're asking about,

right?" Jamira's voice is flat now. She starts picking up loose items on the deck with more purpose. Toys and swim gear. "My best friend in the entire world besides my mom and Titi Lucy. Anyway, why do you care? I thought you were above all that gossipy shit and caring what people think of you."

She doesn't want to talk about it. But she also doesn't know. I start to put the conversation back down like everything else I'm supposed to get over, but the need is too big. It's not fair.

"How long did you work at Duke's before you got fired?"

She freezes, her shoulders drooping. A pair of goggles and a few miniature soccer balls tumble to the deck floor, but she still doesn't move.

"Three years," she says.

"How long has Jordan worked there?"

Jamira sniffs and tilts her head, her shades fixed on the surface of the sunset-colored pool, though it might as well be a hundred miles away.

"Two years," she whispers. "Not even." She knows where I'm going and refuses to look at me because of it.

"And who's going to be assistant manager," I say, "when Eli leaves for college?"

She doesn't answer and takes an extra-long hit from her vape pen, lost in new thoughts about her own best friend casting her aside. I suspect she does it on purpose, obscuring her face in white vapor even if for just a few seconds.

Her next words catch me off guard.

"She didn't get into much detail." Jamira licks her lips, vape lowered. "A little while ago, she thought you might be up to something. She said she hopes Anthony fires you. That she would do it herself if she could."

The confirmation is like a block of ice pressing into the

middle of my back. Jordan's been watching me, and she wants me gone just like Sierra. But not because I'm a threat to her becoming assistant manager (which, who would anyone be kidding with that notion?). Jordan wants me gone because I know about the money. Because she's in on it.

She knows or at least suspects I broke into the Ice Creamery that first night—maybe she was even there—but she couldn't tell Anthony for fear of getting in trouble herself.

Jordan knows about the money.

"Well?" Jamira says. "*Are* you up to something?"

I open my mouth, but she cuts me off.

"Never mind. If you are, don't tell me. I don't want any trouble. It's, like, the one thing my parents taught me that was right." She rolls her neck and shoulders and starts gathering pool toys again. "You'll stay out here?"

"Yeah, sure. As long as you need."

"Thanks." She shoots me a look over the sunglasses, and for the first time I see something like nerves. When she says my name, there isn't a hint of a question. "Minerva."

"Yeah?"

"Whatever's going on with you"—her thick lashes move fast behind the lenses, and I know her eyes are drilling into mine—"just be careful."

CHAPTER THIRTY-FOUR

At CeCe's, a few people have crashed and set up her projector to YouTube. Two girls are laughing next to Large Marge, whose grayish fur makes her disappear into the dark, her eyes glinting like buttons. One of them lifts her ear and whispers into it.

No, blows smoke.

"Hey," I start, but the look the girl gives me is so cold I just whistle for Large Marge to come over. She rises and follows me on wobbling legs to the bedroom, where CeCe's on her mattress watching *Shark Tank* on her cell phone.

"Did you know some girl was trying to get your dog high?" I ask.

CeCe's eyes twitch when I tell her about Large Marge but otherwise remain fixed on the phone. Here and not here.

"Is that all?" she asks. "If you're here for bud, there's no point." She wears a loose-fitting pair of beach trunks, white tank, and no bra. I don't think she wears one usually, but the cotton is so old it's almost transparent. Candy wrappers, blunt leaves, and random disconnected cords crunch beneath my feet. Balled-up socks lie in every corner.

CeCe rolls from her side to her back, armpit hair flashing.

This isn't the CeCe I know, who gets life advice from movies like *Scarface* and usually wouldn't be caught dead in something see-through. It feels like months have passed, or years, instead of days. And now I don't know who this person is in front of me.

I clear a space on the floor and sit down. "I found something out."

She claps, facing the wall. "Congratulations."

"What's *your* problem?"

She gestures weakly around the room. "Can't you see that I'm broke as well as dry?"

"Well, snap out of it. There's shit going on."

CeCe doesn't answer, still facing away from me.

"Jordan's in on it. If we—"

"No."

"No?"

"I'm done." CeCe sits up on the mattress, drawing her knees to her chest and facing the wall. "You know why? Because it's just another dead end. Just another pile of limp balloons."

So this counts her out of my new plan.

"Eli's related to Anthony," I say at last.

Long pause from the wall. "Huh?"

"Eli's his nephew."

"It's weird they wouldn't tell people that," she says. Then, just as fast, she shakes the interest from her mind. "Nope. I still don't care."

I stand up, taking the opportunity to tower over her. "I don't believe you don't care."

She laughs manically. "What are we even supposed to do? Come on, man. They won. *They always win.*"

"That's not true." My voice sounds pathetic in the near-empty room, so I say it again. "It's not true, CeCe."

"You ever heard of the term *sunken cost fallacy?*"

"Obviously not—"

"It means that just because you've put work into something doesn't mean it's always worth it to keep going. It means sometimes you have to cut your losses and walk away."

She flops back down as if the words have drained the last of her energy.

I chew my lip. "Where's Mary?"

She shrugs, back to staring into space. I've seen Mary behave like this before about girls, but never CeCe. I feel partially responsible. I look down at my palms for the hundredth time, wishing money would appear like in some kind of fable. They say money isn't everything, but that's for people who have never worried about how they're going to sleep, or drive to work, or buy a fucking piece of fruit.

I have to find that money.

I have to go back.

I bring CeCe some water and leave her where she is. I don't tell her about the plan that's gathering in my head now, since I'm pretty sure it wouldn't make her budge.

On my way out, something cold and wet bumps my leg. It's Large Marge.

We stand there, the two of us, in a stare down by the apartment door. CeCe once told me it was a sign of aggression for dogs to stare, and for Large Marge I guess it translates into a kind of guilt-inducing sassiness.

"I can't take you," I say. "CeCe would kill me."

She wags her tail. I bend down to scratch behind her ears, and she licks me on the nose. CeCe also said a lick on the nose means good luck for a day. I hope more than anything she's right.

CHAPTER THIRTY-FIVE

I wait for closing time on Friday night. When I arrive at Duke's, the Boat's clock reads 11:22 P.M.

Driving past, I spot Jordan, Eli, and one of the new girls. The window's still open, the customers scattered and doing their usual menu-gaping. Behind the counter, one person handles the customers while the others start cleaning.

My usual incognito parking spot down the block is currently lined with cars, so I keep driving around the corner. The next option is near a bar named McCarthy's By the Sea. But the bar doesn't have a direct view of Duke's—and is a bar—so I turn around, desperate, and settle on the gas station and park at the pump with the best view.

The clerk grumbles when I slide over a crumpled ten-dollar bill from the Probable Orphan Fund, because the pump outside won't take it, along with an oversized bag of sour gummies.

I look past the clerk and off to the right at the coffee station. The window above it has a clear view of Duke's.

"Give me a coffee, too." I peel off another couple dollars from the dwindling stack of bills in my wallet.

"It's self-serve. Also, it's, like, ninety degrees out." He sounds like Nicole.

"Well, I need to stay awake."

I don't drink coffee, but I pretend to be interested in all the choices at the coffee station, where I prepare it the way Mom did—black with sugar—and wait.

The lights in Duke's are finally clicking off. The girls and Eli start filing out one by one, followed by Anthony. Even though his office is air conditioned, the sweat has already gathered at his hairline and on the back of his doughy neck. I stare hardest at him, as if his sweat were lighter fluid and my look could spark a flame.

Jordan's is the last car left. The lights are off in the stand, which means she's still in Anthony's office. And a few minutes later, miraculously, the white pickup truck arrives, idling for a couple of minutes before Jordan comes out and speaks to the person at the driver-side window. She carries a box inside.

The truck leaves. I can follow it or stay and see what it dropped off. And hope that one of them leads me to where the money is. My hands are sweating so much that my paper cup of coffee has become soggy. My eyelids start to ache from looking at the same spot this long.

"Your pump's still open," the clerk interrupts from behind the counter. "You need something else? I can't hold it for you."

I squint at him because he knows damn well there isn't anyone waiting for that spot. I take a small, demonstrative sip of coffee. Then I take my phone out and pretend it isn't dead. Because if I've learned anything from others about having a cell phone, it's that the whole world stops when you're checking it. He scoffs and picks up his own phone out of habit.

When I turn back to the window, Jordan's car is gone. Dammit.

I swallow a real mouthful of coffee and run out, shoving the soggy cup into the overflowing trash on my way.

Jordan's gone, but I still have the copied keys. I might as well see if that box is in there. I peer into the road, empty as expected, then double back to pump the gas I almost forgot I paid for. I leave the Boat in one of the available spots behind the station.

Avoiding the bright rectangles of gas station lights, I cross the street to Duke's and slip inside.

I'm still not used to the Ice Creamery in the dark. It feels like someone else will appear at any moment and tell me to take an order, refill the cones, switch out the rocky road.

It takes me a few tries to unlock the door to Anthony's office. It's quiet except for the purring of the computer equipment. I lift the desk and pull back the rug with all the energy I have available.

If I find the money, Nicole won't have to pay for everything. She can go back to living her own life and not pretending to care what happens to me. If I find the money, she won't sell the Boat. If I find the money, CeCe and Mary will talk to me again, and to each other.

I open the door cautiously enough that it doesn't make a sound. The last time, I scrambled. Not anymore.

I see it as soon as I reach the bottom of those weird, short steps. The box from earlier, sitting in the middle of the floor. I cut the tape with my keys and desperately open the flaps to reveal a shrink-wrapped object. I sink the keys into that, too.

Uninflated balloons spill out of the plastic wrapping to the floor.

A familiar voice hits the back of my head. "Hi, Min."

Jordan has taken a knee at the top of the steps. She grips the door with one hand. In the other hand is a square, shiny-dull object. She lets it dangle, and when the light hits it, I see what it is. A padlock.

I'm about to make a run for it anyway when she says, "Don't think about it. There are people right outside who'll just toss you back in."

Is she bluffing? It's hard to tell with that visor casting that shadow over half her face.

She purses her lips. "I knew you were the one trying to steal from us. I can't believe I was right."

"Did you trick me into coming in here?"

She juts her chin. "You came in here on your own." She was waiting for me, just as I was waiting for her. "I saw that weird car you drive. You're getting sloppy."

"You've been watching me?"

She holds up her phone. *EasyCam Connect*, says a cartoon font at the bottom of the screen. It shows the same angles as in Anthony's office, now empty. "I know you've been coming in here. You and your friends. Even with those ridiculous masks, I knew."

"So what? Why didn't you say anything before?"

I have to keep stalling. Find a way to distract her so I can make a run for it. Whatever idea comes first.

"He wouldn't believe me if I just told him. Now I have the proof."

"And then what? He'll go back to watching you on the cameras?"

Jordan slinks back from the opening, almost as if I've hit her. "Do you *always* have something to say?"

"Yes. I do."

Her voice hardens. "You're sneaking around in things that have nothing to do with you."

"I'd say me standing here means it has something to do with me." She hasn't yet closed the door. If I don't take advantage soon, I'll get stuck in here.

"The money," I yell. "Just tell me if I was close."

Jordan rolls her eyes. "Just like those stupid guys who robbed us a few weeks ago."

Now, I think. *Now I can knock her over and get out of here.*

"They had it all wrong, too. There hasn't been any money down here for a while. So give it up." She checks her reflection in her phone.

"So let me go."

She pauses. My hopes soar, so high I become dizzy. Like when Mom talked about getting a new heart and our lives starting over. Like whenever I think about the future lately.

"Why would I do that?"

"I don't know, to be decent?"

"Give me your phone," she says, like this is somehow a logical response.

Without a word, I toss up my dead phone. A second later, she laughs and lets it fall back down. "You're a mess, Min. Anybody ever tell you that?"

"All the time." I pick up my phone from the dusty floor. An idea comes to me. The only idea left. "Wait!"

She sighs but doesn't speak or move.

I rise as slow as I can. "Is it true?"

"Is what true?"

I sprint up the steps so fast that the door slips from its lightly propped position and falls backward to the floor of the office with a deafening slam. Jordan backs away, but still close enough to kick me in the shin. The pain comes in sparks. Showers of sparks. I buckle down to the floor. Then I vaguely recall hearing that Jordan did gymnastics all through middle and high school, until graduating last summer.

"Is *what* true," she heaves. She stands over me, her face flushed.

I clutch my leg, the pain going from sparks to a dull, spreading ache. "Is it true that nothing will make him treat you or me or anyone like a human being?"

"Fuck you," she says and pushes me back down the steps.

CHAPTER THIRTY-SIX

It turns out there's a light in the cellar, one big old fluorescent light the length of a small person. Not like the ones upstairs meant to keep us awake and alert for the customers all day and night, but the kind that gave up a long time ago. The color of piss or stained teeth. The color of rot.

The old buzzing light feels worse than the dark, but I can't bring myself to turn it off. I take in the expanse of nothing in great, excruciating detail. All the dust in its various shades of gray and brown. Dirt, crumbled cement, paint chips. There are old paint cans I didn't notice before, and the faint, chemically sweet smell of bug spray.

In and out. There and back.

I sink back against the wall, defeated. My only choice can't possibly be to wait for Anthony to find me here, and either turn me in to his cop friends or have me killed for trespassing. I could tap around, find a hollow space in the wall. But I don't have anything on me to break through the wall with. What would I even use, another brick? Not to mention, I don't know how much time I even have.

Even if I made it out, there'd be nowhere left to go, no

one to help me, because my friends think I only care about myself and what happens to me.

And it's true. I *do* only care about me. I never visited my mother enough, not when she was in the hospital and not now that she's in the ground. I deserve to lose it all.

I laugh so hard that I start crying, folding in on myself. I forget that I deserve to be alone, and then I remind myself again. I cry all over again. Everything becomes clear, like the boardwalk after a hard rain.

I lose track of time this way, in my own personal hell within hell. An hour later—maybe more, maybe less—I'm startled back to reality by the sound of a door slamming overhead.

Fuck.

I'm practically gulping down the dusty air, trying to catch my breath.

What follows is a terrible, repeated banging. Is someone being beaten? Do they know I'm in here? Is this a preview of my own fate?

Even if I wanted to make a sound, my vocal cords are desiccated. I wouldn't be able to hear myself above the banging. It fills my skull and eclipses everything in a way that no drug, legal or illegal, ever has before.

After about a minute of this, the cellar door lifts.

I still haven't figured out if I'm going to aim for Anthony's face or balls when a disembodied voice I can't believe I'm hearing rings down.

"Minerva?"

I look up into the harsh center of a flashlight. The light tilts to the side, and Nicole's face materializes in the dark. Then, miraculously, CeCe's and Mary's, too.

A sound escapes me that I can only describe as hideous with relief.

"You okay?" Nicole calls down, her voice off without its usual animosity.

"Yeah. Yeah, I'm okay."

Mary says, "Will you please get out of there already?"

They step back while I climb out. "How did you know I was in here?"

"The cops found your mom's car all the way out in Montauk a couple hours ago," Nicole says.

I whip around to face her. "Because you called them?"

Nicole points back at me in the dark. "Hey, *I* gave you a warning—"

"Enough!" CeCe says. "Shit, you two are like little kids."

Nicole flinches at CeCe's choice of words but turns back to me. "They had no idea where you were in relation to the car. So I—"

CeCe interrupts. "She came to me."

I'm almost impressed. "How did you know . . ."

Nicole rolls her eyes. "Quit acting shocked. I told you I'm supposed to watch you."

Maybe I did underestimate her.

"So how'd you end up down here?" Nicole asks. "And by the way, what is that basement-type room? What's going on?"

Nobody answers.

She snaps her fingers in the dark, first at me, then at all of us. "Hello?"

"It was a stupid practical joke," I finally say. "That girl Jordan did it."

"The white one with the cute bangs?"

I nod.

She considers this, then scoffs. "How gullible do you think I am?"

"We don't," Mary says weakly.

"Okay. Well." Nicole turns on her heel and motions toward the door. "We're talking about this tomorrow. For now, let's get out of this crap hole."

Crap hole, Cece mouths to me in the dark. I cover my own mouth with my hand to keep from laughing.

Nobody speaks as we cross the parking lot.

Until Nicole, who seems to miss the sound of her own voice, says, "You know, it's funny. When I was your age, there was a rumor about money being stashed right in the freezer."

A current passes through all three of us. Mary pauses in her walking and clutches my hand. On the other side of her, CeCe starts coughing.

"Money?" I ask, too tired to mask my interest, bordering on desperation. "Do you think it was true?"

"Nah," Nicole says, mistaking our reactions for interest in the story. She shrugs. "To me, it doesn't make any sense. Why put money in the freezer when the bank is right there?"

Mary digs her nails into my forearm, but I ignore that. Maybe it's finally being free from the cellar, or maybe it's because it's the middle of the night, but in talking to my mother's cousin, I feel strangely calm and still and patient.

"I don't know," she says, yawning. "It just doesn't sound realistic."

We've reached the cars, hers and Mary's. The Boat's absence knocks the wind out of me.

Nicole unlocks her door and climbs into the driver's seat as if we're driving home from the grocery store.

"Can I ride with Mary?" I suggest, still standing in the dusty lot. Mary and CeCe have already taken their seats in Mary's car. Both engines are on.

Nicole pauses at the wheel. "God, I'm too tired for this."

"Hey. You said the Lord's name in vain."

She shifts the car into reverse, replying seriously to my attempt at a joke. "I never said I was perfect, Min." Before I can reply, she backs up and drives out of the lot.

CHAPTER THIRTY-SEVEN

It's that mysterious time between the witching hour and what's officially considered morning. The sky above Duke's Ice Creamery is the darkest possible shade of blue. We unlock the biggest freezer at the very back, a walk-in. Each of us chooses a wall and starts going through the boxes and crates. But my wall is solid blocks of vanilla, chocolate, and a few strawberry.

"This doesn't feel right," Mary says after a while. "I'm not finding anything, and from what I can tell, I don't think I will."

"I know," CeCe says. "Mini-Mart, is there anything else you can think of?"

"I would also love to get out of this freezer," I say. "But there has to be something to what Nicole said. I know there is."

Mary touches my arm, the pads of her fingers surprisingly warm. "It sounded right because you wanted it to."

"No." I look around the closet-sized space and at the two of them. The expectation in their faces, combined with the physical cold, makes my teeth ache inside my skull.

Then the answer comes.

I back out of the freezer. They follow me, flashlight off now. One of them lets the freezer door close, a plunking sound that magnifies in the quiet. The heat rushes back in around us until I cross the room to the sherbet freezers. I bypass the one holding lemon and cherry and find the one I had in mind in the far corner. Cantaloupe, honeydew, and sour berry. Our absolute least popular flavors.

So unpopular I can't remember the last time someone ordered any of them.

So unpopular they aren't even on the menu.

I grip the sides of the freezer, breathing up the cold.

"Min, hurry up," CeCe says. "We're kind of pushing our luck here tonight, don't you think?"

I lift the lid. Mary turns her flashlight back on. The rectangular, barely dented surfaces of these sherbet flavors glow in the small amount of moonlight hitting this corner of the store. Each one is coated in a thin layer of frost. I reach down and lift out the boxes one by one. There should be spare boxes underneath to replace the flavors when they run out.

Instead, a plank of wood, or maybe particle board, has been laid beneath the freezer-damp boxes. I knock, and the sound that comes back is hollow.

The board is wedged in there, but loose enough to try. CeCe takes out her knife from her boot and pries it loose, and Mary shines her cell phone closer.

I lift and tug at the board, which is heavier than I expected. I manage to pull it out all the way and set it lengthwise against the wall.

The bottom of the freezer is lined with flat, clear packages of something pale and solid. They could contain the ingredients for those famous milkshakes—they *could*—but I've never seen this ingredient in my life.

CeCe coughs hard. "Jesus Christ."

"Leave him out of this," I murmur. It's supposed to be a joke, but nobody laughs, of course.

"That's not cash," Mary says in a dreamy voice.

"What is it?" I ask CeCe. "I mean, what do you think it is?"

"Heroin? Maybe fentanyl. I really don't know." She licks her lips again and again. "I never seen either up close like this."

She starts to reach into the freezer, but I hold her arm back.

"What are you doing?"

"We should go to the police."

"Don't be stupid. They already know. It's *us* he's hiding it from."

"It just seems like a bad idea," I say. My skin itches. I don't really believe in signs—Mom didn't—but this feels like one.

Then Mary says out of nowhere, "We got this far. Maybe there's a reason for it."

"Really? You, too?" I edge back in the direction of the door. "CeCe, do you even know what to do with this stuff?"

She sucks her teeth, offended. "Of course I do."

"No. *No.* This is completely fucked."

"Why?" Mary shoots back. "It makes sense. If it's just one time and it helps both of you out of some very real problems, I don't see why not."

"Because it's dangerous. This shit kills people."

CeCe points her knife down into the freezer. "Well, guess what? It's already here. So either they make money off this, or we do."

The way the two of them stare me down generates yet

another alternate universe I can't see beyond. My best friend and my neighbor/dealer, the opposite ends of Nautilus personified. I can't believe it took me this long to see it.

"Okay, kids," CeCe says, "we've gotta move. We can't stay here."

When no one says anything, she grabs as many of the packages as she can fit into her bag. Maybe three or four. I'm not sure, because I'm not looking, as is usually the case when I'm around for her "business transactions," as she calls them.

After what feels like an hour but is maybe less than fifteen seconds, we're back in Mary's car on the way to the Beach Blossom, tied together in an early-early-morning silence, the empty sidewalks and overpasses and swamp yards of Nautilus the only ones doing the talking.

CHAPTER THIRTY-EIGHT

"Good news."

Nicole stands in my bedroom doorway. The late-afternoon sun burns orange in the corner of the window. The rest of the view is blocked by the dresser and the clothes piled on top instead of inside. I'm supposed to be cleaning my room, but my main priority is waiting to hear from CeCe.

I sit up at the words *good news*. It feels like a trick, but I'll take my chances.

"They made an offer on—" Nicole clears her throat. "The . . . your mom's . . ."

"The Boat?"

"Yes."

I bunch the comforter over my mouth.

"We have to, Min."

The first hours of this morning rush back to me. By the time we called it a night, CeCe looked awake enough for the three of us. Like she might turn around and try and sell the stuff right then.

I fight the urge to push past Nicole, put on flip-flops, and run downstairs to find out what happened with CeCe.

Nicole holds out a plate with a toasted half-bagel thick

with cream cheese and a handful of strawberries. I follow her out of the room and eat at the table like a person, so grateful for the food and her silence that I don't even complain when she tells me to sweep and mop the floor and would I please look at some boxes stacked in Mom's room to sort for garbage and donation?

"I thought you'd want to move into her room," she says without looking at me from the TV stand she's in the middle of dusting. "It's bigger."

"No. I'm okay with what I've got."

I watch as she gradually stops dusting, until the cloth she's using falls to the floor. She dabs her eyes with the back of her hand. I fight back tears of my own. The tears haven't stopped much since that day in the car with Eli, like my body is making up for the absence. "I think you should have Mom's room."

"You sure?"

"I can't," I say simply. "You can."

She nods.

"Hey, um." I stand up to clear my plate. "I'm not trying to be an asshole or change the subject. But I really did think you had your own place. Weren't you married or something?"

"Engaged," she says, her hand now wiping faster and smaller circles on the side of the TV stand. "I was. Until a few months ago."

"Oh." I think about the past few months, which feel like a single second and a hundred years at the same time. "Was it around the time—"

"That Sunny died? Yeah. It's funny how everything seems to happen at once." Nicole stops wiping and looks up. "You know what? I can't think of anything that makes more sense."

I go into the bathroom and turn on the faucet, as if I'm

preparing to rinse out the mop in the tub. Really I'm trying not to sob in front of Nicole.

All of a sudden, she calls me from the front of the apartment.

"Min! What'd you do now!"

And just like that, I'm rid of the impulse to empathize with my mother's cousin.

Nicole stands at the apartment door, talking to someone on the walkway. I catch the tail end of whatever she's saying to them, something about how if she had known I was shirking my responsibilities, she would've never something something something.

"You skipped out on work, didn't you?" Nicole says when I reach the front door. She shoves it wider to reveal Eli, looking equal parts amused and terrified.

"I wasn't on shift today!" I protest.

"Oh," she says, then mutters to Eli, "sorry."

"No worries," he says. "I did have to ask about work stuff." He's trying to appease her. For obvious reasons, this is much easier for him than it is for me.

Nicole glances back and forth between us, a glimmer of understanding in her eyes. "Would you like to come in? We're just cleaning, but—"

I step out between her and the door. "We can talk out here."

On her way back inside before closing the door, Nicole gives me a look that I know means not to take too long. I can't believe I'm finding myself in a second consecutive moment of mercy from her. I guess chores aren't a complete waste of time.

"You left," Eli says as soon as the door is closed all the way.

"Yeah."

"You didn't say anything." His voice is calmer, more serious than I've been used to.

"Neither did you."

He purses his lips as if wounded. "Caroline told me you saw the family photos."

I nod.

"It's just embarrassing," he says. "To be the only guy at Duke's. But then to be the boss's nephew. They thought it'd be easier that way. And I needed the money. My parents wouldn't pay for any of that equipment, the records." He looks down at our feet on the cement. My bare, dusty ones and his well-kept sneakers. "I got used to not telling anybody."

"I can relate to that."

We're standing closer. I'm not sure how it happened. I must not have noticed with all the space in my brain taken up by him being here, and CeCe not answering the phone, and Nicole being my guardian, and always always always Mom being gone. Space Cadet strikes again.

"Besides," he says, "would *you* want to tell people you're related to that guy?"

"Good point."

It occurs to me I might've taken Nicole for granted. Not that I'd go announcing it across the island tomorrow, but enough to give her an easier time.

"You did skip out on a shift, you know," Eli whispers. "I just didn't want to make you lose the fight with your cousin."

"Yeah." I smile. "Thanks for that."

"So." He licks his lips, nervous. "You're not coming back, are you?"

"I think that might be out of the question."

And even if I didn't unintentionally reveal myself to Jordan, I couldn't. I can't. Not mentally, emotionally, or physically. I can't entertain the thought of being in that space again after last night. Not without panic taking over. I wonder if my friends feel the same way.

Especially CeCe, wherever she is.

"That's too bad," he says. "But it's also kind of awesome."

I sit down on the walkway floor. He does the same. I don't care who could be watching us now. I want to stay like this more than I anticipated when I opened the door. The sky over and beyond is more shades of gray than I can count, the clouds spreading in thick curls like the sky in a picture book.

I say, "I still don't understand why you never said anything about Anthony."

"I thought you'd stop talking to me. I mean. You're right; he made me assistant manager just to be fucked up. He didn't have to do that. But he did."

I don't know how to respond. Maybe because I already know this.

"Everybody else hates working there, hates him," he continues. "Even *I* hate him. But you're the only one who really says it. It's like you're not afraid of him."

Hearing Eli say he hates Anthony isn't as sweet as I'd have expected. But that's because it's not about him.

It's my turn now. Since we're telling each other everything. I think about diving into the pool with all those kids the other day. "I have something to tell you, too."

He shifts his foot closer to mine and looks over at me. Water drips steadily from the trees and the eaves and the railings, from one of those secret summer rains that nobody's around for but happen anyway.

And for a second it seems like he knows, and he's just been waiting for the truth. "What is it?"

I tell him everything about what we were planning, what we did, and what we found. And how I haven't heard from CeCe since early morning and it's well into the following day.

He doesn't say anything at first. His face and body look like they're still paused to listen a minute after I stopped talking. My own body starts to reject the whole situation, my calves poised to stand and carry me back inside, where I can look for a job, anything that isn't Duke's or the heartache of working so close to someone about to leave.

"Wow." He stands up and leans on the railing, not realizing or caring that his clothes are getting wet.

"That's it? 'Wow'?"

He looks out over to the sliver of water, the view people can't resist once they notice. "I've heard stuff, but I always thought he was too dumb to pull any of it off."

"Who says he has?" I join him at the railing, fall into the view of the clouds over the water.

I tell Eli what Jordan told me, about how she's been watching the stand on an app and that the cash the robbers were looking for that night isn't there *anymore*. At first I thought she was just lying. Turns out Jordan just wanted to rub my face in the fact that I was wrong about where to look.

"Well," Eli says, "that money could be anywhere around here."

"Right."

He laughs. "I wish I could just ask. I bet Nana would tell us if she knew."

"I'm not interrogating your grandma."

A cold breeze, a hint of fall to come, wraps around our legs. The comfortable silence I've come to appreciate with him.

"So when the keys disappeared—" He rubs the back of his neck, his hair. "That really was you?"

I nod.

"I'm a very bad assistant manager for not noticing any of this."

"Yeah, you're pretty bad." I smile. "I'm sorry I got you in trouble."

"It's worth it," he says. "I'm sorry I didn't tell you Anthony is my uncle-*in-law*." He stresses the last two syllables the same way I tell people Nicole's my second cousin, and it makes me laugh and cry at the same time, because Nicole is nowhere near as bad as Anthony and didn't deserve some of that.

"I was terrified, you know," I clarify. "The whole time. Even before we knew what he was up to."

Eli has turned around now, holding the railing with some distance. Water drips onto his knuckles. He seems to be focusing on something in the parking lot.

"She can't have that," he says.

I shake my head, not getting it. "Who can't have . . . ?"

"That stuff you found. The drugs." He watches a faraway boat braving the unpredictable weather. "Anthony will find out, and he'll be pissed."

"What do you mean, pissed?"

"Like he'll have her arrested, fair or not." He licks his lips, which may or may not be shaking. "I've seen him do it before. Get people arrested. It's, like, nothing for him."

I start to explain that I tried to stop her. But even as I'm talking, I have to ask myself if I didn't try hard enough.

Because I wanted to benefit. Because I knew I would, if she succeeded. "I need to find her."

"You want a ride?"

I zero in on his lips saying that word. My understanding of the moment is a wind tunnel. CeCe's in trouble. He's offering to help me find her.

"Yeah." I pause in my tracks. "I just have to tell my cousin real quick. Wait here?"

I slip inside the apartment. The second the door closes, Nicole pulls me to the couch. A basket of laundry teeters on the edge of the cushion. "You're just going to leave him on the landing like that?"

"Huh? Oh." All I can think about is CeCe getting caught, but there's no way I can tell Nicole any of that. I shake my head.

"What is it?" she presses. She mutes the TV, set to a reality show called *The Situation-Ship* (about a group of single people on a ship).

"I have to go find CeCe," I manage to say. "Eli's giving me a ride."

"Is that so?" she snaps. Except this time, there's a glint of something like pride, or maybe even happiness, on my behalf. Maybe all I needed in order to gain Nicole's favor was to act blatantly heterosexual around her.

But she says, "I'm glad you're getting out."

I hesitate. "Shut up. And thank you."

CHAPTER THIRTY-NINE

We try Mary's house first. She hasn't been answering the phone, either. I bite my nails the whole ride, which feels longer than usual. This time, I can't relish the scenery, the water changing color, the boats clustered at the edge like schoolkids.

Mary meets us at the front door.

"Thank every goddess," she says. We're not allowed to go inside—she's on punishment for coming home late the last time we were together. Glenda, though nice enough to not slam the door in our faces this time, gives her five minutes to talk to us, max.

"I'll get to the point," I say. "Have you talked to CeCe?"

"Wait, is *this* Eli?" Mary interrupts. "Oh my god, he sort of looks like Spider-Man, huh? The cute one, not the old rapey one—"

"Mary, focus. Have you talked to CeCe?"

"No, I haven't heard from her. I haven't been allowed to use my phone all day. I don't even know where it is, honestly." She glances over her shoulder as if to look for her phone again, but more likely to check that no one's listening. "Why? You think something went wrong with . . . ?"

She trails off and shoots Eli a guarded look, and he takes an involuntary step back onto the Zen cobblestoned walkway.

"He knows everything," I explain.

"Why? How?"

"It's a long story."

She sighs. "You say that about everything. But okay." She's not wearing any makeup, not even eyeliner, which makes her look younger and even more earnest. I wish I could stop everything and hug her tight.

"So CeCe's in trouble?" Her tone is begging me to say anything but yes.

"Maybe. She didn't give any indication where she might be?"

"For the thousandth time, no." She looks down at her bare feet and blushes. "We're taking things slow this time."

"That's great," I say, genuinely meaning it. But it doesn't exactly help me right now.

I've run out of nails to chew and move on to my thumb. Mary smacks my hand away from my mouth. "Minerva, what's going on?"

"Nothing, I—"

"*Nothing?* No more hiding stuff, remember?"

Barred from chewing on my nails, I fold my arms, which works well against the random chill. "I have to find CeCe before she makes a huge mistake."

Mary stares back at me, her eyes wide.

"If anybody would know where she is, it's you."

Just then, somebody calls her name from inside the house.

"Be right there!" She turns back to address me and, as an afterthought, Eli. "I wish I knew more. Promise to let me know when you find her? That is, assuming I get my phone back?"

I do, and she gives each of us a hug and a wave just as her name is called another, louder time. The door *clicks* shut.

"She seems nice," Eli says when we're walking back to his car.

"She is," I say. "I still can't believe that she and CeCe are together. I mean, one's my best friend and the other one is my neighbor. I can't describe it, but it just feels weird. Nice, but weird."

"Like the different parts of your life are crashing into each other?"

I turn and look at him. He's half smiling, playing with his keys. "Yeah. That is what it's like. CeCe, Mary, you. All of it."

"Not the worst thing in the world."

"I guess."

We get in the car. He reaches for his phone to pick the music and sets it back down with a thought. "You keep calling CeCe your neighbor, but she seems more like a friend. Kind of a close one, actually."

He turns on the stereo, and I don't answer, because the music briefly takes over. This time, it's Nina Simone, who Mom loved. At least our terror has a decent soundtrack.

So CeCe's my friend. Fine. All this means is that my friend—my kind-of-close friend—might be in trouble. Because I didn't stop her from getting into this mess when I should have. Because I was hoping to get something out of it, too. While we're calling things out today.

"Hey, speaking of change, I wanted to tell you something," Eli says. He's checking his blind spots as we turn onto the main road.

"Well?"

He grins.

"Come on, what is it? Stop drawing it out!"

"Fine. I got into NYU off the wait list. I found out this morning."

"What about the fruit school?"

"Huh?"

"Nothing. What about the plans you already had?"

"I can change my mind."

"Why did you?"

"Because it's what I wanted." At first he speaks carefully, his eyes on the road. But the longer he talks, the more excited he sounds. "Their music technology program is just amazing. There's this paid internship in the city I think I might have a shot at getting. And it's closer to home." He reaches over and squeezes my hand. "It's what I want," he says again.

I wish I could ask if I had anything to do with that decision, but I wouldn't dare. Not everything is meant to be found out, anyway. It's enough that he'll be closer and that maybe we won't have to stop seeing each other after all. Maybe.

"So where do we go next?" Eli asks.

"I have no idea."

But I'm lying. Ever since we left Mary's place, my gut has known exactly where to go next. Well, there and one last place. But the latter thought is so outlandish I'm afraid even forming it in my mind will make it true.

"Actually, I do know," I say. I close my eyes and lean back in the seat. "Neptune Heights."

CHAPTER FORTY

CeCe once told me that my sense of direction is one of the top five things about me. She never specified what the other four were, but it was still one of the most satisfying compliments I ever received. It doesn't take me long to find the house once we're within the area generally known as Neptune Heights.

I ask Eli to park around the block from the house, remembering how they searched me last time.

"Now you have to wait here," I tell him. "Sorry."

"Are you going to tell me where you're going?"

"I can't." When he starts to protest yet again, I cover his beautiful mouth with my hand. "*I* barely even know where I'm going. But trust me. It's fine."

He sort of slumps and lowers my hand. He seems like he's going to ask if I'm sure, or something else along those lines, but he only says, "At least tell me where it is, so I know where to find you in case—"

"In case I don't come out?"

He nods.

We drive back around the block one more time, and I point out the house with its washed-out color and dead plants in the windows. Eli's mouth is a line, and he very much seems as if he wants to stop me from going in, but he just parks the car in the same spot. I give him a long kiss on the lips.

Then I open the door and start walking.

It's twilight. At this very moment, the crowd at Duke's is starting to swell again. It'll peak in an hour. Every other person will order chocolate or vanilla. No one's going to order the sherbet.

The air in Neptune Heights smells like salt and gasoline. A stoop's worth of kids grows quiet as I pass, watching me open the gate and walk up the rotting steps of the run-down house. There's no bell or buzzer, so I knock on the door. It opens too fast, as if the person on the other side already saw me coming.

It's the boy from last time.

"It's Celina's girlfriend!" he calls behind him.

"I'm not CeCe's—"

A voice deeper inside the house yells back something in a Slavic-sounding language.

"You can come in," the boy concludes.

"Do I have to take off my shirt this time?"

He answers plainly, already halfway down the hall toward the light and sound of the gigantic TV in the living room. "Not unless you feel like it."

The same old guy from before leans forward when I walk inside, bathed in the light of a Yankees game on low volume. "Mini-Mart," he croons. "Welcome back!"

"Sorry to, uh—" I get distracted watching the boy crawl onto the far end of the couch. "Sorry to show up like this. I just wanted to know if CeCe was here today."

The old guy chuckles. "Why do you ask?"

"I just need to find her."

"If you don't know, do you think maybe she didn't want you to?" He lights a cigarette and blows the smoke to the side.

"Look, man, I just need to find her."

"Maybe whatever you seem to have to tell her . . ." He gestures as if he's impersonating the Godfather, from another one of CeCe's favorite movies. "Maybe she already knows?"

This shit is getting nowhere, and it's obvious that the more frustrated I become, the more it amuses him.

I sit down. "Can you at least tell me if she was here?"

"No," he says, tapping his cigarette in what looks to be a cereal bowl on the table.

"Why not?"

"She's my family, and you're not. Very simple."

I should have figured this part out ahead of time. I run my hand over my face, and they both watch me, the boy with no emotion whatsoever and the man with great interest and a tiny smile.

"Don't worry about my stepdaughter," the old guy says. "She was going to be in trouble, but I helped her."

"I don't know what that means."

I mean, I think I do, but it doesn't make me feel better.

"Because it isn't your business," he says, the slightest hint of sharpness in his voice.

I stand up to go.

His voice melts into a chuckle. "You think I didn't tell her what a bad idea it was to go and try to sell those bags?"

I turn to face him. "What?"

"Sit. Relax. Stop looking so uptight. I know girls like you. You always think you know better than a man. Always."

"You don't know anything about me."

"I knew you were Sunny's kid, didn't I?"

My silence doesn't just answer him—it amuses him.

"Well. Then I know you." He sort of grunts, reaching for a jar of tobacco on the table. He rolls another cigarette while still smoking the one in his mouth, then lifts the wrap, with its mound of tobacco in the center, in my general direction. "I know you because your mother was the same way. I was sorry to hear she died."

"Don't—" I start, but instead of telling him to shut up about my mom, I notice he just said *died* instead of *passed away* or *no longer with us* or *up in heaven looking down*.

"I used to own this restaurant on the bay. Nice place. I had to move on from it, though." The old guy licks the paper, rolling it between his thick fingers. "Your mama, she was about your age, maybe younger. She comes in looking for a job. I ask her why she wants to work there. She says, 'I need to save up money and leave this piece-of-shit place.'"

The words chill me to the bone. "Did she get the job?"

"No. I already hired somebody by then. I just forgot to take the sign down. But she made an impression. I'll say that."

"Great story," I mutter, though I wish I could ask more about what my mom was like back then. There aren't many people left who could tell me what I don't already know.

Then I remember he was the one who told us about the money in the first place. Did he tell us all that just to mess with us? Just to see what we'd do?

"You're supposed to be CeCe's family, but have you ever been to see her?"

He opens his mouth to answer, but I cut him off.

"No, you haven't. You should be ashamed."

He clears his throat for many seconds. The sound is like something dying in the street. "Definitely Sunny's kid."

"Fuck off," I say and walk out.

When I hear padding behind me in the hallway, it turns out to be the boy, who I almost forgot about. I bet he does that on purpose—just disappears, because it's so much easier.

"She said she was going to get something of hers," he says. His voice is so low I almost miss it. "Something that belongs to her."

"What's that mean?" I demand, but he just blinks at me like a cartoon character from that first night, that same TV light playing on the edge of his cheek. The sound is back on. "How long ago was that?" I soften my voice, hoping it'll get him to cooperate. How do people like Jamira do this, make kids trust them—besides committing amazing feats with swimming pools?

The boy sort of shrugs, appearing to regret that he said anything in the first place.

"An hour?" I ask. "A few hours?"

"In between. I think."

Poor kid is so fried he's lost all sense of time.

"Hey," I ask. "Are you okay?"

His face reshapes itself in anger. He frowns, tipping back on his heels. "Yeah. Are *you* okay?"

Fair enough.

I leave, my mind racing over what I just learned. Where would CeCe get what belongs to her? I know and I don't know where CeCe has gone, as sure as my worn-out sneakers slapping against the sidewalk.

The horrible possibility that occurred to me earlier, the one I hoped wasn't real, is now my last option. On the other hand, if I'm wrong, then at least it can be ruled out.

Eli's sitting on the trunk of his car when I walk up. He hops down when he sees me. "How'd it go?"

I shake my head.

"She wasn't there?"

I take a deep breath. "She was here earlier today. The good news is that I think she changed her mind about trying to sell the stuff."

He relaxes. "That's good. That's great, actually."

"Yeah."

He studies me, doubt creeping in. "What is it?"

"Nothing," I lie. "There's nowhere else to go."

CHAPTER FORTY-ONE

On the way home, I watch Eli's hands on the steering wheel, wishing they were my hands. A song called "California Soul" plays on his stereo, all soaring strings and a singer's voice bursting with hope they can't seem to keep down.

"Will you at least try to take it easy?" he asks.

We've reached my street—the farthest I've ever let him drive me. He doesn't comment on it, which makes me like him even more.

"All these questions, DJ Quandary." But I don't even try to force a smile. "Sure, I'll think about it."

But I can't go for even one more day. I can't afford not to, either, but I have to finally admit that it's over.

No more Duke's Ice Creamery. No more money.

When I sneak back in, Nicole has fallen asleep on the couch, phone at her feet. Next to that, a romance novel Mom and I brought home from a church basement, along with dozens of others we picked without checking. I experience a flashback of Mom in that same spot, one I feel in the pit of me. If I stand in this spot in the semidark, it's like she's still here.

Nicole leaves her car keys on a flowery-looking plate near the front door. It's familiar, like something shoved in the back of a closet years ago. Something Mom never would've used. But Mom kept her keys close to her at all times, not sitting out like this. She was always ready to run.

And yet the plate works. The car keys feel like an offering. Of course, I'm not a god, but I was sort of named for one. And that's enough of a sign for me.

Nicole's car lurches when I try to back out of the spot, and then I remember how I'm used to being heavy-footed with the Boat, such an old beast of a car. It's smoother, though, and doesn't take long for my foot to learn.

Please don't let CeCe be there. Please don't let CeCe be there.

My thoughts blink along with the highway lights, the cars hurtling around me on the road. My heart beats higher in my throat, two seconds from thumping onto the dashboard, still beating messily.

Just a few exits away.

Please don't let CeCe be there.

Fog rolls across the road, which darkens the second I turn off the highway. The usual question: do I park and walk, or try to get close?

What if I'm too late? What if someone sees me or the car?

Visions of jail time descend on me again, this time for me as well as CeCe, for breaking and entering. Maybe another charge or two thrown in for good measure by Anthony's cop friends.

I shake my head and focus on staying inside the lane.

If CeCe's there, who knows what might've happened already?

I park what feels like far enough from the gated community entrance to not draw attention. My body moves on its own. I think it's still floating somewhere over the highway.

The wind rushes through the cover of trees, stronger than it's felt in a while and growing stronger. It's officially hurricane season. The leaves, entire branches, jump and shake as if possessed. Somewhere, bamboo or something clacks together. Frogs and cicadas and crickets shout at one another. My clothes feel damp all over, and whatever's on them extends to my skin.

I'm close to Anthony's house.

I jog along the road to the entrance. As I pass by, I try to see through the trees on my right to find that view of the bay, as if this will confirm I've found the right place. Not that I need the confirmation. I feel it in my gut.

Then I find it: the wide, sweeping view behind the trees placed strategically to block and protect the people inside. Between here and there, houses more beautiful than any of us could ever imagine. Like a soap opera, or one of Nicole's dumb reality shows. Rooms that go on forever; you could throw a button across the smallest one and never hear it land.

The road slopes and curves, both sudden and familiar. The houses in their wide circle. The pool, inside its own fence and beside its own house, glowing blue.

So fucking blue.

I start toward the pool on instinct and then remind myself that CeCe might be here somewhere.

The houses are too silent. It's like walking through a movie set, a kid's dream of a normal life. Then I see it, not too far ahead of where I'm standing in the road: CeCe's bike sideways on the wet grass.

I drag the bike to the bush at the border of the yard. I wish Large Marge were here, and then I remember how attention-seeking she can be. How impaired did CeCe have to be to leave her bike all out in the open like this? And to *ride here* in the first place.

Or how desperate?

CHAPTER FORTY-TWO

I try the front door. It opens right away. The first thing I see on the other side is the ocean, stretched across the biggest window I've ever seen, lit up under a near-complete full moon. It's obvious the window is meant to be seen straight through from the front of the house. The closeness of the water is surreal.

I imagine a giant hook lowering from the sky, piercing through the top of the house, pulling it up and away.

"CeCe," I say, barely able to whisper. My heart is wrapped around my lungs.

Silence answers.

Then, so low it could've been a hallucination, the sound of something falling to a bare floor. A single faraway *click*.

I think I'm following the sound, through a dining room bigger than my whole apartment. Into a kitchen full of shiny and serious-looking appliances. Everything swallowed in the light from the moon, the ocean. The brightness is almost violent on its own.

As I climb the stairs, I make out a sound, something like a purr. Rumbling.

Snoring.

"CeCe," I say at normal volume. It echoes softly in this house, with its giant rooms and forever-high ceilings.

The sound from before—the click, or snap—starts up again, like an answer.

"CeCe."

I follow the sound to a bedroom.

Inside, Anthony is asleep, snoring. CeCe stands at the foot of the bed, opening and closing a knife. If I had to guess, it'd be the knife her cousin gave her. I remember what she said when he went to jail. *That was a rough time.*

I hadn't thought to ask what she'd meant.

Anthony is sprawled across the bed, his head tipped back on a pillow too small for his stupid head. He's wearing a T-shirt and boxers. His snores crash over us like waves.

"What are you doing?" I hiss.

CeCe says, "It took me, like, half an hour to ride my bike here. Felt like longer."

I believe it; her hair is drenched, fanned out across her shoulders. "We have to *go.*"

"Everything seems so far away," she says. She opens and closes and opens and closes and opens and closes her knife. *Click, click, click.*

I can't lose CeCe to this.

"We'll figure something out," I say. "But we have to go. Now."

She startles as if only now seeing me here.

"CeCe, please."

She closes the knife and holds it out to me, handle first. It's shining black on one side and bone-white on the other. When I reach for it, she psyches me out and clutches it back to her side, then shrugs.

The snoring rises again between us. If this were a beach,

it'd be full of black sand and sea urchins. Evil. Mom told me about a beach like that she saw once, somewhere in the Caribbean.

"Please," I say. I reach for the knife. But I'm too late, and she's back to opening and closing it dangerously above what may be Anthony's Achilles tendon.

"There's a way to do it that's almost instant," she muses. "The death. It's only fair. You know it'd only be fair."

"It's not worth it," I say. But part of me wants to know what "almost instant" means. Whether Anthony even deserves that.

"They're just gonna get me on something else," she says. "I might as well make it count. Everybody in my family does time. Even Bonnie did."

The name Bonnie startles me. CeCe hates talking about her mom just as much as I do.

"So you're just going to force it now because you've convinced yourself it's inevitable? This is stupid."

I'm hoping the tough love will snap CeCe out of it. It occasionally works for me. Maybe bring the light back into her eyes. But my being here only seems to make her more determined.

Click, click, click.

I remember, of all things, what Mary told me about Eli. About love but also letting people in. Or letting yourself out. Being pleasantly surprised.

All I know is, it turned out to be good advice.

"It doesn't have to be true," I tell CeCe, louder than I mean to. "None of it has to be true."

She peers over at me, as if trying to recognize the words. Then she screams.

I jump back. I expect a gush of blood to spring out in front of us, but there isn't one. Anthony is scrambling, coughing in the strange light that comes from the moon—a mess of sheets and body hair in his shirt and boxers in the middle of the bed. He squints at us.

"What the fuck? Who the fuck?"

"Where's the money?" CeCe asks.

"Money?" he repeats, eying us blearily. "Who the hell are you?"

"You know what I'm talking about," CeCe says, flashing the blade. Maybe she's not out of it at all.

Maybe she knows exactly what she's doing.

"I'm calling the goddamn cops." He still hasn't moved from his spot in the bed, however. "I don't know who you are, but you're gonna pay for this."

"The money. The valuables." She says *valuables* like a swear word. "Whatever it is you're moving for people much smarter than you, tell me where it is."

He swallows hard, shifting into some kind of understanding. Sweat pools around his eyes despite the central air. "Okay," he says. "Fine. I'll give you what you want."

"Now," CeCe barks. She slightly tilts the knife in my direction. "Tell her where it is, and she'll go look."

"Can't I just show you?" he asks.

"No. You're staying here."

He opens his mouth. The sweat has tumbled down his face, mixed with tears. "You're gonna start in the kitchen. There's a door—"

"Anthony!"

CHAPTER FORTY-THREE

A woman walks in behind her own booming voice. She's dressed in a blazer with piles of gold jewelry, her hair French-twisted on top of her head, and thick, shiny-dark tortoiseshell glasses. She flicks on the lights, and everybody except her flinches.

She can't be anybody other than Anthony's wife.

Even though Eli said they were related by marriage, part of me must not have believed this person truly existed. If I had, I might've pictured somebody different. On my own, I could never come up with someone who looks like this. Someone so rich you can see it in their skin, in the molecules of air around them.

"You're bringing them into our *house* now? That's it, I'm done."

She's yelling at Anthony and pointing at us. She refuses to look in our direction.

Anthony stands up and backs away from the bed, the moon shining as bright as ever behind him. "What are you talking about?" His gaze snags wildly on me and CeCe. "I didn't bring them here."

"Like hell you didn't," his wife says.

"No," CeCe blurts over everyone. "He definitely did not."

"It's you," Anthony says to me, his eyes hot with recognition now that the lights are on. I was hoping he couldn't tell without the uniform. "What in the hell are you doing in my house?"

"Hang on a minute," his wife says. She turns her attention to me. "Do you work at the ice cream stand?"

"Yes," I croak.

It's very quiet in the room until she explodes. "Again, Anthony? *Again?*"

They start a brand-new fight as if we aren't there.

"For Christ's sake, Jen, there are trespassers in our house right now." He points at me. "Did you come here to steal something? Don't think I forgot you creeping around near my office. Your ass is going to jail. Jen, call the cops."

His wife ignores him, having turned away. She seems to be taking a moment, consuming great breaths through her nose.

She turns back to CeCe and me. "You two, this way," she says, then *clicks* back down the hall. The scent she leaves behind is pine or something else evergreen.

Money. The scent is money.

We follow her down the hall, first me, then CeCe, who slips her knife back into her boot. Both of us marvel at the house with the lights on. It's even more beautiful.

We end up in a glowing kitchen, just one corner of the giant room lined with windows. Somewhere nearby, a landline rings, but Anthony's wife ignores it and unzips a gigantic wallet.

She says, "You're obviously not hookers, so how much so you don't go up and down the island, blabbing to folks about what happened?"

"What?" I say.

At the same time CeCe answers, "Ten thousand."

Anthony's wife takes out a checkbook. "I'm not giving you ten thousand dollars."

"Five thousand," CeCe says.

"One thousand for the both of you." Anthony's wife—who I keep having to remind myself is also Eli's aunt—sets the checkbook down on the counter and starts scribbling. His earlier reluctance to discuss this part of his family is making more sense.

"No," I say. "Stop. Gross. Keep your money."

She stops writing and looks at me like I'm a leaf that's fallen into her food. She's about to pick me off her plate and forget about me forever. I try to hold the gaze that seems like it could pry open just about anything. There's something familiar about it.

It's that she reminds me of Mom. How I'm scared of her and want to be like her at the same time. How I want her to like me. There's also the fact that CeCe hasn't mouthed off to her yet, which only confirms it.

Maybe everything really is about money.

When Anthony's wife speaks again, her voice is calm and singsongy and terrifying. "I don't think you understand. This is a *courtesy* to you. For dealing with my soon-to-be ex-husband. If you try to *sue*, you will *lose*. And be stuck with legal fees that will take decades of your miserable lives to pay off."

Sue? The word sucker-punches me in the gut.

I look to CeCe, whose eyes are glazed with fear and awe, then right back at Anthony's wife. Her bright red nails resting on the counter, near the checkbook clipped open with some kind of contraption only rich people have or need.

Jennifer Duke, the checkbook says in the top-left corner.
"Hold on," I say. "Your last name is Duke."

"Yes."

"Duke?"

"Yes," she says. Then she smiles, understanding. "You thought I'd be a man?"

"I guess I did."

"All right. Well." She clears her throat and pulls the checkbook closer. "I'll make it out to one of you. Which one?"

All of a sudden, multiple phones start pinging at once. Or what sounds like multiple but is just one, Jennifer Duke's. It looks like she's receiving a flurry of messages, with at least three unique notification sounds.

When an actual phone call comes a few seconds later, she excuses herself to the other side of the room, where of course we can still see her reflection in the walls.

"He did *what*?"

Now CeCe's phone buzzes. "It's Mary," she says, swiping at the screen. "Wait just a second now. Holy shit."

"What is it?" I ask.

CeCe's typing furiously into her phone. She pauses and waits for something to load. When it does, the result seems to paralyze her. "It's real," she breathes.

"Can you tell me what *it* is? Please?" I know better than to crane my neck. Once she almost elbowed me in the nose to keep me from looking at her screen.

She holds up her phone.

The headline reads: NAUTILUS ICE CREAM STAND VOYEUR CAMERAS REVEAL MORE THAN EXPECTED. There's a photo of a blurred face over a curved gray body. From that angle, it's hard to tell who it is. Maybe one of the new girls. The article explains that an anonymous source tipped off the local news about the cameras as well as years of illegal activity. As of right now, the story is spreading to bigger news outlets in the area.

"Is that little fucker going to pay my lawyer?" Jennifer Duke yells. "Is he there right now?"

Jennifer Duke—formerly known to me as Mr. Duke—has drifted away and back down the hall, seeming to have forgotten us. "What do you mean, 'who'? Eli, your *son*, my *nephew*. Put him *on*."

Hearing Eli's name causes time to stop. Again I look over at CeCe, who might be even deeper in shock than me. But I push past the shock. *Come on, Space Cadet.*

"Hey," I say to her. "Let's get out of here. I don't think we want to be here when she gets off the phone."

"But . . ." CeCe stares longingly at the check, which so far only has the date and *one thou* written out for the amount. Jennifer Duke's handwriting looks like a font, crisp and upright with a hint of cursive in the edges.

"It's wrong to take that money, and you know it," I say. "Besides, you really want her to know your name?"

This does the trick.

"Dammit," CeCe says, and when I pull her toward the door, she doesn't even try to fight me on it.

For the first time all summer, we both just want to go home.

CHAPTER FORTY-FOUR

Duke's is closed the day after the news comes out about the cameras. Since I have no other plans or excuses, I finally let Eli pick me up at the Beach Blossom. Over French fries, pizza burgers, and one strawberry shake, he confirms that he figured out how to sign into Jordan's camera app and make recordings for the express purpose of leaking it to the news. He calls it the Ultimate Snitch's Media Kit. I call it the most romantic gift I've ever seen.

Eli's family is furious with him for going to the news.

"Pretty obvious it's because of the feds coming around," he says.

I nearly choke on my fries. "What?"

"Most of us had no idea just how bad it was." He holds his shake tumbler and looks out the window with a sad smile. "Turns out my uncle, and possibly also my aunt, were up to a lot more than paying people under the table."

The only person who isn't upset is Nana, who also hates Anthony and is overjoyed to watch him punted from their family and general society. And Caroline just doesn't care.

The stand is closed the day after that, and the day after that, too.

It reopens a full week later to protests. The majority are well-meaning people from the city who have flooded the trains, then walked or taxied over just for this purpose. When the protests don't stop right away, Duke's closes again.

In that time, a couple of miraculous events take place at once.

After Jamira's boyfriend proves he didn't commit that first robbery, it's finally revealed who did: a couple boys from Montauk who were squatting in the abandoned condos. When the news comes out, I recognize one of them as the guy who ordered all those coffee milkshakes. Predictably, they're sentenced to a few days of community service.

The next occurrence is that a woman closer to Nicole's age comes to the Beach Blossom saying she's with an advocacy organization in the city. She shows up while I'm home alone looking for new jobs and Nicole is on a date with some poor idiot. The woman from the organization, whose name is Shawna, doesn't look much older than me, although her words belong to someone who's studied them for years. Mom would've let her in.

She explains that they're working to file a class action lawsuit against all of Duke Food Corporation, and could I help them prove the illegal use of surveillance cameras and other malicious activity?

I like that she doesn't seem to change her usual language for me, as if she expects me to keep up. That can be rare in adults.

Even though I mostly get it, I interrupt to ask, "Can you come back when my cousin's here? She's a paralegal or something."

Note to self: give a shit what Nicole does for a living, since it might come in handy now.

It's an odd sensation, wishing Nicole were next to me. But the truth is, I'm also scared of how big the issue has gotten. And I'm scared of the questions and the possibility that nothing will change in the end, for me or anybody else, no matter how big it gets.

Shawna tosses—no, rearranges—her braids over one shoulder. Palms open, she says, "Frankly, I'm appreciative that you let me get this far."

She hands me a business card. *Shawna Quisqueya-Guerrero, JD*, it reads in glossy, raised letters. *Senior Community Advocate.*

"Just making sure," she asks, "you *are* open to working with us?"

"It's what my mom would've wanted."

Shawna smiles. "I need an actual yes." Her response is equal parts empathetic and no-nonsense and almost makes me feel guilty about not answering right the first time. Which must mean she's very good at her job. "It helps me figure out what sort of paperwork we should be bringing to you and your family."

"Okay," I say. "I mean, yes."

"Great." She turns to go.

"Hey, wait. Can I ask you something?"

She nods. "Yes. Of course."

"Can you look up a girl named Sierra who used to work there? I don't know her last name. But it was about a year ago."

Shawna types the name quickly into her phone, her gaze sharpening as I tell her the little bit I know.

"We'll be looking into this as soon as possible," she says. "I mean that."

I call Eli as soon as Shawna Quisqueya-Guerrero's car pulls away.

"Oh, yeah," he says. "She stopped here a little while ago. Had a ton of questions. It's good that it's happening, though, right? I don't see how it could be bad."

"Why didn't you tell me?"

He laughs. "Will you take it easy?"

"No. Never. Don't you know that by now?"

"I was going to tell you. I promise. It's just . . . still not the easiest thing to talk about. Also, I'm doing chores."

"A likely story."

His voice lowers, wavering like he's changing locations for privacy. "You around later?"

My eyes settle on the dining table, no longer cluttered with weeklies. The only object is Nicole's laptop, which she made me promise I wouldn't use for gambling or porn.

"I'm job hunting," I say.

"Nice. I have to do the same thing."

"You're looking for jobs in the city?" He's been mentioning school more and more, clearly excited. I try to sound as supportive and non-clingy as I can, per Mary's and CeCe's advice.

"Yeah," he says. "I saw a few I like. You want to maybe job hunt together?"

It's frankly embarrassing how fast the blood rushes into my face every time Eli says he wants to be around me. But at the same time, I don't mind it. In fact, it's one of the top five feelings in the word. I bet I'll even get used to it.

I look around at the apartment Nicole transformed after moving in, even though our longer-term plan is to find a place closer to school. There are curtains on the windows, a tablecloth and an actual bowl of fruit on the dining table. I keep pretending not to hear Nicole's unsubtle hints that I should eat some, but it does still look nice. There are framed photos all along the wall, mostly of Mom and me. One of the pictures is the two of us in front of Niagara Falls that a stranger must have taken, and that I didn't even know Mom had developed. I'm clutching her like a little kid, arms around the waist. Behind us, the falls are a giant, frozen memory. Unreal. Neither of us are smiling, but both of us manage to look happy.

Although I didn't recognize the photo when Nicole hung it, I can't let a day pass without staring at it now. It's not better than having Mom around, but it's a new thing I don't hate.

"Okay," I say to Eli, "your house or mine?"

CECE TELLS ME to meet her in that creepy spot under the boardwalk. She makes me promise to come alone—no Eli and not even Mary.

She didn't offer directions even though I've been there just once before. But I do find the spot on my own, partly because I remembered the entrance was past the playground and through the second gap in the sand beneath the board-walk. And partly because I know this place as if it's a part of my own body.

I have to crouch in through the lip of the entrance in the sand, making myself smaller and smaller until I'm down to crawling army style.

I call CeCe's name, and she answers with a whistle. I haven't told her I know her name is Celina, but I plan on breaking it out the next time she calls me Mini-Mart.

In the room of sand, she's sprawled in the last beach chair left intact, playing with a lighter. The light streaming down from the world above is minimal—it's too cloudy today. At least there hasn't been a hurricane yet.

"You're late, Gutiérrez."

At least she didn't say Mini-Mart. I dust myself off. As always, the sand down here is eerily cool to the touch. "What's going on?"

"I wanted to get your opinion on something."

She opens her backpack and takes out a flat, compressed package of off-white powder. The fentanyl or heroin or whatever it turned out to be. "It doesn't matter anymore that I have it. I can't sell it. I was thinking of dumping it into the ocean."

"You were what!"

"I know, I know. You don't have to get all—" She flips her hand in a gesture of dismissal. It's a mannerism of Mary's. A warm feeling passes through me. "I knew it was a bad idea. So what do I do? You're the smart one. Tell me."

"No," I say.

"No, you won't tell me?"

"No, I'm not the smart one. You are."

She grins in the pale light. "Thanks."

"You're welcome."

"I gotta tell you something," she says. "I'm leaving."

"What?"

"Norwalk, Connecticut." She shakes her head. "It's far as hell, but I have some family there. They're letting me stay with them as long as I go to school. There's a community college up there."

I nod. I can't think of a single useful word.

She says, her voice breaking on the first word, "For once in my life, I can actually afford to leave."

"Wait what?" I ask. "What do you mean, you can afford to leave?"

She holds up a hand and waves me closer. She kneels on the sand and unzips her backpack between us. I kneel, too, in order to see better.

Inside her bag, at least halfway through, is a beautifully tangled mess of gold and silver and gems shining deeply, secretly.

There is so much of it.

"Maybe I went a little overboard with the Jennifer Duke souvenirs," says CeCe, hand to her chest. "Before I met her, of course. That woman is my hero. Except for the whole being *evil* thing."

"When did you do it?"

"When I first got to the house," she muses. She holds up a bracelet made of what I assume are real diamonds. "Anyway, this is just whatever I haven't sold yet."

I can't take my eyes off all the jewelry. Although the idea of touching any of it's too much, as if it could burn my skin off. "So you wouldn't want to stay here?"

Just then, a helicopter decides to pass over the conversation.

I have to start laughing. CeCe doesn't, but she doesn't seem bothered by it, either, which is different for her. She's screamed at more helicopters than anyone else I know.

"There's a good couple thousand dollars for you," she says when the helicopter is far enough away. "Maybe more. But only when you're ready. You have my word. I already opened a separate bank account and added your name to it."

"Are you serious?" The tears well up and break. I pull her into a hug.

And yet at the same time, in the back of my mind, I am *in fact* wondering how I might find a way to mess it all up.

I let the voice talk and talk and talk, not unlike how I've dealt with Nicole, and then I pretend there's a sound-proof glass between me and the voice. If it works on a real, flesh-and-blood person, it must work on a figment of my imagination built out of my weakest parts.

Anyway, I have money now. Before this, I had almost nothing.

"When you're ready," CeCe reminds me, as if she can read my thoughts, "we'll talk about it."

"Deal," I say. "What are you going to study in school?"

She stands up and crosses her arms over her chest, eyeing me. "You already know."

Business.

CeCe and I end up burying the drugs right there, filling a good portion of the hideout with surrounding sand. We wrap the package in a tarp she pulled off a house she insists nobody's worked on for over a year. Now I understand why she didn't bring Large Marge. It turns out she'd planned to do this all along. She even brought shovels.

By the time we leave, the space under the boardwalk feels less like a room now, which is probably a good thing.

One of our phones starts to ping for attention. It isn't mine, which is only a few days old and also in need of a recharge.

"It's Mary," CeCe says. "She wants to know what time we're leaving tomorrow."

CeCe finally got her car fixed. In celebration of that and everything else, we're going on a trip to Mary's family cabin in the Catskill mountains.

"We leave whenever we want," I say, distracted from all the sand in my sneakers, which CeCe advised keeping on during our project earlier.

CeCe taps an answer, smirking. She and Mary are starting over as friends, but everyone in Nautilus—probably even Jennifer Duke herself—can see how into each other they are.

"Hey. Mary says to make sure you charge your phone for the trip."

"Yeah, yeah." I grin to myself, wondering if I'll get to drive. I've already examined the map, which roads I want to take. We're driving west, then north. Not as far as Niagara Falls, but closer to the stars.

CHAPTER FORTY-FIVE

It's not necessarily what Mom wanted—not that she ever said, but I know more than anything she would've preferred cremation and to be scattered. Not to be kept in some vase, growing dusty on our nonexistent mantel.

I think she would've wanted her ashes to end up somewhere important. Out in the world. Moving. Free.

Even though I already know I'm right about this, I ask Nicole what she thinks.

We're standing at Mom's grave in the city cemetery. The stone reads *Cassandra Gutiérrez*. No other information. No middle name, like me. Not even her nickname, Sunny.

Nicole sets down the marigolds fresh from the florist. The grass on the plot is delicate, like hair, still new and easily crushed. I'm surprised to see she just leaves them in a pile on the ground like that. No vase or cloth or anything—just a stone the size of a softball to keep them from blowing away in the next storm. She tucks the previous flowers into a paper bag she brought with her.

"Your grandparents are here." She points to two slightly larger tombstones I recognized earlier, just a few feet away. "It was for them more than anything."

"Why?"

"It's just not that big of a deal to her." Nicole bends down to pick at a few stray flowers from one of her previous visits. As usual now, I don't pick on her for using present tense. "But it is to them. Sometimes we just have to make decisions that way."

I think she's going to launch into some kind of lecture, but she doesn't.

"You're right, though," she says at last. "She would've liked to have her ashes scattered in the bay."

Nautilus Bay, where the trip started in real life. Where everything begins and ends for both of us.

That's what Nicole and I end up doing with the flowers from before. It's what she has been doing this whole time—buying fresh flowers, switching the old ones out, tossing them in the bay as if they're ashes.

When we're back in the car, I check my phone—Nicole made me silence it while on cemetery grounds—and find a voicemail from Shawna Quisqueya-Guerrero. I play the message on speaker, Shawna's clipped, solemn voice filling the car.

"Minerva. Shawna here. I just wanted to let you know I got in touch with that young woman you mentioned, Sierra Campos. I thought you might want to know she's currently a student at Stanford University. She was . . . very receptive to aiding our efforts. It sounds promising. More soon." She pauses and adds with a touch more warmth, *"You take care, all right?"*

It's funny how everyone suddenly cares if I'm taking care of myself.

Okay. Fine.

Maybe one day soon I'll admit it's not so sudden.

CHAPTER FORTY-SIX

My favorite part of swimming is the web of light across the floor. Beach or pool. I could sink and touch the bottom, or I could shoot forward, lighter and faster than the water itself.

I spent the first three years of high school wishing I'd tried out for the girls' swim team, and at the beginning of senior year, I finally did it. Right before the school year started, Nicole showed up at the main office and threatened to sue them for expelling a child in mourning. It took all of two minutes for them to put me back in the system.

It's the second swim meet of the season, and fewer than two dozen people have collected in the bleachers that are old and grim and big enough to fit an army. Coach Whitaker, a history buff, told us all the story. The building is a product of the Works Progress Administration, when the president had pools and parks and libraries built to give people jobs and make them feel better about how the world had gone to shit. I think Mom would've liked Coach.

When I'm in the pool, the chatter blends into a buzz I can tune out. The tiny crowd makes the place feel even bigger. Through my goggles, I search for a familiar face. Mary's taking extra classes—the college-level kind, not the kind I'm taking to catch up—and Nicole has to work. I told them both there'd be plenty of other swim meets, and I meant it. But still.

I spot Caroline sitting alone on the top bleacher. She waves, embarrassed—either about the waving or being here at all. After Eli left for college, she warmed up to me so fast it was a little scary. Then it was kind of nice.

I try not to ask her about Eli. Mostly I don't have to, since he and I talk on the phone about every other day, even more so after Nicole gave in and agreed to unlimited minutes and a better phone.

Sometimes he and I are on the phone until early morning, both of us mumbling and half asleep. Once I woke up to music playing on the other end of the line. A present he left for me.

Sometimes he calls and it hurts so much I don't answer.

"He has to work a lot," Caroline tells me when we sit together at lunch, and the other kids at the table who don't know Eli veer on into other conversations without us.

"What else is new?" I try to joke.

She says, "I think he wants to come back to Nautilus."

I just nod, knowing that it's wishful thinking on her part. A little bit on mine, too.

"Maybe you can convince him to come back," she said once. "I keep telling him someone's going to steal you away."

To change the subject from Eli, I'd interrupt and ask her how math was going. She'd say, "Crappy," and I'd go over some problems with her right there in the cafeteria or on the bus to Crystal Cove or wherever we were.

"See?" I'd say, "not every problem is a problem."

I asked Mary to give me a buzz cut—what's left is all dark

brown. I still have to wear a swim cap, but there's relief in starting over.

Nicole came to the first swim meet. Afterward, she took us to dinner (I made her drive to the pink and chrome diner) and chatted about the law firm where she'd gotten a new job.

At some point, she paused and said, "I'm proud of how good you were."

I was looking out the window at the diner parking lot and the village street beyond, at the clusters of people walking in the cold. Some seemed happy. Some didn't.

I wondered if strangers ever wondered about me when I was at my worst. I bet someone had.

"Sorry, what?" I said to Nicole before stealing one of her fries.

"I said your mother loves you so much."

Love. Far from all I need, but more than I could ever hope for.

It's time to take our marks. I've gotten lost in a thought within a thought, which is funny because the team motto is "Think or Swim." When Coach first yelled it at tryouts, I swore it was the corniest thing I ever heard. But there was something to it. If I don't leave all these thoughts behind, I might never get to the other side. Let alone back to where I started.

I fold my body at the edge of the pool, ready for the buzzer.

There and back.

Dear Reader,

When my mother was very young, she underwent open-heart surgery for a rare defect she'd had since birth. It was the 1970s in the Dominican Republic. Living still wasn't guaranteed, and childbirth was basically prohibited for her due to the possibility she might not survive.

She fixed her heart temporarily, and then she fell in love, and finally she took her chances and had me (and later on, my little brother). Her pregnancy terrified people.

When I first had the idea for *What's Coming to Me*, I was only a couple of years older than Minerva, its protagonist. I had grown up—was still growing up—with a chronically ill parent and seeking books about kids with chronically ill parents. I was also very poor, very brown, and very angry.

I didn't know it at the time, but what I was looking for was a book on anticipatory grief. It's a subset of grief, the type we feel in advance of the actual ending. When we can see it coming, even if it's far away. Since my mother was seriously ill for most of my childhood, grief was around just as long, not so much a friend but a companion, sometimes a co-conspirator and other times an opponent, one more worthy than anything made of flesh.

People familiar with grief are likely to also be familiar with this complicated dynamic: its infinite faces; how we perceive it, interact with it, and are influenced by it. We know that every instance of grief is unique because every life and relationship is unique. I craved a reading (and later, writing) experience that would give voice to this.

I concluded that I'd write about all this "someday" and then set it aside. When I returned to it years later, my mother had passed away. The idea solidified.

And so, this book is about every kind of grief. About how once it happens, it's always happening. I didn't mean to write about anger, or being young and poor and brown in the suburbs, either. But this book became about all of those things, too.

The final piece for me was its escapism—and, ultimately, its joy.

This book is a whole voyage, and I'm really glad you're here for it.

Francesca M. Padilla

ACKNOWLEDGMENTS

First set of thanks goes to my family, immediate and close extended. You never once doubted my ability to get here, and you gave me time and leeway and patience. There's no chance I could've accomplished any of this without you.

Endless thanks to my literary agent and friend, Kate McKean. You called me the real deal years ago, and it meant way more than you knew. To Alexa Wejko, my editor (and also friend now, sorry!), for being more than a champion of my writing. I learned so much from both of you about how to write a good novel. For real. Massive gratitude to everyone at Soho Press for your help bringing this book to the world. Professionalism is mostly a tool of white supremacy, so I'll just say, sincerely, that you've all been lovely to work with.

To my absolute first readers, when this was a completely different story with the same set of players: Alissa Dufour, Amelia Kahaney, and Nova Ren Suma. Your incredibly close reading, excitement, and support is how I knew I had something on my hands, even if I didn't quite know what it was yet. To Adalena Kavanagh, a brilliant writer and photographer and a dear friend, who read my work in the beginning and bravely wrangled me for a fantastic author photo toward the end. To Dasha Fishman, my invaluable beta reader and first consumer: your genuine excitement kept me going.

To the members of the Writing Shoppe and Empanada Emporium (aka my first real young adult/middle grade writing group): Jessica Balun, Jeff LaGreca, Laurie Smollett Kutscera, Colin Riley, Melissa Ross, Samantha Rowan, Marjorie Sweeney, and of course Miss Kate again. I know most of you didn't read this story while I was writing it, but you were the best cheerleaders a writer could ask for at the beginning of their publishing journey. Can we go sailing again? Just kidding. Or not (let me know). To all my other lit besties, whom I will not name specifically for fear of leaving anyone out: I appreciate you, learn from you, and am in constant awe of you every day. Honestly.

Many thanks to the Studios of Key West, Peyton Evans Artist Residency program for giving me additional time and space to work on revisions in one of the most beautiful places in the United States. Mil gracias also to We Need Diverse Books for awarding me the Walter Dean Myers grant in 2016/2017 and for your continued support for this book. Again and again, it means the world to me!

To the professors at the SUNY Purchase College Creative Writing program way back when I was around Minerva's age: shout-out to Catherine Lewis for sending that acceptance and helping me get the hell out of Brooklyn. Love to Brenda DeMartini-Squires, a truly badass writer and educator and friend.

Not least of all, thanks to the readers whose sadness looks like anger to the outside world, especially brown and Black and queer and grieving kids. To anyone who has feared losing a loved one and realizes the fear doesn't go away once they're actually gone. To anyone who reads this book and gets it. What more can I say? Thank you, thank you, thank you.